THE SMALL FLYER CAME TO A SUDDEN, WRENCHING STOP . . .

. . . then began to fall. Commander Riker tried to take the controls, but the air was suddenly thick as wet sand against his chest, and he could not move. From the edge of his vision he saw dim, gray rock spiraling upward toward the port window.

Then everything went black, but Riker could still hear the whine of air rushing against the flyer. The whine ended with the crunch of metal collapsing against rock.

Riker felt sharp pain ripple through his body. Then . . . nothing.

Look for STAR TREK Fiction from Pocket Books

Star Trek: The Original Series

Star Trek: The Next Generation

Star Trek: Deep Space Nine

STAR TREK
THE NEXT GENERATION®

FOREIGN FOES

DAVE GALANTER
and GREG BRODEUR

POCKET BOOKS
New York   London   Toronto   Sydney   Tokyo   Singapore

This book is a work of fiction. Names, characters, places and incidents are products of the author's imagination or are used fictitiously. Any resemblance to actual events or locales or persons, living or dead, is entirely coincidental.

An *Original* Publication of POCKET BOOKS

POCKET BOOKS, a division of Simon & Schuster Inc.
1230 Avenue of the Americas, New York, NY 10020

ISBN: 0-671-88414-X

First Pocket Books printing August 1994

10 9 8 7 6 5 4 3 2 1

POCKET and colophon are registered trademarks of
Simon & Schuster Inc.

Printed in the U.S.A.

To Diane Carey,
holder of the elusive pebble
(Think *Kung Fu,* folks)

Roused by the lash of his own stubborn tail,
Our lion now will foreign foes assail.
                                    —*John Dryden*

FOREIGN FOES

Chapter One

"If the Klingon moves, *kill him.*"

For a moment, no one moved. The Hidran ambassador's order crashed off the meeting hall's stone walls and into the ears of the *Enterprise* officers. His breathing mask muffled the threat, but made it no softer, no less a demand.

Captain Urosk crushed his phaser into Worf's chest.

If Worf moved, he would die.

He tensed, his wide shoulders tight, his dark face clenched in anger.

"Hold it!" Commander William Riker yanked up his phaser and took a step toward them. Close enough to smell them—not to stop them.

He motioned Data forward from the other side.

The hall had grown uncomfortably large. What had been a meter between them now seemed much more. The only thing within reach was Riker's regret at having brought Worf when judgment should have told him better. Klingons and Hidran never mixed.

Urosk and Ambassador Zhad glanced at Riker. It was long enough for Riker to see their eyes, dark green marbles set under brows of wet red leather.

Worf seized the moment of distraction and swung his arm, slapping Urosk's weapon away.

But Urosk's tall frame gave him advantage, kept him on his feet. He whipped the disrupter back around.

"I said stop!" Riker jumped forward and wedged himself between his own security officer and the two Hidran.

Riker was tall as well—tall enough to shoulder the Hidran captain back in a sweeping motion. Why hadn't he seen this coming?

"Kill him! *Kill him!*" Zhad shouted to his captain.

Lieutenant Commander Data came up beside them, the android's gold-skinned hand gripping his holstered phaser, ready for Riker's order to draw.

"You insult us with the presence of this animal!" Ambassador Zhad spat, his glare intent on Worf, his voice gravel beneath the breathing mask that shrouded half his face.

Urosk took only one step back. The Hidran's long scarlet fingers anxiously pumped the handle of his weapon, waiting to finger the trigger.

"How dare you?" Zhad growled, his tall body shaking, his red hue darkening in anger.

Riker looked from the Hidran to Worf and back. "How dare *we?*" Staggering audacity. To demand that the Federation help the Hidran people, then act as if they were doing the Federation a favor by accepting such charity . . . Riker had to restrain himself from explaining to the good ambassador just where he could stuff his vainglorious attitude.

He took in a settling breath, then regretted it as he choked on the Hidran's musty odor. He should have been ignoring the stench—humans probably smelled to a number of alien races—but that was easier said than done when the alien next to him reeked like mold and wet burlap.

"What do you know of seventy years of oppression?" Zhad roared, his voice shaking the hall, his dark eyes burning with contempt. "Or twenty years of war? And twenty more of harassment?" He pounded a ruby fist on the granite table next to them. Rock on rock. "When was the last time your comrades were killed in cold blood? Was your family murdered in your home?" He angrily wagged a dripping crimson limb at Worf. *"He* has done this to us! *He* has ravaged our homeworld, and strangled our future!"

Worf straightened stubbornly. *"I* have done nothing."

The Klingon's deep baritone and skyscraper posture were a reminder of just how intimidating he could be.

Riker stepped back. "Your war was with the Klingon Empire, gentlemen," he said. "Not the Klingon race."

"That is a matter of opinion." The Hidran ambassador turned his head away. "I will speak with your captain now."

"He'll be here, Zhad." Riker couldn't force the anger from his tone. His body held it too—fists clenched, jaw tight.

Data moved his hand away from his phaser.

Not yet. Riker shook his head once, and the android gripped the weapon again.

Zhad was too unpredictable, too irrational. Every ambassador was a creature of rhetoric, but Zhad was also a bully who coerced his way to victory. His reputation said he twisted facts to suit his purposes, freely perverting his opponents' arguments, all despite the breathing mask that distorted his voice. He was a rooster who announced the dawn with such arrogance that he convinced every ear he'd created the sun himself. It had worked for him and his race, and was why he was present.

That thought stiffened Riker's spine, for if Zhad had a purpose here, so did Urosk.

And Urosk was a soldier. Riker had watched the Hidran captain's eyes as he surveyed his situation and summed it up. There was little Urosk would do without reason. Captains were all alike in some ways. At least the ones who survived were. And that was why the Hidran captain was the danger. Loudmouths with fists were annoying—clever thinkers with fists were dangerous.

Riker assured himself he would not be caught off guard again.

Nothing ever went quite as planned. Riker had been ordered to keep the Hidran occupied—diplomatically. *Can't be done.* And adding Worf to the mix hadn't been the wisest move. He'd hoped it might show the Hidran how Klingons *could* be. No such luck. Now it looked as if an argument was the only way they would communicate.

"We'll not wait much longer." Zhad's face twisted into what Riker assumed was a frown.

"Ambassador, we're here because your planet is dying," Riker said.

"Interesting lie!" Zhad spat. "Agreements are signed over subspace. Why has the Federation brought us to this godforsaken planet, where we are met by our enemy and forced to wait at his bay?"

"Lieutenant Worf isn't your enemy, and this god-forsaken planet was the only one your government would agree to," Riker said.

"Enough!" Zhad axed Riker's platitudes off with a bark and turned back away. He slithered the perimeter of the table, spying every corner of the large hall.

"We *are* the only ones here." Riker gestured for Data to follow the ambassador.

Zhad flashed an unamused eye at Riker and ran his palm along one of the tapestries that lined the high walls. With two quick tugs he tested the strength of its hold on the ceiling. He lifted it and looked behind.

"Klingons don't come that thin," Riker grumbled dryly. "And their assassins don't hide in the cracks of walls. If we had brought you here to kill you, you'd already be dead."

"Perhaps I was interested in the rugs," Zhad said.

"They are quite old, Ambassador." Data motioned to the tapestries. "They are believed to be the work of the ancient Velexians."

Zhad shot a glare at all three Starfleet officers. "Who cares?"

Data began to answer, but Riker shook his head again.

The ambassador stomped back and stood next to Urosk. "Summon your captain or we leave now."

"Ambassador, Captain Picard said zero-eight-thirty hours, and he meant zero-eight-thirty hours." Riker squeezed the grip of his phaser and felt the tension grow. It had smothered all diplomacy since the first weapon had been drawn, and now it threatened to spoil what civility was left. "In fifteen minutes—"

Captain Urosk's communicator screeched wildly and he yanked it off his belt. A voice crackled from the small speaker. *"Sir, a Klingon warship enters this sector. Its weapons are charged and it cruises at battle speed."*

Riker groaned. *Great. Just great . . .*

Urosk pulled his disrupter up again and roared into the communicator. "Shields up! Arm for battle! Pull out of orbit."

"Understood, sir."

Zhad grabbed Urosk's arm and yanked the communicator to his mask. "Destroy the Klingon vessel!"

"No!" Riker stepped closer, but stopped himself from jumping on Urosk's weapon. Instead, he nodded Data back behind the Hidran and held his own ground. "The *Enterprise* is up there! Let them handle it!"

Zhad wheeled around and rammed the butt of his disrupter against Riker's shoulder, knocking him to the ground. Riker's phaser went clattering across the marble floor.

Pain arched Riker's back as he pushed himself up on his elbows and stared at the ambassador's weapon, which that had come from . . . where?

Towering over him, Zhad aimed very deliberately at Riker's head.

"So, this is the Federation's 'word of honor.' As much a lie as Klingon honor." He turned to Urosk. "We've been betrayed. This *was* a trap! They have brought us here to die!"

"Status report!"

Captain Jean-Luc Picard marched onto his bridge. The lift doors whispered closed behind him.

"We're on yellow alert." Lieutenant Anderson vacated the command chair and returned to her tactical station. "Sensors indicate Klingon battle cruiser— this sector—armed. The Hidran have raised their shields and moved out of orbit. They are transferring power to weapons." She paused, checked a readout on her sensor board. "The Klingons are on an intercept course."

Picard nodded and surveyed the approaching disaster on the viewscreen. The Klingons were early. Too early. He'd wanted time to deal with the Hidran, time to explain that the Klingons would be coming. Time to explain to the Klingons as well.

Explanations were no longer an option.

"Shields up. Battlestations."

Alert panels flashed red and the captain could almost sense his crew racing to their stations throughout the massive ship. He shared a brief glance with Counselor Troi who sat to his left. The thought that she might be feeling his tension crossed his mind. He was sure the rest of the crew believed his calm demeanor. Deanna was the only one who could know better.

"Ensign DePotter," Picard said, his attention now squarely on the Klingon vessel that steadily retreated on the screen, "take us out of orbit, heading two-ten mark six. Put us right between them."

"Aye, sir." The young man's fingers flew over the navi-console, pushing *Enterprise* gracefully out of orbit, placing her steelgray hull between the Hidran ship and the now closing Klingon battle cruiser.

Under Picard's order, *Enterprise* hovered there. To the other ships she must have seemed to dominate space. That was as Picard wanted. His ship could be a looming reminder of just how powerful power could be.

"The Klingons are trying to maneuver around us, sir," Anderson said.

"Crowd them out, Mr. DePotter," Picard ordered.

The Klingon vessel turned and twisted, and *Enterprise* echoed each move, barring them from the Hidran ship at every angle. Picard watched the starscape shift wildly across the main viewer and was annoyed by the Klingon's tenacity. He fought the urge to remove his ship from this nonsense, and leave the Klingons and Hidran to the violent fate they coveted.

The captain pulled in a deep breath, and let it out slowly. "Patch me in to the Klingon vessel, Lieutenant."

"On screen, sir," Anderson said.

The forward viewer image of the battle cruiser washed away, replaced by the harsh features of a Klingon commander.

"I am Kadar, commander of Imperial Cruiser HIv SuH. *Captain, we assume you are under attack by what we identify as a Hidran warship. We offer assistance. Move, so we may destroy them."*

The Klingon's manner was cool, his tone measured. Despite that, Picard saw through to piercing anger. With revenge in the pot, Klingons had poor poker faces.

"This is Captain Picard of the Federation *Starship Enterprise."* His voice was calm and hard.

"Sir," Anderson interrupted, her voice low, "Commander Meliosh of the Hidran ship is signaling."

Picard nodded and thumbed a button on the arm of his command chair. "Captain Kadar, I appreciate your concern, however, none is necessary. I assure you we are in no danger. Please stand by." The captain motioned to the screen. "Put Meliosh on."

The bridge of the Hidran ship came onto the viewscreen. Meliosh sat in a command chair that could hardly be seen for the water vapor that filled his ship.

"This is Captain Pic—"

"You have broken your word, Picard!" Meliosh bellowed.

"We broke no word," Picard said. "You asked our help. Conditions on that are *not* yours to set."

"You claim aid, yet summon our enemies to murder us. No, Picard, you have lost our trust!" Meliosh's color glowed ruddy and his lips curled around sharp little teeth. *"Remove your vessel from our path. We have an enemy to defeat!"*

Picard rose and stepped closer to the viewer, hoping his compact stature would appear more imposing as he filled the Hidran's screen.

"You won't defeat anyone, Meliosh," he said, his voice firm and even. "You don't want to risk another war."

8

Meliosh raised his head proudly. *"We've beaten back the Klingons before. We will again."*

Abruptly, the starscape returned to the screen.

"Transmission cut, sir," Anderson said. "I'm reading a power surge on the Hidran ship. They're moving off—locking torpedoes on the Klingons."

"Tactical," Picard ordered sharply.

A corner of the forward viewer flashed a graphic display of the sector. The Hidran ship warped out of the solar system with the Klingon battle cruiser turning to follow.

Picard frowned and frustration gnawed at his will to help those who so vigorously rejected it.

"Shields on maximum." Picard leaned down to the helm. "DePotter, do *exactly* as I say."

The Hidran ship twisted about and fired a spread of torpedoes. Wicked orange bolts flashed across the viewer as they rounded toward the Klingon vessel.

The young ensign looked up. Picard gave him a reassuring nod and ordered: "One-one mark twenty. Warp one . . . now!"

Enterprise jumped into warp, forcing herself into the path of the salvos.

Picard glared at the main viewer. One after another, the torpedoes pounded against the shields, cloaking the starscape in a blur of electrical flame. Each explosive sizzle of energy rattled the *Enterprise* and jolted her a little off her course.

The captain gripped the back of DePotter's chair as the bridge shook around them. Fingers of electricity crackled across the screen as the *Enterprise* was gripped and wrenched to one side. "Stabilize," Picard ordered over the din of every deck reporting in. "Hail those ships, Anderson. Request a three way conference. Demand one. If they refuse, force it." He pointed at the navi-console. "Full stop."

"Minimal damage to engineering decks three

9

through seven, sir," Anderson said. "Shield strength holding at eighty-seven percent. Commander Meliosh and Captain Kadar standing by on three-way."

"Damage control teams, Lieutenant." Picard smoothed out his tunic and glared at the viewer. There was a rage that filled the captain when he was forced to put his ship and crew in the line of fire. That anger narrowed his eyes and clenched his jaw.

"Put our *friends* on," he said slowly.

Meliosh appeared on one side of the screen, Kadar on the other. Picard could see by their expressions that they also could now see each other.

"Commander Meliosh," Picard said, his voice a hammer. "You've fired on a Federation vessel. That is an act of war. Stand down from battlestations and resume orbit around Velex."

"We'll not lower our shields with an armed Klingon warship at our throats!" Meliosh raged.

"Commander," Picard said, "perhaps you could defeat the Klingons in a war. Perhaps even the Federation. But certainly not both."

There was silence as Meliosh considered the threat.

The Klingon captain smiled.

"There's nothing to smirk at here, Kadar," Picard snapped. "You haven't won anything. Your peoples need each other. You *will* work something out."

"We do not talk with Klingons," Meliosh said.

"You will, if you want to live," Picard corrected. "And I don't refer only to your suffering homeworld. I'm willing to overlook your attack on my vessel, but only for the moment. Picard out." The captain gestured toward Anderson, and Meliosh faded from the main viewer. Now only Kadar filled the screen.

"Scan them," Picard ordered.

Anderson jabbed at her console. "Hidran moving back toward Velex, sir. An orbital maneuver."

Picard nodded and pivoted back to the screen.

"Kadar, disarm your weapons as a show of good faith."

"Out of the question, Picard," the Klingon chuckled darkly. *"Your quaint little tactics may work with the Hidran. I am a different matter."*

"When it comes to the needs of your peoples, there is no difference."

"You dishonor us, Picard. We were lured here with a lie."

Picard pressed his lips into a thin line. That was true. He had wagered that there would be enough time to prepare the Hidran to talk with the Klingons and vice versa. He'd gambled that he could keep both sides in the dark as to the other's arrival. He'd lost.

"An arguable point, Captain, but you *are* here, and your government has asked the Federation for assistance that only the Hidran can supply."

Kadar lost the grapple with his anger and growled at Picard. *"I will not talk with them! You are fools to trust the Hidran! They do not kill for honor or for game. They just kill. Without thought. Without reason. We will not stay!"*

"That's your choice, Kadar. I cannot force you to stay." Picard turned his back to the screen. "Lieutenant Anderson, inform Starfleet Command we request another Klingon delegation for discussion on the Hidran matter. One that *can* handle the situation."

The main viewer shimmered back to the starscape view. Picard glanced at Deanna.

"Anger and frustration clashing with intense pride," the empath said. "I think you have him where you want him, sir."

A corner of Picard's mouth drew down. He wasn't quite ready to believe that.

"Captain," Anderson called, "the Klingons have signaled that our message to Starfleet is 'unwarranted.' They're entering orbit around Velex."

Picard glanced at Deanna. His brows went up, a little surprised that a failed plan had so quickly given way to one that had worked—for the moment.

"Well," Deanna sighed, "that was more difficult than we thought."

Picard shook his head and lowered himself back into the command chair. "That, Counselor, was the easy part."

Chapter Two

"PHASERS DOWN!" Data leveled his weapon at the two Hidran. "I would not want to injure either of you."

Zhad and Urosk laughed, a loud mocking growl that could not be mistaken for anything but ridicule.

Riker accepted Data's glance. There was no annoyance in the android's features. How often had Riker looked for a flash behind Data's gaze that could not be dismissed as merely electrical? The android shouldn't have liked to be laughed at, if even just a little, but that didn't play on his face, behind those bright sulfur eyes.

Suddenly Urosk tensed and launched himself forward.

Riker snapped his attention back. "Data!" he warned.

The android twisted to one side and with his free hand sent Urosk stumbling across the floor and into Worf.

Ambassador Zhad aimed his disrupter and fired.

Riker rolled away, then skidded to his feet as the orange bar of energy scattered on the marble floor. He wasn't sure if it was the weapon blast or anger, but he felt a flush of heat rise in his face.

Worf seized Urosk, spun him around and rammed a knee into the small of the Hidran's back. The Klingon pulled Urosk's elbows together with his right hand and wrenched the weapon away with his left.

Riker squinted as Zhad targeted him again. At the edge of his focus he saw Data grab the ambassador's leathery wrist and bend it back—Zhad cried out in angry pain. The android holstered his phaser, ripped Zhad's own weapon away, then released the ambassador from the vice with a quick shove.

Zhad stumbled back, crumpling like so much musty laundry, a mound of damp limbs against the cold stone wall.

Data reset the ambassador's disrupter to stun and trained it on its owner.

Riker spotted his weapon on the floor, snatched it up, and aimed it at Urosk. With a nod he gestured for Worf to release the Hidran captain.

The Klingon loosened his grip. Urosk jerked himself away, spun around, and faced the one who'd humiliated him so. Dank burgundy fingers tensed over an empty holster.

"That's enough!" Riker said.

The Hidran captain braced himself, but did not move forward.

Worf stood in front of him, looking like an Old West gunfighter—a phaser in each fist.

Furious and insulted, Zhad dragged himself up and over to Urosk. "I will see that you all die for this." He pulled the communicator from his captain's belt and growled into it. "Meliosh, tell me you have defeated the Klingon ship."

"Ambassador, I regret to report . . . a stalemate."

Zhad sharpened his glare on Worf, but spoke to Urosk. "Relieve Meliosh as first officer. He does not deserve the rank!" He held the communicator before the captain's face.

"He is a competent warrior, Ambassador," Urosk said in a tone that Riker almost recognized as one he'd often heard from Picard.

"Do it!"

But Urosk hissed at him in the Hidran tongue and pulled him toward the far end of the hall.

Riker rubbed his tender shoulder and croaked out an order for Worf to keep an eye on them.

Nodding, Worf handed the Hidran weapon to Riker. The Klingon shifted his own phaser to his right hand and set out to follow the two Hidran at a distance.

The comm badge on Riker's uniform chirped. He tapped a channel open. "Away team."

"Picard, here. Report, Number One."

"The Hidran are a bit . . . resistant, sir, but all's under control down here. They're off sulking, hopefully ready to bargain."

"Don't be too sure, Mr. Riker," Picard said. *"These are a hard people, by necessity. In their experience, those who bargain are those who die. It's going to take more than one threat to change that. I'll be down shortly. Picard out."*

Riker rubbed the knuckle of his thumb against his lower lip. He wondered if Picard meant there would be more threats, or that threats were useless. And he wondered where his part in the next move would lie. If one thing was true it was that Picard could still pluck surprising rabbits out of hidden hats.

Unfortunately, thanks to the Klingons' irritatingly early arrival, this plan of Picard's had failed. Originally the captain had hoped to talk the Hidran into accepting a conference with the Klingons, who were to arrive after Picard had a chance to make sure they understood the conditions he'd worked out with the

Hidran. The fact that neither side knew the other was coming was supposed to assure no one would cause an incident that would "politically require" the other side to drop out.

Riker shook his head. *Nothing ever,* ever *goes as planned.*

"That was a nice move with Ambassador Zhad, Mr. Data," Riker said, still keeping one eye on Worf and the Hidran across the hall. "You acted very quickly. In fact, you saved my tail."

Data nodded a salute. "Thank you, sir. However, I was surprised by Captain Urosk's attack. I did not expect him to underestimate my abilities."

Examining the Hidran disrupter he rolled in his palm, Riker chuckled. "You assume it's obvious that you're an android, don't you, Data?" he asked, thumbing the weapon's safety.

"I have never considered it, sir. I suppose so."

Riker looked up. "Why wouldn't he think you were human? Because you don't look *exactly* like other humans?"

There was silence as Data considered.

"Let me put it this way," Riker continued. "Would you notice minor variations in a Hidran's appearance?"

"I believe so, sir."

Riker swallowed a sigh. "All right, would *I* notice?"

Data paused and considered that too. "I do not think so, sir," he said finally.

Riker shook his head, a chuckle rising in his throat—

"Drop all weapons!"

Riker swung toward the unfamiliar angry voice. A woman's voice.

Who was she? And why was she pointing a phaser at him?

As she stomped toward the *Enterprise* officers,

silver-blond hair brushing her shoulders, she kept her weapon high in spite of the two armed security men flanking her. "I said drop them."

"I'm Commander Riker—" he tried to explain.

"I don't care if you're the president's personal shoe stretcher! There was phaser fire in here, and that wasn't part of the bargain. You're the ones holding the phasers. *Put them down!*"

Riker looked from her to the security men and back. Hired help. One of them had his weapon's safety on.

"Okay." He shrugged, holstered his phaser, and nodded for Data to do the same. "They're down. Now, who are you?"

She took another step toward him, her phaser angled down only slightly. Impatient hazel-green eyes blazed with a steady determination. "What's going on in here?"

The rent-a-bicep security men were less resolute. They wanted to be behind the woman, not next to her. There was probably nothing in their three minutes of extensive training that mentioned anything about pointing phasers at someone in a Starfleet uniform. Starfleet personnel just weren't the bad guys. They were the ones called when the bad guys showed up.

"I asked you first," Riker said.

"Barbara Hollitt. I'm in charge here."

Yes, you are, aren't you? Riker suppressed a smile. She was not gorgeous. Not a vision. But she was exciting somehow, attractive.

"What happened in here? I was assured there'd be no problems."

"I'm sorry, Ms. Hollitt," Riker said, gesturing to the dark smudges where Zhad's disrupter had scorched the floor. "We had a little trouble, but it's under control."

She glanced from the floor back to Riker. "See that it stays that way, please."

17

"We will," Riker said. "And something tells me that if we don't, *you* will."

Barbara smiled and a spirited flash glinted in her eyes. "Indeed I will, Mr. Riker."

"Not less than twelve men, Picard," Kadar said.

Picard tapped his communicator off and leaned his compact form against the meeting hall's granite table. "Mr. Riker, what about the Hidran beaming down twelve crewmen?"

Riker turned to Data who shook his head.

"Impossible, Captain." The first officer clasped his hands behind his back. "Their landing party is only outfitted for six."

"Then have them add six more to their regular team, gentlemen."

"It is not that easy, sir," Data said. "The Hidran need to breathe one hundred percent humidity with a substantially higher oxygen mix. The masks they wear are surgically implanted and only a few members of their crew are so equipped."

The captain let out a short breath and touched his comm badge. "Captain Kadar, you will beam down only six crewmen, including yourself."

"Twelve," Kadar insisted.

"Six. Not twelve. Not seven. *Six.* Picard out." The captain hit the communicator again and it signaled off. "Everything is a struggle," he muttered. "If the Hidran have six men, the Klingons want twelve, and then the Hidran want twenty."

"I'm afraid I sympathize with the Klingons on this one, sir," Riker said. "The Hidran are a tough lot. Anyone who can win a war with the Klingons . . . Their *ambassador* eats Klingons for breakfast."

Data's eyes widened. "Sir?"

"Don't be so literal, Mr. Data," Picard said.

The android lowered his gaze. "Sorry, sir. They are

a curious people. Early contact with them by Federation surveys classify them as combative, but hardly as hostile as they are now."

"Seventy years of war might change that, Commander," Picard said, taking on that professorial tone Riker knew too well. "The Hidran had to be harder, stronger, to survive a war with the Klingons. The Hidran may not have won, but they certainly did not lose."

Riker stood straight by his captain's side, but his focus was not on his duties. Barbara Hollitt had entered the hall by the far doors, and his thoughts faded away from his responsibilities. He shut his eyes, tried to listen to Picard—the man whose control he envied, whose demeanor he wanted to emulate.

". . . you too would find that which was necessary to survive."

"I am fascinated, sir," Data said.

Picard nodded. "Splendid, Commander, because I want you to do a little research into the Hidran side of this conflict. We're quite familiar with the Klingons' history. All we know of the Hidran is that, like the Klingons, they claim both victory and victimization. Find out what you can. Perhaps the Hidran will allow you access to their computer banks."

"Aye, sir. That should give us a different perspective."

"Indeed." The captain raised a finger. "Also, I want a frequency shield to block unauthorized transporter and communicator use during the negotiations. I need no last-minute maneuvering by either side. But we will want to keep access for ourselves."

Data nodded. "We could blanket the planet in a white-noise transmission, sir. That would mask out their frequencies but leave certain coded ones available to us."

"Good. I want that within the hour."

"Aye, sir. I believe that from the sensor array we can transmit a——"

Picard cut him off with a wave of his hand. "Yes, yes. Work now, explain later, Commander. Dismissed."

"You Klingons know nothing but death. You should taste of it yourselves!"

"You, Zhad, are not fit to be killed!"

"And a Klingon is not fit to kill me!"

"I'd like to test the truth of that statement."

"Are you calling me a liar, Klingon?"

Twelve faces, wrenched in anger, sat at opposite ends of the large table.

His hands hidden beneath that table, Riker gripped his holstered phaser. He flexed his fingers, trying to cool his sweaty palm. He wanted to shift the weapon to his left hand but refused to take it from its holster if it wasn't necessary. And he just knew that in the one moment when the phaser was out of hand, he'd need to use it to stun a violent delegate.

"Make sure no one dies," Picard had ordered, giving Riker the most difficult task of all. He knew they had weapons—security couldn't very well frisk-search official government delegations. They'd be insulted and, *boom*—the talks would be over.

No, this was the only way. Riker just had to be sure his timing was right. A shot too soon, and the Federation would be taking sides. A shot too late, and someone would die. The line was painfully fine.

He clutched the phaser handle tighter, tense fingers squeezing the perspiration from between his knuckles. He was a raw nerve, with nothing to rely on when his moment to act might be, if at all, except for Deanna. She sat at his right and had promised to touch him, mentally if necessary, if the feelings of hate in the hall grew to the point of murder. His eyes would shift between her and the delegates, and he prayed he wouldn't be looking one way when he should've been looking the other.

He glanced at her, and lingered too long. She wrung her trembling hands, all the emotions biting at her, twisting her heart as well as her head, while Picard sat on the other side of her, relaxed, withdrawn. The only thing missing from the picture was a book in his hand and his legs outstretched over the table.

"You will stay away from our mining planets or we will destroy you!" Zhad spat.

Kadar pushed himself half out of his seat, pressing his palms flat on the tabletop.

Riker stretched forward a little, ready.

"Those planets are ours! They are the spoils of war!" Kadar roared.

Picard looked from Kadar to Zhad, waiting for a response.

The Hidran ambassador's color grew ruddy with anger. "The treaty we were forced to sign was a one-sided piece of rubbish. We have the moral obligation to deny its edicts."

"You were forced into nothing!" Kadar pounded his fist on the table and the vibration sent a computer clipboard clattering onto the floor. Riker forced a flinch inward.

Zhad hammered the table with both fists, as if to one better the Klingons with his own storm of anger. "You assure us no alternatives and call that choice?"

Picard said nothing, but this time looked up with intent. There was something more than insult there. With the Hidran insulting the Klingons, the Klingons insulting the Hidran, and both threatening death for what had seemed like hours, finally they'd grown weary enough to deal with actual issues. And Riker knew that had been Picard's wager.

Kadar rumbled to the captain, "The Hidran lies

about a treaty that is one-sided in *their* favor. It is obvious that nothing will come of these . . . discussions."

"We lie?" Zhad bolted from his seat.

Riker moved his thumb on top of the phaser's trigger.

"Sit down, Ambassador," Picard ordered.

Zhad remained on his feet, his thick legs pressed against the table, his fists tight rocks against his thighs. "Do you not hear these lies? Do you listen to your 'trustworthy' allies?" he hissed.

Picard's eyes hardened and he stood abruptly, his chair grinding the floor as he pushed it back. The captain paced over to Zhad and pulled out the ambassador's seat. *"Sit down."*

Indignant and offended, Zhad sat back down. "I will be talking with your superiors, Picard," he muttered. "You have ruined these negotiations."

"No matter. The negotiations are over."

A brief roar fell into mutters, then into death-like tacitness as Picard's glare seemed to strike every eye—except Riker's.

"You've had the chance to talk. You chose to argue instead. Kadar, the Hidran need aridium shielding for the power reactors you left them—"

"That they *took* from us—" one of the Klingons bellowed.

"Irrelevant!" Picard hammered down the outburst. "They have the reactors, they need the aridium. Only you can supply it. You will."

Kadar folded his arms and sat back. "Really?"

Picard ignored him and pivoted toward the Hidran. "Ambassador Zhad, the Klingons need the vaccine for the virus they contracted on your planet."

"A virus they were blessed with while *destroying* our planet!" Zhad interrupted.

"That's all in the past," Picard said. "The treaties were signed twenty years ago. The war is over. Perhaps

22

that is what distresses you. So much hate, so much anger . . . and no one to kill."

"You are mistaken, Picard." Zhad burned Kadar with a glare. "I *have* someone to kill."

"Not here, Zhad. Not on this planet, and not in Federation space."

"Velex isn't a Federation colony," Urosk countered. It was the first time the Hidran captain had spoken in more than an hour. Riker had expected him to be one of the more vocal delegates, but he hadn't been.

"Velex is a Federation protectorate," Picard corrected firmly, "and there is a starship in orbit."

With that threat Picard let the anxiety grow. That the delegates weren't human didn't matter—apprehension showed on every alien face.

Picard began moving around the hall, stalking, closing in on each side as he spoke. "This is the way it's going to work, gentlemen. The Klingon Empire will supply an amount of aridium that will be determined and collected by the Federation. On the Hidran side," he said, holding the back of Zhad's chair, "Ambassador, your government will give the vaccine to us, and when both sides have contributed, they will receive the supplies they need."

Zhad twisted around in his seat. "What is to gain by these talks if we get nothing but the aridium? Will they stop raiding our outer planets' mining colonies? Will they continue to harass our vessels?"

"I don't know, Ambassador," Picard said frankly, "and I truly do not care. I *can* tell you that you gain your life, and the lives of your people. Your power plants will safely produce the energy your society needs."

"And Kadar gains the health of his people," Riker said, a more relaxed thumb over his phaser's trigger. The captain hadn't really needed his help, but two rational voices were always better than one.

Picard nodded. "The Klingons will get the vaccine for a crippling disease that neither kills nor is curable."

"We will not consent to this," Kadar said. "They must agree not to attack our mining ships."

Zhad gripped the arms of his chair until his fingers were a bright pink. "The mining ships that destroy the planets of our system! We will not agree unless they arrest all mining!"

"Enough!" Picard barked, moving back to the head of the table. "The only terms of this agreement have already been stated. The Hidran get the aridium, the Klingons get the vaccine. That is all. It is agreed."

"It is not agreed!" Zhad wailed. "You have no right to delegate terms to us, Picard."

"Really, Picard! How dare you presume to tell us when we agree—"

"To what, Kadar?" Picard asked. "To survive?"

Kadar and Zhad exchanged a hateful look, then turned it to Picard. The captain appeared to be struggling to keep a smile from his lips. He had achieved his goal and angered the two parties into working together—against him. They were finally joined in something, Riker thought—their resentment of the captain.

"You will agree to these terms or the Federation will not help at all," Picard said as his comm badge sounded. He hit it immediately. "Not now," he snapped, and stabbed it back off.

"Perhaps the Federation's help is bought at too high a price," Zhad hissed.

"Perhaps," Picard agreed bitterly. "Perhaps it will take your cities growing dark and your people freezing before you put behind you the prejudice of a war twenty years passed." The captain then spun about toward Kadar. "And perhaps it will take a disease destroying your fleet before you can do the same."

Kadar averted his gaze.

Zhad looked down at his ruby fist for nearly a full minute. Then, in his first calm moment since his arrival on Velex, he said, "You seem to leave us without alternative. But let me tell you this, Picard. You and the Federation have much to learn. You think that because you have had a form of peace with the Klingons for some time that they are like you. You are wrong. You may be worthy of trust, Captain . . . but it is naive of you to think the Klingons are the same." The ambassador rose slowly, calmly. "I suspect you will regret your dealings with the Klingons, Picard. I know I will."

Chapter Three

"I APPRECIATE THIS, CAPTAIN," Barbara said. "Private operations so far out just don't see state-of-the-art equipment."

She gestured to the small cluster of makeshift buildings that made up the Velexian industrial colony. Except for the ancient meeting hall, they were sparse boxy structures, built more for function than form. She gave Riker and Picard the grand tour, all five minutes of it, and diminished her accomplishment at building it all in a week's time. That wasn't what she was here to do. Anyone, she thought, could dig a hole and pitch a tent—colonies had been popping up everywhere for hundreds of years.

But Barbara was supposed to be investigating the planet's native crops, not just starting a colony. She wanted to get past building labs and opening boxes. She'd run into difficulty, and she worried about explaining her problems to those who had hired her—at her insistence—to market the Velexian grain.

"We set up a few labs with some basic equipment," she said, "but resources are tight. I'm hoping the reason we can't scan the indigenous flora is because our equipment is inadequate."

Captain Picard looked over the colony as if he himself were scanning it with sensors. "My science department reports that we are unable to scan your grain as well. It may contain some native compounds that evade traditional scans. Commander Data wanted to do a crust/core sample before we left to see if we could isolate the substance."

"Perhaps we could work together, Captain?"

"We're always willing to share our facilities as time provides, Doctor," Picard said.

"If your facilities can help me figure *that* out, I'll be indebted." Barbara pointed toward the rolling saffron-colored grain that could be seen at the eastern edge of the camp. Where the dirt path ended, grain began, and ran into the horizon. It waved her forward, stalks of jasmine swaying and calling in the breeze. They paraded down to the edge of the camp, where the field began suddenly, an army of wheat marching to the tune of the wind.

Picard plucked a stalk out of the ground and turned it back and forth in his fingers. "It looks like normal grain. What's so mysterious beyond the sensor problem?" He handed the tawny stem to Riker.

Hands behind her back, unwilling to touch it herself, Barbara said, "Well, it grows in soil that has few nutrients. We tried transplanting on our second day here, to see if it would grow on other planets, in systems closer to the trade routes. It withered and died the next day." She lowered her voice and glared out at the field. "As far as we can tell, it shouldn't be growing here at all. Nothing should."

"I'm afraid I haven't done my homework," Riker

said. "What's so important about this particular grain?"

"Everyone wants it, Mr. Riker. I admit I didn't believe the myths and stories myself, but I tried it personally earlier this week. It has the strongest medicinal effects of any unprocessed naturally growing flora ever discovered. When ingested . . . well, it has a measurable effect on your health."

"You mean it makes you feel better," Riker said.

"No," she corrected. "You actually get better. Nothing miraculous that we've found yet, but we've measured some physiological improvements. The effect varies from person to person and species to species."

"How does it work?"

"I honestly have no idea," she said quietly. "That's why I agreed to host this circus you call diplomacy. I need your computers, Mr. Riker. I need your technicians. I need your assistance. And if I can't solve this one little problem, I'll need another job."

"I'm sorry. I hope we can help." Riker pressed her shoulder and guided her away from the grain. He preferred her spirited smile to the frown that touched her lips now. "We should be getting back."

She nodded and they started toward the meeting hall, three pairs of boots plodding along the gritty stone street. "Captain, I can set up some simulations and tests and leave them running, if you'll allow. Once the initial data is in, I'll return for the feast we're having tonight. Despite little to celebrate, I've been talked into commemorating our first week here. You, the delegates, and any members of your crew who wish to, are welcome to attend."

"I appreciate your hospitality, Doctor," Picard said. "It might be just the thing to keep our friends occupied while we await final treaty confirmation from the Hidran government. I only hope the use of our research labs can return the favor to you."

As Riker held open one of the thick wooden doors to the hall and allowed Barbara and Picard to enter, she smiled, that certain kind of glint in her eye again. "Perhaps Commander Riker will return the favor."

Riker flashed his best "little-ol'-me?" grin. "Whatever I can do . . ."

"Be my escort tonight?"

After the slightest nod from Picard, Riker said, "I'd be honored."

She turned smoothly on a heel, her silver-blond hair swinging softly behind her. "I should be back by three o'clock. Anyone here can tell you where my home is. Will you meet me there?"

Before Riker had the chance to answer, she was back out the door, and he and Picard were alone.

The captain crossed his arms. "Three o'clock is closer to teatime than suppertime, Number One."

Riker shrugged and his brows went up. "Would *you* argue with her?"

"Deck twelve."

Data's order to the lift barely allowed Barbara to slip between the doors before they began to close.

"I am sorry, Doctor. I did not realize you might be unaccustomed to the turbolifts."

"I'm not usually. I should have been watching," Barbara said, trying not to stare at him.

There wasn't a scientist in the Federation who hadn't heard of the android who'd joined Starfleet, but relatively few got to meet him. Sure, there were interviews and early studies, every once in a while "A Discussion with Lieutenant Commander Data" would be the cover story of some tech journal, but he was hardly at the beck and call of anyone with curiosity.

What surprised her so was that he hadn't anticipated her hesitation into the lift. Wasn't he an advanced calculator with legs? Wasn't he supposed to consider *everything?* That's what computers were for —to search out possibilities and run them down to conclusions. It was the reason she was begging time from a Starfleet supercomputer. So that nothing would be left out.

She averted her gaze from him—it?—and studied the slit between the lift doors. What did one say to an android? Did computers do small talk?

Anything was better than silence.

"I appreciate all your help, Commander."

The lift doors opened and this time he waited for her to exit. "I am happy to assist you, Doctor. The captain ordered me to investigate the Hidran side of the Klingon-Hidran conflict. I have downloaded their own history texts and can easily view them from the research lab you will be using."

She smiled, a bit more nervously than she would have liked, and they started down the corridor. Happy. He was *happy* to assist. Just using an expression?

"How close are you to marketing the grain," Data asked.

Barbara looked up at him curiously. "You know about our plans to harvest for marketing?"

The android nodded. "I requested information from your company regarding Velex when we were ordered to this sector."

One thing was clear—Data learned fast: at the research lab he held his hand over the open door and waited for her to enter.

The android waved her in. "Right in here, Doctor. This should suit your needs."

Beyond his pale hand was the finest, brightest computer Valhalla that Barbara had ever seen. She was impressed not only with the bank of computers and equipment that was now at her fingertips, but that such things, like the android next to her, were possible. She felt as if she had been years away from such new technology. And she wasn't likely to see any soon. They just didn't risk new equipment on long-shot colonies in the middle of nowhere.

She stepped into the lab, unable to imagine any problem being insoluble with help like this at her fingertips. This was what she needed. This was why she had risked having time-bomb negotiations in the middle of her burgeoning industrial colony. With these—the brains of a starship—she might make it all work out.

"Thank you," she murmured.

"My pleasure, Doctor."

She looked at him, and at the bright canary-yellow eyes that were not even supposed to connote emotion, but seemed to. "Wrong, Mr. Data. The pleasure is all mine."

"It is safe, is it not?" Data poked at the pellets of grain that rolled around his palm.

Barbara hesitated. "It's safe," she said flatly.

"You do not sound quite convinced."

"I would be more convinced if I could find out *why* it was safe." She dabbed at the station's panel, turning herself away from the thoughts of past tests, and toward future solutions.

Data looked from the grain to her, then back to the grain. "What exactly will it do?"

An android looking for a cure-all? She chuckled at the thought. "To you? Probably nothing. With most people it's highly therapeutic. I mean, it's no fountain of youth, but it does have a measurably positive effect. It brings about a homeostatic condition in the body. Race or species doesn't seem to matter." She cocked her head toward the grain. "Go ahead. Try it."

"Species does not matter?" Data asked. "But races can differ so widely. One race's nourishment can be another's poison."

"There are seventeen races in my colony. All tested and all reacted favorably. That's the mystery, Commander." She smiled. "I don't think it would hurt you."

Data brought his hand to his mouth, tossed in the grains, and swallowed.

Barbara lowered her gaze back to the console, then looked back up when he spoke again.

"Interesting," Data said, pressing his lips into a thin line. "I am unable to determine its molecular makeup."

"Pardon?"

"That is how I taste, Doctor. I suppose you might say I have tasted better."

He *tasted?* Then what was it about him that wasn't human? Or did he just "say" he tasted? Why did this android, in form and function created to be like a man in every way, have those bright yellow eyes and that sallow color of lifelessness? The ship's computer spoke to her in a similar tone. What was it that made him different from the computer she was programming now? The thought distracted her, made her uncomfortable, curious.

But every moment she spoke to him, every moment he spoke back, that discomfort melted away.

The android's face fell blank for a moment—blanker than usual anyway. "I detect no change in my internal systems."

Barbara smiled. "I'm not surprised. The bread it makes doesn't affect my toaster, either."

"I am far from a toaster."

Her smiled faded and she felt her face flush. "I'm sorry. I didn't mean any offense—"

"I cannot be offended," he said. "How long does it usually take to affect someone?"

"Well, it depends on the person. Sometimes immediately, sometimes a few hours. But you're an android . . ."

"I do have certain organic fluids," he said. "Perhaps it will only take more time with me."

With a pat on Data's hand, Barbara said, "I wouldn't hold my breath."

Perplexed, Data shook his head. "Neither would I."

It was blinding light and a small pang of irritation that brought Lieutenant Commander Geordi La Forge from the *Enterprise* to the planet below. He always avoided directly blaming the prosthetic VISOR that allowed him his sight. Doing so seemed . . . unappreciative. But the transporter could sometimes cause such a flash, especially when a strange frequency was being used, or extra power was added to the matter push. And both were happening thanks to the captain's order of a transmission jammer.

When his vision cleared and the pain dulled into a normal ache, he saw Captain Picard near the meeting hall's large table and walked toward him.

"Glad you decided to join us, Mr. La Forge," Picard greeted.

" 'Us,' sir?" Geordi scanned the room and saw only a few colonists setting up small tables at the far end of the hall. "I hate to be the first to break it to you, Captain, but you're alone." The chief engineer smiled. "Where is everyone?"

"We have two security details keeping the delegates separated until the dinner," Picard said. "The Hidran government's approval should come through any moment and we can sign the documents after dinner."

One of Geordi's brows shot up. "Hidran and

Klingons eating together, sir? Sure you're not asking for too much?"

A corner of Picard's mouth turned down and Geordi assumed the captain had been wondering the same thing.

"You'd think that a race intelligent enough for space travel would be rational enough to use discussion to settle differences," Geordi said.

"One would think so," Picard said sardonically. "Wouldn't one?"

Sunlight streamed through the windows and folded itself over the pillows scattered across the floor. Riker lightly brushed Barbara's cheek where the butter-colored rays caressed her milky skin. He couldn't remember feeling so comfortable with anyone . . . not since Deanna.

"I don't usually fall into bed after I've just met someone," he said.

"We're not in bed," Barbara said, rising. She smiled and as she rose, the brightly colored throw that had been around her collapsed into the bars of sunlight. The brilliant reds and forest greens of the blanket caught the light and tossed it throughout the room. "But that is good to hear, even if I don't believe it," she added as she walked into the next room, her nude form also catching the light as she left.

Riker pushed himself up against the overstuffed chair that held his empty uniform. She disappeared through the doorway and he chuckled softly. He didn't know what it was about her. All he knew was that she either understood that social graces were left floating near the dock when you spent your life tearing through the galaxy, or she didn't care about them in any case.

From the folds of his collapsed uniform, his communicator sounded. He dragged the red tunic toward him and pressed the arrowhead comm badge. "Riker here."

"Deanna here, Will. The captain wants us to report to the meeting hall as soon as possible," she said.

"On my way," Riker said quickly.

"Where are you? I'm on the western side of the colony. I could pick you up on my way."

He and Deanna might not be together anymore, but they tried not to rub each other's nose in the fact.

"I'm *far* on the other side. I'll meet you there. Riker out."

He jabbed the communicator off.

School teachers and empaths, they could always tell. Never lie to either.

"Trouble, sir?"

Riker was all business. He stood laser-straight between Deanna and Barbara, and looked only at Picard.

"Possibly." The captain raised a silencing finger and spoke into his comm badge, his voice low. He wanted to assure neither the Hidran nor the Klingons across the hall overheard. "Repeat for Commander Riker what you just told me, Mr. Data."

"Aye, sir." Data's voice seemed to boom from the communicator's speaker and Picard quickly thumbed the volume down. *"The white-noise transmission blanket is taking considerably more power than it should. Sensors indicate the source of absorption is somewhere on the planet's surface."*

Riker moved forward and asked into the comm badge, "Any ideas as to what's causing it?"

"Nothing concrete. However, I am formulating a hypothesis."

35

Picard allowed only a brief pause. "Well?" he prodded.

"I suspect the Klingons may have some covert operation under way, sir. They may have found a way to breach the transmission blanket. It would explain the energy drain. Or perhaps they have a cloaked base of operations somewhere on the surface."

"Activity from the Klingon ship?" Picard asked.

"Nothing at this time, sir," Data said.

"Any indication that they have another landing party on the planet?"

There was a pause, then finally Data answered. *"No, sir. But the transmission blanket is interfering with the accuracy of our own sensors."*

Picard felt his brow furrow. No proof. He could hardly go accusing without evidence. In fact, he could hardly go accusing *with* it. The last thing they wanted was to upset either delegation. And both the Hidran and the Klingons were ready to welcome any chance to scuttle the progress that had sailed so calmly until now. Calm being relative—no one had been killed yet. "Very well, Mr. Data. Do what you must to get to the bottom of the situation. Commander Riker and myself will see what we can find out down here. Picard out." He tapped the communicator off and nodded toward the delegates. "Mr. Worf and the security detail can handle the dinner, Number One. I want you to see if you can find the source of this energy absorption Data is talking about."

"Aye, sir." Riker tried to relax his posture, his muscles.

Picard hadn't noticed the man was a knot of tension until the tightness began to fade.

"Captain, do you still think it's a good idea to have Worf around?" the commander asked. "It didn't work well this morning."

"I do," Picard said. "The Hidran need to see that the Klingons have indeed changed in some ways. Worf is an excellent example of that."

Riker nodded.

Perhaps it was for the best. He seemed pleased with the order that would take him away from the dinner. And Picard could send Deanna as well. He wouldn't have to keep considering the effect of all this hatred on her. Neither delegation liked having an empath present, and it was exhausting for the empath as well.

"You and Counselor Troi can take one of the low-atmosphere craft the colonists use." Picard turned to Barbara and quickly added, "With your permission, Dr. Hollitt."

"Of course, Captain," Barbara said.

Picard smiled a thank-you and looked to Riker.

Once again the first officer was a clenched fist, his spine beam-straight.

"Picard to *Enterprise*."

For all the festive noise that filled the hall, all the laughing and talking and chattering that came from a hearty dinner, it was the silence that was irritating Picard. The silence of the Klingon and Hidran delegates who sat brooding at each other across untouched plates. The silence of a ship that refused his call. *His* ship.

The captain pursed his lips and shook his head at Commander La Forge. He tapped his comm badge again, searching for a better channel. "Picard to *Enterprise*."

Finally: *"Data here, sir."*

"What the devil took so long?" Picard demanded.

"Sorry, sir. I am the only one with clearance to override the transmission blanket. I was occupied for a moment."

There was the slightest delay in the android's response. Probably the fault of the white-noise blanket.

"I didn't order restricted clearance to communications for *Enterprise* personnel. Why isn't Mr. La Forge's communicator working?"

"I took the prerogative of deactivating all communicators on the surface aside from yours and Commander Riker's, sir. In case someone were to appropriate them."

"I see," Picard said. "I want them *re*-activated, Commander. If Mr. Worf or another member of the security team needs to reach the ship, I want them to be able to."

"Aye, sir," Data said in his normal, even tone.

"Stand by to beam Mr. La Forge up." Picard turned to the engineer. Geordi's coffee-brown features were twisted into a pained mask. The captain grabbed the man's elbow, waiting to lend him support at any moment. "Is it worse?"

Geordi struggled to force a smile. "Well, bad enough to get me to leave a meal halfway through."

"Report to sickbay as soon as you're aboard. And no matter what the doctor says, I want you to rest that stubborn head of yours."

Geordi gasped and pressed the heels of his palms against his throbbing temples. Agony, spikes of it, ripped through his head and down his spine.

Eyes that never saw the warmth of light now burned as if open to the sun. He thrust his VISOR away, far way.

Aching knees wobbled and gave, and he crumpled toward the transporter pad.

Hands grabbed him before he hit the floor and he felt his cheek against a body he could not see.

"Emergency medical team to main transporter room! Hurry!"

The universe was a blur of pain, until needles of white and sharp yellow finally melted into blackness.

"No, thank you." Captain Picard placed the flat of his hand over his glass and nodded the waiter off. He looked down the length of the main table and nearly sighed. Twelve beings, two races, and not a damned thing for them to agree on. For two hours they had just sat there, not eating, not talking, not finding any common ground as Picard had hoped they might.

"This isn't going well, Mr. Worf," he said, leaning toward the tall Klingon standing at his side.

Worf looked from the stoic Hidran Ambassador Zhad to the somber Klingon Captain Kadar. They headed their separate delegations of dark, angry comrades.

"It is not, sir?" Worf asked wryly.

Picard suppressed a smile. "I've been to more joyous funerals."

Worf glanced down to meet his eyes and tried to force away a smile.

"Perhaps 'funeral' is a poor choice of words," Picard added.

"Indeed."

Picard nodded. "But not wholly inaccurate." He looked up at his security officer and wondered just what it was that allowed Worf to joke about an issue that had his Klingon cousins ready to start another war.

"What do you make of all this, Mr. Worf?"

The tall Klingon leaned down, as if he wanted to be sure only the captain heard his deep voice.

"I expected as much. From both of them."

Picard's brows drew up in surprise. He knew it was a look that demanded Worf elaborate.

"The Hidran are quick to anger, sir," Worf continued. "You have forced them into an agreement, the benefits of which they do not yet fully understand. Captain Kadar on the other hand is more enraged at the dishonor. His hand has been forced. Through his indignation, he can barely see it was in the only direction he could move."

"You don't side with the Klingons on this matter?" Picard asked.

"They are wrong," Worf said in that matter-of-fact tone that no one would dare take issue with.

Picard pushed out a short breath. "They're being stubborn."

"Stubbornness is a Klingon trait. Being wrong is not."

Nodding, the captain said, "Prove it to the Hidran."

Worf thought for a moment. "How?"

The captain's eyes thinned and he studied the Hidran delegation across the hall. He looked smartly up at Worf and gestured toward the ambassador. "Distrust passes with familiarity. Why not show them who you are?"

With forced gentility and a dozen Klingon eyes burning into his back, Worf awkwardly lowered himself into the seat adjacent to Ambassador Zhad. Not in front—not across from him. *Next* to him.

It went against his grain, and he had to force the tension from his muscles and wrench a casual look onto his face.

The Hidran turned his head and hammered Worf with a glare. "What is this?"

"It is a dinner, where honorable beings may meet and break bread together," Worf said calmly. Maybe too calmly. It was a strange balance for him: his tone had to be severe enough to warrant respect, yet soft enough to broadcast appeasement.

Zhad said nothing. He stared. Everyone was staring —the Hidran, the Klingons, Picard. Another knot in Worf's spine.

Worf reached out for the platter of grain-bread in front of them, and as his fingers touched the handle of the knife, one of the Hidran began to rise.

The Klingon stopped, let his fingers fall to the table. He looked up to see Urosk gesturing the Hidran soldier back down.

One slice with the knife and Worf had a large piece of the Velexian delicacy. He made sure he held the knife not one moment longer than necessary.

Tearing the bread into two chunks, he dipped one into a dish of gravy and held the other out to Zhad.

The ambassador looked away. "Better to die than eat with a Klingon," he spat.

It was Worf who remained silent this time. He would not prove Zhad right about all Klingons by speaking in anger. His race was inflexible—he did not have to be. He had the cushion of a Terran upbringing to support him, and he could use that hereditary Klingon obstinance to make sure he did not slip into impulsiveness.

"Do you fear me so much that we cannot have a meal within the same walls?" Worf finally asked.

Zhad turned so quickly he nearly spun out of his seat. He grabbed the bread from Worf's hand and pushed it through the electronic field in his breathing mask. A loud gulp and it was down—whole.

They locked eyes, Worf and Zhad. Klingon and Hidran. Enemy to enemy.

No, not enemy. Worf knew he was not the enemy. Neither friend nor foe, he was a symbol, and the irony of that nipped at him. He would never feel fully Klingon, yet here he stood to represent all Klingons. An alien on Earth and *Qo'noS,* he fit only in Starfleet, and now found himself the embodiment of two cultures that would never completely accept him. That *he* could never completely accept.

"If we can have a meal in common, perhaps we can share a trust," Worf said slowly.

"We will share *nothing!*" Zhad pushed back his chair and sent it grinding across the floor. He turned, his slick black cloak twisting around him as he stormed through the nearest door.

Worf glanced back at Picard, but did not wait for an order or even gesture. He rose, and followed the ambassador out.

The gall of these animals.

Zhad angrily paced the dim corridor. The only thing worse than an arrogant Klingon was an insufferably condescending Starfleet Klingon.

He wondered if even Picard fully trusted Worf. Or was it just another of the Federation's tricks?

How could he learn to fight the urge to crush those ridged skulls? How had the Federation? It was no secret—Starfleet had been at odds with the Klingons for decades. How did Picard now trust a phaser to a Klingon on his own crew?

"Ambassador?"

Zhad pivoted toward the deep baritone he knew was Worf's. His muscles tensed and he readied himself for the attack.

"I have not come to antagonize you," Worf said.

"Your existence antagonizes me—as your people have done for a hundred years," Zhad sputtered.

His throat felt tight and he adjusted a control on his mask to allow himself more air.

"War is a fire that can rage out of control, Ambassador," Worf said. "But only when both sides feed the flame."

"A Klingon saying for every occasion, *Starfleet*

Lieutenant Worf?" Zhad snorted. He took a step closer to the Klingon he nearly towered over. "You slip into stereotype. Do you know the Hidran reply to your saying? How many times must we be blistered before the flame is finally smothered?"

"I am sorry," Worf said. "I did think there was some hope for you. I see I was wrong."

"Don't you pity me, Klingon mongrel!" Zhad balled his fists and leaped forward. If anyone needed a few hard jabs of pity, it was this pompous Klingon.

Worf jerked up his arm and belted Zhad away.

Pain knocked Zhad off his feet and pinched his eyes shut. He fell hard on his knees, then rolled forward, his hands covering the breathing mask that had been pounded into his face.

"My apology, Ambassador," Worf said as he turned to the door that led back to the main hall. "I hope in the future we can both learn to feed the flame a little less."

The Starfleet Klingon left, abandoning Zhad in a puddle of pain and awe.

Zhad's throat was parched with anger and hate. Still somewhat dazed, he straightened his tall frame and worked his way to his feet. If Worf had stayed another moment, *he* would have been on the floor now. And there would have been no getting up.

Too much of a coward to even finish what he starts, Zhad thought.

Taking a deep breath, Zhad felt the scratchiness of dry air. He adjusted the mask control again and felt a twinge of pain ripple through his body.

He sucked in another breath. Dry. Too Dry. Like the grit the Klingons filled their own lungs with.

Frustrated, Zhad snapped at a dial on his mask. "More moisture," he muttered, then found himself doubled over in agony.

He gasped, tried to suck in a breath. Any breath. Couldn't!

His hands flew back up to the mask and grabbed wildly. No air! His chest heaved, his lungs sharp and tight. He struggled to tear the mask away—to gulp any air if not his own.

Wet fingers clawed at the tubes that now burned his skin. He yelped in pain and twisted them out. Anything! *Anything to stop the pain!*

He felt warm blood drain from the holes in his cheeks down his shoulders and into his skin.

Staggering forward, he looked at the air tubes that had once fed him life. They now dangled useless in his hands. He coughed a dry hack . . . and knew he was dead.

The Klingon! He'd known just where to strike the blow! Just where to snap the mask and force it to destroy its owner!

Hatred took over where panic left off. Zhad drew the dagger hidden in his cloak. His throat closed and his chest ached for freedom from its desert grave. He scrambled up, determination the only wind his lungs could feel.

He nearly fell through the doorway and into the hall, a trail of blood pouring from his exposed mouth.

Where? Where was the Starfleet Klingon? Where was Worf! *He* did this thing! *He* would pay!

Vision began to cloud into a mesh of color, and the ambassador cursed himself a fool for not killing Worf when he'd had the chance.

He held the dagger close and squinted across the room.

No one moved toward him. The hall was alive with noise, yet all he heard was the silence that was his absent breath. Worf was too far across the hall, and Zhad knew he would not reach him.

Another Klingon—closer. *Any* would do.

He would avenge his own death, and prove to his people that the Klingons could not be trusted.

He croaked out a puff of air, and took in the alien breath that was sand in his lungs.

A moment passed, and felt an eternity.

Zhad fought to focus . . . feet away . . . one Klingon . . . alone . . .

Slowly, the Klingon delegate began to turn. Zhad saw his victim's eyes. It was his due, to see the look on the Klingon's face as they met death together. *Everything has a price, Klingon! That you shall learn!*

Zhad drew back his arm, and with all the strength he had left, with all the strength his people had left, plunged the blade down.

The Klingon's hands moved too slowly to stop the dagger from piercing his armor and cutting through his rib cage. Zhad reveled in the feeling of sinew tearing against steel, bone cracking against hate. A gush of alien blood warmed his cold fingers.

The Klingon's grunt shook the room, and he fell back, pulling Zhad down with him.

What a sight! What a shadow they would cast, both of them collapsed into a heap in the center of the hall's floor. His death . . . his victory . . . how the legends would be!

He struggled to raise his head one last time, to taste with his eyes the Klingon's blood that gurgled round his blade.

Zhad saw, and savored his success for a final, fleeting moment.

Slowly, his hand fell away from the dagger that triumphantly stuck in the Klingon's chest: a flag beckoning on the brink of war.

Chapter Four

"EMERGENCY STRETCHER to main transporter room! Stat!"

Beverly Crusher lifted Geordi's head gingerly off the transporter pad with one hand and ran her medical scanner over his tearing, sightless eyes with her other.

"How'm I doin', Doc?" Geordi croaked out softly, droplets of perspiration streaking down his skin.

"You're going to be fine," she told him.

It was a lie. She didn't know that. She wasn't sure of anything right now. It was just what doctors told patients when they were critical . . . what doctors told themselves when those patients were friends.

Beverly glanced at her hand-scanner for the third time in as many moments, then gazed at Geordi again.

Not a brain hemorrhage. Not an aneurysm. Not something simple. Nothing she could just give him a pill for and make go away. And no magic technologi-

46

cal wand to wave. This was the kiss-and-jab of being a doctor to her closest friends: she could cure them when she knew the answer, but had to watch them suffer when she didn't.

Setting the scanner down, she slipped her hand into Geordi's and held it tightly.

Suddenly he convulsed, every muscle pinched and shaking. He writhed forward, plunging off Beverly's lap and onto the transporter dais.

She dived for him, scooping up his head, keeping it from cracking against the hard deck.

Pain seized his body—a hot poker of agony that jerked his muscles one way, then the other. She reached around and hugged him—half motherly instinct, half medical training—keeping him from hurting himself.

The readout on her tricorder told her nothing she couldn't see for herself: Heartbeat—rapid. Breathing —shallow. Perspiration—by the bucket. The pain indicator on the graph might be malfunctioning, but not as badly as Geordi was.

Did she dare give him a pain depressant without knowing the cause?

His neck was a knot in her hand as he pitched back and forth. He cried out, and his hands flailed back up to his temples, fingers scratching at the glowing implants.

She yanked her head up to the nurse and pointed at the medkit. "Four CCs zenapantocene!"

Geordi's trembling body went slack as the hypo hissed into him.

She pulled his limp body back onto her lap and slipped her hand back between his slack fingers and squeezed.

"Come on, come on! Where's that damn stretcher?"

* * *

The turbolift droned upward. Rushing was always too slow when life was at stake.

Beverly Crusher bounced on the balls of her feet, as if to lighten the drag on the lift or get her closer to the deck . . . *something.*

She hung tightly on to Geordi's hand, her thumb lightly brushing back and forth against his clammy skin. Too clammy.

The lift released them, but the door to sickbay was still an endless corridor away. They hurried, Beverly's long red hair an annoyance in her eyes as they ran.

People . . . walking . . . in the way . . . "Move it!" *Doctor's orders.*

They exploded into sickbay, Doctor Crusher barking commands. The room became a beehive, with Geordi its center and goal.

"Lifesign indicators at minimum, Doctor."

"Get him into the bio-bed—activate a sterile field."

"I want that cart over here. And move MacCaffy out of the way!"

"Where?"

"Post-op."

"Set up cranial scan!"

Beverly ushered the medical team over to the diagnostic bed in the middle of the room. She had to pull her hand free of Geordi's—not from any grasp of his weak fingers, but from her own.

"Set up the O.R.," she ordered the young medic who'd closed Geordi into the diagnostic table. "I want a complete neurosurgical team standing by. Dr. Peiss to assist."

"Raenna is already on her way."

"Good."

Beverly paused a moment, looked down at the stretcher that held only Geordi's VISOR now. The eyes without their master. Or was the VISOR the master here? Was it the reason he was now in sickbay?

She turned away from it, looked back to Geordi, and frowned at the sight of his unconscious body. So lifeless . . . with that bright, humming diagnostic equipment enveloping him. It flashed, pulsed, clicked . . . as if it were alive for him.

Fumbling with the bio-bed control pad, Beverly cursed her fingers for not working right, not knowing the places on the console that would be second nature if . . .

She ordered another doctor over, and pushed herself toward the wall comm. "Sickbay to Bridge."

"Yes, Doctor," Data replied after a moment.

"We're running tests on Geordi," she said quickly, turning to the screen next to her, taking in the initial data from the more comprehensive scans of Sickbay's sensor bio-bed.

"How is he?" Data asked.

Beverly shook her head. "Not well." She poked something into a control panel on the wall, shook her head, cleared the screen, and tapped it in again. "He's sedated, but still in a great deal of pain."

"Cause?"

"I don't know yet," she said, and cursed the fact. "I can't seem to relieve the pain. Maybe a viral infection." She pressed her lips together and frowned, dissatisfied with her own non-answers. "I don't know," she repeated quietly. "The area around his neural implants is inflamed."

"Diagnostics are running on the transporter systems to discover sabotage, if any. Have you found such evidence?"

Beverly's brows wrinkled in confusion. "Sabotage? No." She shrugged, wondering who would do such a thing—and why. "I'm going to have Bioengineering look at the VISOR, though."

"Understood, Doctor," Data said. *"Contact me when you know more."*

The channel beeped closed and she pulled in a breath, her brow wrinkling. "Your concern is underwhelming," she muttered, and looked back to Geordi. *For godssake, Data, what could possibly be more important than your best friend?*

"Computer."

"Ready."

"Request access to primary and secondary communication frequency controls."

"Access denied. Command security code required."

"Override command security code, personal authority."

"Confirm authority."

"Lieutenant Commander Data, currently in acting command of *U.S.S. Enterprise.* Reference ship's log stardate 47511.3"

"Pro tem command only. Access denied."

He tapped quickly into the control panel.

"Access denied."

He paused a moment, thought, then typed again, longer this time.

"Restriction released."

"Re-restrict primary controls, my personal code."

"Complete."

"Encode all secondary frequencies with encryption procedure in file 'Commander Data two-zero-three point five-nine-three.'"

"Encryption complete."

"Computer, link all frequencies through my console."

"Complete."

"Function switch, main database."

"Database ready."

"Search all sub-bases, Klingon military tactics. Topic: covert operations. Subtopic: espionage. Cross-reference: Hidran-Klingon conflict of twenty-two ninety-two."

"Searching . . . Complete. Four hundred thirty-six files found."

"List topics."

Data glanced over them rapidly, then pecked a few orders into the console.

"New cross-reference: current Klingon tactics based on military reports."

"Complete. Seventy-seven entries found under Tactical subtopic, one-hundred fifty-one entries found under Federation/Klingon Liaison sub-topic."

"List entries, maximum speed."

"Stop squirming!" Deanna snapped.

Riker pulled away, more from her tone than from the pain in his leg.

She pulled the bandage back around his calf and twisted. His hand lurched off the control panel and the small shuttle rocked. Deanna found herself jammed between Riker's leg and the small alcove under the console.

Flying manually by choice was exhilarating for Riker—*having* to do it was just nerve-stretching, and his injured leg wasn't helping.

She pulled herself back up, grabbing the ends of the makeshift bandage again.

"Watch it!" He reached down, flexing his toes and feeling the caked blood that had stuck his uniform to his calf. He wanted to rub at the wound but couldn't bring himself to reach any farther than his knee.

Deanna slapped his hand away and the *flitter* shook again.

"Just let me do this, and you fly the ship," she said. "Why not try to get the autopilot working?"

"Can't be fixed for the same reason we can't reach

the captain. *Enterprise*'s white-noise blanket must be having some effect on it." He stabbed at the autopilot control, then felt the ship shudder and lose altitude. He quickly turned it off. "We'll just have to continue manually."

She twisted at his bandage again and he grimaced. "That's a little too tight, Deanna," he said, squinting at the console in pain.

His only answer was a bandage that pinched even closer around his leg.

"You're cutting off my circulation!"

"You're 'circulating' all over the deck. I'm trying to stop the bleeding."

They'd been sniping at each other since takeoff and he was ready to let himself circulate to death if it would quiet her up. She'd wanted to turn back when the ship had lurched and he'd crammed his shin into the jagged edge of the console panel. He had decided they'd go on.

Riker didn't believe that their minor disagreement was what edged Deanna's emotions, though. Maybe she hadn't released the tension she'd absorbed from the delegation. . . . He didn't know, and he might have cared more, *if* she hadn't been taking her anger out on the gash in his leg.

What kind of transport doesn't carry a med-kit? Riker glanced back around the small shuttle the colonists used for short-distance surveys. It was old and small, with barely enough room for the two of them and their tricorder. A thick layer of gray dust covered every surface. Riker had wiped down the controls before powering up, but that had only removed a decade of grime.

Dust—and the sight of his own blood. Things he usually enjoyed living without.

He sneezed, and his leg pulsed with pain. The small

ship jostled again and he and Deanna grunted as she bumped against his leg.

The pain and the frustration weighed upon him, with her anxiety a mound on top of his own. He struggled to keep his glare on the small craft's controls and off her as she worked on cleaning and dressing his mangled shin and calf. Well, maybe not mangled, but it *felt* that way.

"We should turn back." she said.

"No," he growled, burying his thoughts in the console, pounding at the controls. Too minor a reason —he wouldn't turn back just because he was in a little pain.

He looked down at the strip of uniform that now acted as his bandage. A laser suture on board *would* have been nice, or even a roll of gauze, but the lack of either wasn't enough reason to squelch a mission.

"We have our orders. I'm not going to let this stop us."

Orders. He bent his lips into a frown. The captain had asked the impossible—not unusual for Picard— but this time Riker saw no reasonable way. Thousands of square kilometers of land couldn't be surveyed in a flying dinghy with a souped-up tricorder.

Deanna gave a final tug at the bandage and pulled herself out of the small crevice she had been folded into. "It's not a small injury, Will. No one's been on this planet long. We don't know what kind of microbes . . ."

She let her sentence trail off.

"What kind of microbes what?"

She settled into the only other chair, the copilot seat, and looked out the starboard window. A real window. With real blue-green sky and endless fields of grain below.

"Nothing," she murmured.

He pursed his lips and silently fumed, unable to stem the burst of emotion he knew would probably catch Deanna's empathic attention. He could feel her staring—those know-all-tell-nothing eyes of a counselor—and wondered where the intimate eyes of a friend had gone. Or did he even want them?

And what did *Thomas* Riker see when he looked into Deanna's eyes?

There was a strange and confusing turn of events. Recently Riker decided he led a . . . well, an *odd* life. What normal person wakes up in the morning to find that a transporter malfunction years ago had created an exact duplicate of himself? It had been strange to look in *that* mirror . . . to see a man he could have been—*would* have been—had things not happened at certain turns in his life.

Thomas Riker, as Will's duplicate now called himself, had been stranded early in his—their?—career, marooned at an abandoned post. That *Lieutenant* Riker, as he would remain while Will Riker received two promotions, lived his life not among the stars, but scraping an existence from day to day. Thomas Riker only dreamed of the life that *Will* Riker was actually living. More than that, Tom Riker was still in love with Deanna Troi.

Not so surprising, that. So why wasn't Will Riker? And why did he feel those twinges of jealousy and guilt when Tom and Deanna had began . . . or was it continued? . . . where he and Deanna had left off?

Maybe he was still in love, in a way. He still enjoyed her company—more than any woman he had ever known, but he wasn't really interested in rekindling anything at this point, was he? Falling in with Barbara was evidence of that. Then why did he feel those twinges?

It probably didn't matter. Deanna wasn't interested

in Will Riker anymore, it appeared. She was interested in Tom Riker. Even if Will *did* want to rekindle anything . . . well, he didn't know if that was possible. It all depended on Deanna, and she wasn't an open book right now.

What else was new? For a psychological counselor she was a master at uncovering other people's feelings while shielding her own. She could sense, feel and report on others, but so often bottled her passions while seeming to be open.

Right now she didn't even seem that, and it was beginning to annoy. Since when didn't she confide in him?

Since Tom.

The manual control, the frustration of not even knowing what they were looking for . . . it *all* had worn on him. Mile after mile of grain and mile after mile of edged talk was not a prescription to stop the throbbing of his leg *or* to find what on the planet was absorbing *Enterprise*'s energy.

All he was sure of so far was that Velex seemed to be a giant power sponge that soaked up the white-noise blanket with fervor.

Every last bit of the flitter's reserve power had been diverted to sensors to hack through that blanket. That left manual navigation turbulent, and what energy was left being drained by the planet as well.

He gritted his teeth and tried to think about his piloting more than anything else. If he was going to be resentful about something he should at least take it off of her. She could be reading him. Another problem with empaths . . . they'd leave their victims wondering what thoughts had been "listened to."

Each attempt to block his emotions just frustrated him further. Like trying to blow out a camp fire, he was only fueling what he'd hoped to smother—

flagging for perusal those thoughts he wanted hidden. The harder he tried not to be read, the easier he would be to read.

"Sensor penetration?" he asked, knowing the answer was the same as ten minutes ago.

She looked from one screen to another. "Twelve kilometer radius and holding."

Monotone. Distant.

Dammit, Deanna!

He was looking at her, and she snapped her eyes up to his.

"What?" she asked, perplexed.

Riker hesitated, then decided to push forward. "What's with you today?"

She looked at him for a moment, then looked away, back toward the window. "I'm not sure."

Concern thumped around his gut, pulling his jaw tight. His leg throbbed with the pumping of his heart but it seemed the least of his problems.

He stared at the back of her head, then looked out the starboard window, trying to follow her gaze to whatever it was she saw, or felt.

He leaned over, nudged her shoulder.

"Deanna, I didn't mean to snap," he offered a bit softer, knowing it should have been a lot softer.

She shook her head a little, looked up. "You didn't," she murmured.

"You all right?"

"Fine."

But she wasn't.

"I know when you're fine. What's bothering you?"

She turned to him, those mahogany Grecian eyes catching his and pulling him in. There was such confusion pasted on her face . . . pain almost—worse than when she was swept up in a tempest of emotions that were the Hidran and Klingon delegations.

56

She stared at him a bit longer, looking the little lost girl. Perhaps trying to put thoughts into words.

He glanced out the window, made a course adjustment, tried to lose his tension in the churning jasmine fields below. Tried to, but couldn't and swiveled back to her.

They rode up and down an air pocket and she said nothing. Riker got the feeling she was trying. Her knuckles were white marbles on her lap and he half twisted out of his seat to face her.

She inhaled deeply and let it out slowly, folding her hands together thoughtfully on the edge of the console. "I don't quite know how to put it."

Riker tapped the autopilot control, but the white-noise blanket still interfered with compu-nav-sensors and the computer refused his command again. He grumbled something and had to turn back to the console. "Tell me what you're feeling."

"This planet . . . there's something unnerving about it," she said slowly. "It was barely noticeable before . . . but as we get farther from the colony . . ."

From the corner of his eye he noticed she was looking out the port again.

"The planet makes you 'uncomfortable'? What could do that?"

Cocking her head to one side, as if listening to something in the distance, she focused her eyes on a remote point and whispered, "Nothing."

Riker's brows knitted. He shifted toward her, forgetting their mission to scan and just allowing the flitter to travel off in a relatively straight line.

She bit her lower lip softly, then finally spoke. "What do you hear when you go to the beach?"

His brows shot up. "Excuse me?"

"Seriously," she said. "What does a beach sound like?"

57

"People—"

She cut him off with a wave of her hand. "No. Say you're alone."

He shrugged, briefly wondering why he'd be alone on a beach. "Birds, the surf. I don't know. What else?"

"Right." She nodded. "Even blindfolded you'd know you were near the ocean. Entire planets are like that for Betazoids. The millions of life-forms, from insects to people, put out a sort of . . . hum of life. I can sense it. Sometimes I can even tell one planet from another by how it *feels* to me."

"How does this planet feel to you?"

There was a cold silence for a moment, but Riker suddenly realized it wasn't an emotional cold. It wasn't passionless. "Picture your beach without sound," she said. "The tide coming and going silently as if you were deaf. But you could still hear the sound of your own voice and your boots crunching the sand."

The image sent a shudder down Riker's spine. It was the stuff of nightmares.

"Maybe a better way to describe it is like walking down that beach breathing stale air." She was raising her voice now, almost angry at the situation. "It sickens you. Suffocates you."

Riker frowned again. "What do you think it means?"

She gripped his arm, her fingers now talons and her eyes burning with small tears. She was scared. One emotion he hadn't thought of—*she was scared.*

"As sure as we're alive, Will," she said, "I know this planet is dead!"

"Klingon! *You are dead!*"

Urosk's bellow cracked through the hall and yanked Picard to his feet. It echoed as Worf spun to see Zhad's form collapse over a Klingon's. Worf looked up at

Urosk, and the indicting Hidran finger that meant to bore through him.

Picard followed the line of Urosk's arm straight to Worf's eyes. Surprise tinted the Klingon's features only a moment before becoming angled with strength. He bent his knees and braced himself.

Captain Picard vaulted over his table, phaser drawn, and stabbed at his communicator. *"Enterprise!* Beam down emergency security team!"

Urosk, down on one knee, grabbed the dagger in the dead Klingon's chest. The armored corpse jolted up with the blade, then fell back down as Urosk shook the body free. Urosk hurtled forward, toward Worf.

Picard bolstered his foot against the edge of the table in front of him and shoved. It went sliding across the room, grinding toward Urosk. It slammed into the Hidran captain, barring his way to Worf for the moment.

The other Hidran smashed their chairs on the hard stone floor and instantly each one was armed with a strong, threatening club.

Splinters flew as wood cracked against marble and the Klingons suddenly had equally sinister weapons.

The Hidran captain held his blade, clamped tight between rust-red fingers. "I *will* kill you myself, Klingon!"

Picard pulled Worf back and squared off with Urosk himself. A moment more and another security team would beam down around them. Picard would have to hold them off until then.

But no shafts of light and sparkle appeared. No hum filled the hall, and Picard's phaser seemed less and less adequate in his palm. He didn't want to end up with a roomful of stunned carcasses. That would save Worf's life, but lose the Klingon-Hidran peace. Not exactly how his mission orders read.

He looked back at Worf, hoping the Klingon

wouldn't lose his cool in the shadow of Urosk's posturing. Worf was not the only one he had to worry about—the remaining five Klingons came up behind his security chief, flanking him. Protection?

If so, the protection was capricious at best. With five Hidran, five Klingons, Worf and Picard, all crushed into a few square yards in the center of the festival hall, something had to give.

Picard jabbed at his comm badge again. *"Enterprise!"* He heard the dull electrical tone that told him the channel was blocked.

"We will have vengeance!" Urosk cried, grabbing a club from one of his men and shaking it wildly in the air.

Kadar clutched at his own dagger. "We are the ones who shall have that!"

Picard's muscles tensed and he balanced himself against a possible onslaught. His eyes became slivers and he quickly pinpointed the positions of his few security men and Barbara's two guards. If it came down to sheer numbers, he had control. Unfortunately Klingons and Hidran could count as two apiece—their rage turned even odds into poor ones.

"Hollitt!" Picard called, "Get your people out of here! Close off the hall!"

The Klingons closed tighter on Worf to barricade him, yet moved forward toward their foes.

Kadar put his hand on Worf's shoulder. "We will stand with you."

The security chief pushed away. "I stand with my captain."

Picard wasn't sure if Worf was acting out of loyalty or tactics, but he heard and nodded as his officer moved out from between the cloister of his protectors. It looked bad to have Worf with them, as if there had been some conspiracy to kill the ambassador.

The Hidran pushed closer, and the two groups

began to square off against each other, space-faring races who'd clung to daggers in their lust for death by any weapon.

The captain gestured for his personnel to surround them. He hardened his shoulders, looked briefly at Worf, then back to the throbbing mass of hostility that called itself a diplomatic delegation. Civilized pretense had been lost. A pretense he was supposed to have preserved.

"Phasers—on stun," Picard said, rather quietly, to Worf.

Kadar, blade in hand, bulldozed the table between him and Urosk. They were feet apart and Picard thumbed the trigger of his phaser. A brilliant orange rod of power slammed into the floor between the two adversaries. A whine of energy rang throughout the hall, and dark smoke settled onto a frozen audience.

"There will be no more death today!" he thundered.

Every glare blazed rage and hate.

Indignantly, Urosk shook his knife in the air. "We have had enough of your idleness Picard! Let us fight our enemies or become an enemy yourself!"

"You don't want to be my enemy, Urosk," Picard barked. "I will not have this. Cease, and we will find the cause of your comrade's death."

Kadar held his dagger in one hand and gestured to the fallen Klingon with his other. "Will we not see why my first officer died, Captain?" he bellowed.

Picard nodded at the bodies. "His murderer is dead. What more would you seek?"

The Klingon turned toward Urosk, his blade outstretched, his voice a low, threatening growl. *"More."*

Urosk dived forward, crimson arms extended, cloak flowing.

Picard locked eyes with Worf and gave the slightest of nods. Worf fired, and a sizzling lance pinned the Hidran captain.

Urosk deflated, falling back into heap of groggy confusion.

The Klingons seized the moment and rushed forward.

Picard pointed, a threatening motion. His finger marked Kadar.

The Klingon commander toppled to his knees, dazed by the blast from Worf's phaser. Orange rivulets of spark grappled his form, and his knife clattered onto the stone floor.

The captain looked from dagger to dagger, Hidran to Klingon, and wondered how many other traditions they shared but would admit no common ground. Their problem was not their differences, he thought, but their similarities.

He tacked back to the remaining Klingons. Four violent, savage scowls gouged with surprise. Not only had a Starfleet ally phasered down the commander of an Imperial Battle Cruiser, but Worf had fired the blow. Bitterness overpowered his pride in Worf's loyalty, though. The captain nodded and said: "Phasers will now be set to *heavy* stun."

A grating hum filled the hall and pressed into them as every energy weapon sang with more power.

"Shall we go at it again?" Picard asked harshly.

One Hidran officer, his furious eyes defiantly burning into Picard, exploded toward the Klingons.

Worf's phaser came up but Picard pushed the Klingon's hand down and fired his own weapon.

The Hidran officer snapped forward, then convulsed and went flying back, his weapon clattering to the floor.

No one reached to pick it up.

"Well, gentlemen," Picard said, pitiless, "how do we get ourselves out of this bloody mess?"

* * *

"We demand the right to prosecute him! A Hidran court must judge this matter!"

Urosk had unfolded himself from off the floor and now stood before Picard. If the Hidran captain was still feeling the effects of the phaser stun, as he should have been, he wasn't showing it. He pulled the dark cloak around his slick skin and took in a short, angry breath. "Well, Picard?"

A good two feet shorter than the Hidran, Picard somehow managed a glare that looked *down* at Urosk. Worf still at his side, the captain holstered his phaser and nodded a firm chin toward the Klingon. "And then execute him, Captain? I think not."

"We have our rights!" Urosk bellowed.

"And so does Lieutenant Worf, Captain."

Urosk scowled at Worf and ground those sharp little teeth that flashed through his mask. "Murderers have no rights, Picard. Especially Klingons."

"I am not convinced a murder has been committed by anyone other than Ambassador Zhad," Picard said. "I assure you an investigation—"

"Investigation!" Urosk twisted away then pivoted back. "And while you act to protect your security chief, do not think I will not act on my own!"

"You'd better not." Barbara Hollitt came up beside Picard. She held her own weapon, and matched Urosk glare for glare, her green to his. "Everybody in this hall is under house arrest until further notice."

Urosk's face crumbled into a scowl. "By whose authority—"

"Mine," Barbara said coldly and turned to Picard. "My guards will remove the Klingon delegation to the back hall. No one comes in or out without my say-so."

Picard nodded approval, glad the Klingons would be separated from the Hidran, but uneasy with Barbara's guards doing the job. Where were his own?

Why hadn't his communicator connected with the
Enterprise? What other problems were burning elsewhere?

"I will not stand for this, Picard," Urosk said.

"You will," Picard said slowly, darkly, "whether
you wish to do so quietly or not I do not care, but you
will do it." The captain leaned closer to Urosk, over
and up. "I am in control of this situation, Urosk, and
if anyone else gets injured it will not be me or my
people."

The Hidran captain's wide florid lips snarled up
into a smirk. "That we shall see," he said, and spun
quickly on his heel, leaving a swirl of sour air twisting
under Picard's nose.

He and Worf shared a glance as the captain
pounded his comm badge. "Picard to *Enterprise.*"

"Data here, sir." There was no delay.

"Where in hell were you ten minutes ago?" Picard
demanded.

"In sickbay with Dr. Crusher, sir," Data said in
something slightly more concerned than his normal
tone.

"Geordi?" Picard asked quickly.

"Yes, sir," Data said. *"After beaming up he collapsed on the transporter pad. He has been in emergency surgery since eighteen twenty-two hours."*

Picard's brow furrowed, his skin felt tight. "Surgery
for what?"

*"To have his temple implants removed, sir. A total
malfunction of his VISOR bio-circuitry."*

Picard's gut twisted and he suppressed a shiver. His
crisp hazel eyes focused on Zhad for a moment. "Is he
in any mortal danger?"

"No, sir. Not at this time."

"Keep me informed every step, Mr. Data."

"Aye, sir."

Thoughts of Geordi still chewing at him, Picard

pushed on to more pressing matters. "Commander, when I needed communication with the ship—"

"Yes, sir. Sorry for any delay. I was transferring all frequencies to my control for security purposes."

The captain looked up at Worf and shook his head. "Quite inopportune, Mr. Data. We needed an open channel."

"I am sorry, sir," Data said. *"I thought there may be a chance that the Klingons could use our open comm channels if we left them available. They have used similar tactics in the past."*

"Any evidence of unauthorized use?" Picard asked.

"No, sir. But I am pursuing a hypothesis."

Pulling in a deep sigh, Picard nodded. He didn't want to step on any of his officers' initiatives, but Data might have caused problems, even deaths.

"I understand what you were trying to do, Commander, but you'll have to work on your timing. More harm than good might have come of it."

"Aye, sir," came the simple reply.

"Any word from Riker?"

"Not yet, sir."

"Contact him and have them return directly here. A small energy drain is the least of our worries right now."

"Yes, sir."

"Can Doctor Crusher leave Mr. La Forge?"

"Once she's out of surgery, I believe so, sir."

"Have her beam down as soon as possible. There have been two deaths." Picard's eyes narrowed on Zhad's collapsed form, still crumpled over the Klingon's dead body, soaking in a pool of alien blood. "I want to know if *both* were murder."

"Stabilize!" Riker pounded the console with his fist. "Come on! Come on! Get up there!" he scolded the flitter as it pitched forward and down, a burst of power burning through it.

He slammed hard against the console as Deanna toppled out of her seat.

"What the hell was that?" he choked, pushing himself away from the controls, trying to fill his aching chest.

"I don't know," Deanna groaned, pulling herself back up into her chair.

Riker scanned the different computer screens and worked to balance the shuttle further. He wasn't used to roller-coaster rides where he could plummet to his death. He also didn't usually yell at his equipment, but with only Deanna here . . . well, this wasn't the bridge of the *Enterprise.*

"Sensors show we just passed through that anomaly you read. No energy drain down there."

"I'm reading something else." Deanna swiveled away from her console. "There's a sensor beacon here." The tone in her voice was less anxious than before. Telling him what she'd been feeling, getting into words what she hadn't even been able to get into thoughts, must have taken a weight off her shoulders. Unfortunately, all the weight was now on his.

Riker punched up the visual on his screen. A lump of barren rock at the center of a wild grain field stared back at him. He looked out the port window and saw the same: gray-brown slabs of stone chunked together in the middle of all that wheat.

"As if someone dropped their cargo from a quarry ship," he said.

Riker had the *flitter* circling wide around the outcropping. He punched in a command for a tighter spin, then looked up at Deanna. "What do you think?"

"I don't think it's naturally occurring," Deanna said. "It *is* broadcasting a beacon, Will. Weak, and certainly not on a Starfleet band, but on someone's. If we hadn't been looking . . ."

"Maybe someone's trying to hide it," Riker said, thinking aloud. He shook his head and a few strands of dark hair fell over his brow. "But you don't hide something from someone who isn't looking. Anything you want to hide you make sure is hidden when someone *is* looking."

She looked at him for a moment as they were quiet. He angled back toward the port and looked down at the boulders and sheets of stone that were suddenly so out of place on a planet of continuous fields.

"We should report back to the captain," Deanna said.

"Agreed, he needs to know what you've told me . . . but this is too good to pass up. Let's try and take back more information than 'the planet makes Deanna fidget.'"

He rubbed the back of his neck. "That didn't come out the way I meant it to, Deanna. All the tension, now this puzzle . . . Can we forget that comment with a few other choice ones I've made in the last few hours?"

"And I thought I was the empath." Deanna smiled. "You read my mind."

He laughed, reached for her hand.

"Okay," he began, "we'll find out a little more, then head back."

She nodded, gave his hand a squeeze, and turned back to her console.

"Square one," Riker said. "What kind of broadcast is it?"

Deanna shrugged. "Short. One or two seconds, then it repeats."

"Try a standard hail on its own wavelength."

She tapped at the console, then lifted her head. "Nothing."

Riker began to tap his foot nervously, then remembered the pain in his leg. He winced and sucked in a quick breath.

"Computers ask standard log-in questions. Maybe this is some kind of a log-in computer prompt, asking for a response or a command," she suggested.

"That would take forever to find," Riker said. "Try simple codes."

A moment later she shook her head.

His hand dropped back down to his knee and he rubbed. "My kingdom for a bullet to bite on."

Deanna continued to type something into her board but stooped down to check Riker's bandage. "Is the pain worse?" She asked. "You're bleeding through my handiwork.

"I promise to wash it before I return it."

She shook her head. "Why are you so stubborn?"

"You love it," he said, bobbing his brows up and down, giving his bearded face a devilish tinge.

"There goes your rating as an empath. The only thing I'd love right now is a *medical* doctor looking at your leg."

"We'll compromise. We'll try a few more things. If nothing works, we head back."

She nodded agreeably. "Okay. What next?"

"Try anything," he said. "Play back its own signal, transmit a binary request for communication, whatever." He watched her peck away at her console. "Something's down there," he said. "We can't scan under the rocks, yet we get a beacon *from* them. The signal can't be from the rock itself, can it?"

Deanna gave a soft shrug. "Transmitting. Maybe we don't have enough power to penetrate the rock with *Enterpri*—"

Suddenly Deanna was quiet. Riker twisted to ask—
Craaaaaaaack!

Riker slammed to a stop in mid-motion, his muscles straining against air that suddenly was thick as wet sand against his chest. He couldn't move . . . saw Deanna at his side . . . motionless . . . turned to stone.

With all his will he tried to push against whatever fist held him in its grip. What was it? He didn't care. He wanted to turn, to breathe, to move.

His muscles ached, his head pounded with pain . . . there was no give from whatever held him. Riker felt himself trembling against the strain, but knew he wasn't really moving. Frustration held him as tight as the paralysis.

From the edge of his vision he saw the dim gray rock spiraling up toward the port window.

His vision abruptly fogged to black. He could still hear the whine of air rushing against the shuttle, and there was horror when the awful whine began to fade.

It ended with the crunch of metal collapsing against rock.

He felt a twinge of soreness ripple through his body, then . . . nothing.

Chapter Five

HIS FACE LOOKED NORMAL without the glowing temple implants. Eyes closed, no one would have known he was . . . blind. Beverly's mind choked over the thought as surely as her throat would have if she'd tried to speak it.

Blind. *No fooling* blind.

There was no medical reason for her to be there. She could've been checking on Riley's arm or Tsnatsu's fluid intake . . . she should have been. But she left it to others, to be here holding a hand.

Watching the movement of his eyes under closed lids, she wondered what he envisioned in a dream. Did Geordi see as she did—colors, forms, definable lines and shapes, or did he dream in whatever impulses he usually saw through his VISOR?

It struck her that Geordi hadn't really been blind since he was a child. No more than anyone who could turn their sight on and off with a desire. There was no permanence when he took his VISOR off at night, just as there was no permanence when she let her own eyes drift shut.

Now all that had changed. His VISOR was elsewhere, the implants that allowed it to work were gone—and his "eyes" might never open again.

Beverly squeezed his hand and looked up at the vitals screen, more for distraction than anything else, until Data's voice pulled her gaze toward the doorway.

"Geordi?"

"He's still under the anesthetic," she whispered, rising, yet keeping her hand around Geordi's.

Data nodded and glanced up at the monitors. "How is he?"

"Resting easily." She gently released Geordi's hand and joined Data near the doorway. "Let's talk somewhere else."

Data hesitated. He wanted to stay. Should he? No logical reason presented itself, so he turned and followed the doctor out.

In silence they walked to the next door and entered Beverly's office. She let out a long sigh and fell into her desk chair. Beverly looked tired, eyes weary, shoulders weaker.

"I guessed right," she said. "Removing the bio-neural implants worked."

"Guessed, Doctor?"

Beverly looked up at him, then back down. "Without time to review procedures on the operation I had to let the computer lead the way and suggest the answers. We had to make an educated guess as to the problem."

Data nodded. Dr. Crusher had good stamina for a human, but her voice was spiritless and she seemed not to wish to go into the details Data needed. "And that problem was?" he prodded.

She rubbed her forehead—another sign she was

71

tired. "His temple implants were breaking down and inflaming his tissues." She frowned, glowering at her hands as she clasped tightly on top of the desk. "We took them out. Now he's fine."

"Then you acted correctly." Data was trying to be consoling and he wondered if it came across that way.

"Did I, Data? I let a computer be the doctor and ended up taking out a man's eyes because he had a headache. Not exactly a method of which Hippocrates would have approved." She ran her thumb along the edge of her tunic jacket and mumbled, "What's next? Decapitations for dandruff?"

She was being overly dramatic, Data decided. "I would think that out of the question, Doctor."

The slightest smile appeared on Beverly's lips. Why? Surely she didn't want him to take the comment seriously.

Beverly gestured for Data to take a seat.

He did, knowing that humans disliked an inferior position in any discussion. "Do you know what happened to the implants?"

"They looked decayed to me. Something that shouldn't have happened—the implants should outlast the *Enterprise.* Bioengineering is examining them. They've ruled out a problem with the VISOR itself." She tapped a few commands into her desk computer and swiveled the screen toward him.

Data looked down at the screen a moment. The text said nothing she hadn't told him. Why show him? Just for the sake of having done it? Humans were fidgety.

"Prognosis, Doctor?"

"He's stable now. He'll be fine . . . except for his sight."

"Is the blindness permanent?"

Speaking slowly, she whispered, "I don't know."

How was he to react? The injury of a comrade was

serious. That the disability may be permanent made it doubly so.

He knitted his brows in an expression he thought was regret.

Judging by the sadness in Beverly's eyes he probably came close.

"Doctor, I am sorry to ask you to leave, but the captain requires your presence planetside."

Her expression changed to anger without thought— once round brows now arched up. "Like hell. I can't leave Geordi right now—"

"You did just say he was stable, Doctor."

"Yes, but . . . leave? Now? Out of the question." She shook her head. "Under no circumstances. When Geordi wakes up, I have to be here. He's going to wake up blind, Data. Truly blind. Do you know what that means?"

Data thought he did, but something told him that Beverly had another meaning in mind.

"It's going to take more than an order from the captain to get me off this ship right now, Mr. Data. It'll take an act of god."

It *was* an order from the captain. What more could he say? "There has been a murder, Doctor."

Beverly's face became red. Whether from guilt or anger or disgust, Data could not be sure.

She picked up a medical tricorder from the edge of her desk. "I guess an act of stupidity is as close as I'll get to an act of god."

"Captain Picard?"

Barbara was able to catch up with Picard's gait across the hall as he stooped down to snatch a spoon off the floor. He walked so quickly she'd had trouble keeping up with his stride.

She stopped, letting him march a few paces without her. Finally he realized and turned.

73

Picard stood there, slapping the cup of the spoon against his palm anxiously. "Dr. Hollitt?"

She flattened her lips. "I'm sorry—were we supposed to be racing?"

He glared and walked toward her. "Point taken. What did you find out?"

Barbara gave an apologetic nod. She hadn't meant to be so flippant, just wasn't sure how to react to all these Starfleet people. And she wasn't sure how she felt about Riker's disappearance. A few days ago Velex had been a small colony of scientists fumbling in the fields, and she was an overworked and underpaid botany specialist. Now Velex was becoming the battle ground of a war and she was in the middle of it, worrying about a man she'd just met a few hours ago. She'd stepped into that relationship expecting nothing more than the moment, and she couldn't really explain the feeling of loss. All she really could explain was that she didn't feel Picard was doing enough to stop the entire situation from falling out of control.

But what should she do? Assert herself as leader of the colony? Or maybe just sit back and let the soldiers do their jobs.

She looked at the hard line of Picard's jaw and the captain's determined brow.

"We don't show them on scanners, but your transmission blanket makes our equipment pretty useless."

Picard nodded and they continued across the hall again. This time the captain seemed to be watching his gallop to assure she wouldn't fall behind.

He huffed out a breath and clacked the business end of the spoon against his comm badge. "Picard to *Enterprise!*"

"Enterprise, *Data here, sir.*"

"Mr. Data, I want a scan of the planet for the away team's shuttle."

*"It would be necessary to disable the 'white-noise'
transmission, sir."*

"Do so, Commander. Restore when scans are complete."

There was a pause. Too long, Barbara assumed—
Picard was surprised enough to stop his trot across the
hall.

"Acknowledge that, Mr. Data."

Barbara flinched at the bark in Picard's voice.

"Yes, sir. Do you think it is wise considering Commander Riker's failure to report in?"

The captain shifted his weight from one leg to the
other and Barbara saw his shoulders tense. Was he as
anxious to find out about Will Riker and the counselor, or was he just cross at being questioned by a
subordinate?

"Explain, Commander. Quickly."

*"Mr. Riker's unexplained absence may be due to . . .
Klingon interference. Interference that could only increase if the 'white-noise' blanket is disengaged."*

Picard looked sharply back toward the center of the
hall, a clanging noise distracting him.

Barbara followed his gaze. Just someone setting a
table upright.

"I see," Picard said flatly.

Wasn't this news? Wasn't this important? Just a bit
cold-blooded—to discuss a missing crewmen so dispassionately. Which was the android, Data or Picard?

"That's the second time you've made such an
assertion, Mr. Data." Picard was focused again, his
eyes off the table and pivoting around the room.
"Upon what do you base it?"

Barbara opened her mouth to speak.

Picard waved her off.

Instinctively she took a step back. His gesture
wasn't threatening, but was certainly a warning.

75

Will Riker was a kind, delightful good time. How did he get along with this captain? They weren't just day and night—they were separate seasons.

"Evidence is inconclusive at this time, sir."

She frowned. *Damn.* No news was . . . well, no news.

"Then carry out my orders," Picard said.

"Aye, sir."

"How soon can I expect Dr. Crusher?"

"She is on her way to the transporter room now and will brief you on Commander La Forge's condition upon arrival."

"Very well. Alert me as soon as you know something about Riker and Troi. Picard out."

The spoon clanged against the communicator, signaling it off.

Picard glanced back toward the middle of the hall and Barbara's gaze followed.

From here, Zhad's body was nothing more than a long gray blob, his tall form covered with a tablecloth. A few feet away lay a similar blob, the ambassador's Klingon victim.

"None of this is going away," she said.

"No." The captain shook his head. "It's not." He pivoted toward her. "What's the maximum range of one of those flitters of yours?"

She shrugged. "Under five thousand kilometers without refueling I'd guess."

"Spaceworthy?"

"No. Strictly low atmosphere. Captain . . ." Barbara hesitated, unsure she wanted to ask her question. She might get an answer. "What do you think has happened to them?"

Picard began thwacking the spoon against his leg. Was he finally nervous? If he was that may be worse than when he wasn't. Why was he concerned all of a sudden?

"Something's happened," he murmured. "Maybe they found something."

"Disengage white-noise transmission, Mr. De Potter."

The young ensign looked up at the android and nodded. "Aye, sir." He'd been all worked up for first shift duty, which meant posting with the captain on the bridge, and hadn't expected to be under command of the second officer. Not that it was a problem—just that Commander Data wasn't who he'd been ready for. And with a starship under his fingertips he wanted to be more than ready.

He ran his hands along the console. Nonstandard transmissions were always a problem. If he even missed *one* key sequence . . .

"Disengaged, sir."

DePotter looked down at his board to confirm the disbursement of the frequency field. Stay on top of things, anticipate questions, and you look good.

"Sir!" DePotter poked at the board again to make double sure.

Data rose from the command chair. "Report."

"Seismic activity—planet wide! It was there. . . ." DePotter looked up, expecting to see incredulity reflected back at him. All he saw was Data's expressionless face and it startled him. He stumbled. "Then it . . . it was gone a second later."

The android leaned down over the ensign's shoulder and scanned the readouts. "You are correct. Three-point-three-two magnitude for point-seven seconds."

"I know," DePotter said, then quickly added, "sir." Mistake number fifty-two since he had been transferred to his first bridge rotation a day ago . . . and he knew he wasn't the only one counting.

"Unique, Mr. DePotter."

"Yes, sir." *Shut up. Do your job. Say "aye, sir" a lot.*

Data tapped a finger at one of DePotter's console readouts. "A fleeting earthquake of significant magnitude, less that a second in length, with no after shocks."

"Aye, sir."

The last "aye" shoulda been a "yes" and the "yes" shoulda been an "aye." He was overanalyzing, and knew that introspectiveness only led to . . . perspiration.

Data stood up straight. "Ensign?"

This was it—somehow he'd caused the quake and now the *real* boom would be lowered.

"Sir?"

"Was not your previous assignment Geological Sciences?"

DePotter fought to keep himself from cringing. "Uh, yes, sir." Back to the gravel pit he went. Shortest bridge rotation in Starfleet history.

Commander Data looked down at DePotter with a serious expression. "What do you make of the situation then?"

"The quake, sir?"

What a dunsel question! Of course the quake.

The android simply nodded.

"Well," DePotter began slowly, trying to draw out his first moment of real comfort on the bridge—at least this he could answer. "There's no overt volcanic activity of any kind, but sensors have been unable to penetrate the crust. We are assuming a solid core considering the age of the other planets in this system . . ." He looked from Data to the planet's image on the main viewer and back, analyzing what he knew out loud. "I don't think there's ever been an instance of seismic activity occurring simultaneously over an entire planet. Especially one that has no tectonic activity. At least there's no recorded record of one."

Recorded record? What was that? Is that like a yelling scream?

Data nodded. "I concur." He turned toward the science station. "Scan for the away team and the Velexian shuttle, and download all sensor data on the tremor to the science station. Then reestablish the white-noise broadcast."

DePotter poked at his console, and tried to salvage his self-esteem. "Aye aye, sir."

No one could be having a worse day.

Captain Picard had given his version of a sigh again. He'd done it more than a few times in the last hour, and that concerned Barbara almost as much as Will Riker's whereabouts. She decided the outcome of this entire situation rested on Picard's shoulders, and that he was suddenly uncertain . . . well, that was something to worry about too.

Maybe there was no blessing in the captain's asking her to join him in private, but she'd needed to get out of the main hall. There was something unnerving about that room now. Two dead bodies and so little activity—no screams, no weeping, just a lone doctor hovering over them, and even she had seemed rather detached to Barbara.

Barbara wasn't sure which was better: when these people didn't seem to care . . . or when they did.

She couldn't read Picard right now.

"Thank you, Mr. Data. Let me know when you have something more. Picard out."

The wooden chair creaked as Barbara leaned forward. "Well?"

Rising, the captain began to circle the table that filled the room. He barely had room to pace.

"My science officer confirmed the earthquake. What's puzzling," the captain said, his finger whirling in a small circle to encompass all of Velex, "is that it was concurrent planetwide."

Barbara looked up, tensely gripping her hands on the arms of the chair. *"Well?"*

Picard looked at her a moment. If he wondered what she was talking about, it was only for a fleeting moment. "He also said there was no sign of the away team *or* the shuttle within the radius of its presumable range."

She could feel tears beginning to well and she blinked them away. It was crazy—she'd only met him today. It also wasn't just him—that was a lie to herself. The whole situation—what had happened to her simple plan? "Maybe an after-effect of the white noise . . ."

"Unlikely. I'm having the entire planet scanned, but if they've"—he looked down quickly, then back up—"landed somewhere, it'll take time."

She nodded and pushed herself out of the chair.

"Doctor," Picard began, as if he were deciding whether to confide in her, "has a quake like this ever happened here before?"

Back to something other than Will and his companion. Maybe Picard couldn't deal with it, so he had to think about something else. Barbara didn't know what to make of anything anymore. The only thing she did know was that she didn't like Picard's inaction.

"Ever?" She cocked her head to one side. "I can't speak to 'ever.' I've only been here a little over a week."

Picard scowled across the table at her. "What is this annoying tendency of scientists to be so damned literal?"

"That's what science is all about, Captain."

Picard gave a "harrumph" and looked down at the spoon he still held in his hand. "Dr. Hollitt, I appreciate your help so far, but I need serious answers. Has there been a similar quake while you've been here?"

She gave her hair a defiant flip. "I would have told you if so."

A simple 'no' would have sufficed—but maybe that's one of the reasons civilians like her weren't in Starfleet.

"Why do you ask?"

Asking too many unnecessary questions was another of those reasons.

Picard thumbed his lower lip and she thought he was either considering an answer, or considering answering.

"I have a hunch."

She laughed. "Ah, I see. That explains your problem with science." The laugh was nervous and she thought it showed. Here she was depending on this stranger and he had a hunch . . . What did that say about her?

"I don't have a problem with science," Picard said. "In fact, it's because of my disbelief in coincidence that I have this hunch."

"What's your hunch?"

The captain shook his head. "I don't know yet. Some possible connection with the quake and the away team's disappearance perhaps."

"You're right, that *is* scientific," Barbara said dryly.

Picard flashed a glare.

If looks could burn, Barbara would have been a cinder.

"Lieutenant Worf, reporting as ordered, sir."

Five feet from the door, Worf still blocked Picard's view of its polished wooden frame.

The captain looked up at the tall Klingon and

81

nearly said, "At ease," but knew Worf would feel more comfortable at attention.

Picard sat up straight. "Mr. Worf, we have a very delicate situation. You've been accused by the Hidran of murder, and I'd rather not exacerbate matters by keeping you on duty. I must relieve you."

"Understood, sir." Worf yanked his phaser from its holster and placed the weapon on the table. "I stand relieved."

The captain pursed his lips. Worf had spared Picard from making the longer speech he'd been dreading, but that was no real relief. He trusted Worf, believed in him, and didn't enjoy having to relieve him. He just couldn't keep Worf on duty considering the circumstances—it would only serve to anger the Hidran further.

The Klingon, still ram-rod straight, looked down and relaxed the expression on his face. "Regulations require it, sir. I would do the same in your place."

Of that Picard had no doubt. But he wondered if Worf would feel the same regret. What was the Klingon feeling now? The severity of his thick brow and that bony forehead left most emotions masked. Pride was always there. Anger, sure. Loyalty he wore like a badge. But regret? Picard couldn't remember finding regret in those dark, shadowy eyes. And as the Klingon stood there, the paragon of a soldier, Picard knew he couldn't conceal the remorse in his own.

If anything was clear from the events of the past few hours, it was that Worf was no murderer.

"Lieutenant," Picard said, waggling a finger at Worf, "we're going to prove your innocence."

Beverly Crusher closed her medical tricorder and pushed herself up from her half-kneel over Zhad's body.

A disgusting sight. Not the sight of blood or the

scent of the Hidran's wet flesh, but the sight and scent of murder itself.

"Well, Doctor?" Picard prodded. "What do you think?"

"I think they're dead." She spat the words at the captain, and meant to.

Picard shook his head. "You're not being enlightening, Doctor."

"Fine, you want to know what I think?" She crooked a thumb angrily over her shoulder. "I think the Klingon was stabbed and the Hidran had his face ripped off. That is my *official* medical diagnosis."

"Doctor," Picard scolded harshly.

She knew ironic answers where not what the captain had in mind. He never did. But to be here—cleaning up the mess of people who . . . well, who weren't Geordi. She just wanted to be up there, mending the living rather than sweeping up after the dead.

Picard gripped Beverly's elbow with his strong fingers and pulled her to his side. His tone was at once understanding and harsh. "Mr. Worf needs your help as well."

It was as if Picard knew where her thoughts were. A doctor with a ship full of patients had a thousand different concerns for a thousand different crewmen. She'd forgotten that a captain's thoughts radiated farther—the crew, the ship, Starfleet, life, death, right, wrong . . . and Geordi too.

She lowered her gaze and nodded. A little guilt was a good thing now and then, someone once said. Come to think of it, a doctor probably said it.

Worf needed help . . . okay. Maybe she could do something. "I don't know enough about their physiology to determine anything more than the Hidran died of suffocation. Maybe with some files on general anatomy from their ship and sickbay—"

The captain shook his head. "I'm afraid that's not one of our alternatives at this point, Doctor. Diplomacy."

Beverly held up her tricorder. "Science, Captain. And diplomacy has nothing to do with science."

Picard motioned to the two dead bodies. "But plenty to do with murder."

"I am not willing to sit and wait to be murdered!"

"Be seated, Batok."

"You know they will protect their own and we will not see justice! You know we will be killed!"

Captain Urosk rose slowly, evenly. If he'd had a knife it wouldn't be the tension he would cut—it would be Batok's throat. *"Sit down,* Batok."

Batok paused, testing his captain, then angrily snapped back into his seat.

Urosk knew that bringing the young hothead along was going to be problematic. He cursed his own decision. Once in space he could have backed out on his promise to allow the ambassador to choose the security force. He should have known Zhad would favor those politically aligned with him.

"The Federation is different from the Klingon Empire." Urosk spoke more to the other three, less volatile members of his party. "Even the ambassador said Picard was worthy of respect."

Batok twisted away and studied the door. "That was before Picard ordered his assassination."

"We do not know that. Worf is a Klingon. He acts as a Klingon." Urosk forced his tone down, cooler, and began to pace the room.

He had to keep control of Batok. Like Zhad, the young officer was alive for his hate. If allowed to, he would die of that hate—or for it. Urosk's concern was to see that Batok did not pull the Hidran race down with him. It was true that without strength the Hidran would have died by the millions, and it remained true. But reasonability was not weakness, and while such knowledge was common among the masters of ships, it was less evident to a people raised on venom.

"Picard is not Klingon and may not hold their biases."

Batok shook an angry orange fist at Urosk. "Picard is a Klingon sympathizer! He has one in his crew—he has been active in Klingon politics—and he speaks their language!"

Urosk pivoted toward Batok, clamped his long fingers around the young officer's neck, and pulled him up. "How many Hidran speak Klingonese, Batok? A third? More?" He shoved the young tusk back into the chair. "Shall we slit every throat that cracks a Klingon word?"

Shuddering with either fear or anger—Urosk could not tell which—Batok narrowed his gaze and looked away from his captain. The highest insult one could pay a superior.

"Perhaps," Batok hissed slowly, "we should."

No mask could muffle Urosk's intensity, his anger, as he pressed his face down close to Batok's. There would be no looking away. "Then we would've had to kill Ambassador Zhad first."

Batok's angry expression dulled, and Urosk knew he had hit his mark.

The Hidran captain turned on his heel and walked toward the door. He pounded three times, summoning the guards, and took in a deep breath of artificially moist air. He wanted to bathe, to feel refreshed by the waters of his planet, to be out of this Klingon desert.

"I will speak to Picard."

"About?" Batok asked defiantly.

"About justice for the Ambassador *and* the survival of our people."

"Good!" Batok said defiantly, as if he had won his

point. "And what if in his actions Picard proves me right?"

"Then we shall act at the first opportunity. But on my order, Batok. *Not* yours."

"Speak plainly with me, brother." Kadar faced Worf head-on and gripped the other Klingon's shoulders. His grip was tight, his smile one of admiration.

Worf did not shrug off the embrace, but neither did he clamp his hands around Kadar's arms to complete it. "Captain Picard wishes to meet with you and Urosk in private."

Still smiling, Kadar dropped his hands with a fraternal slap on Worf's shoulders. "The Hidran have thought us weak since we left their space. You were right to execute Zhad. You have restored our honor."

"I executed no one." Anger welled in Worf's chest. He could feel his muscles tighten and he balled his fists at this sides. "And you were *driven* from their space."

The words were meant to gouge at Kadar, and Worf knew they had. It wasn't just the truth that was injury to the Klingon captain—it was Worf referring to his people as "you." It was a distance never spoken by Klingons.

Kadar's dark face crumpled into offense and he stepped closer to Worf, overtly making sure not to touch him . . . yet.

"What are you?"

Worf knew the rote answer was to be *I am Klingon.* Silence furthered the insult.

"Are you my brother?" Kadar growled.

Again there was silence as Worf studied the Klingon captain's face. Was this the picture he himself cast? Was his own face this severe and cold? Was he a brother to this one who would gladly kill every last Hidran?

"I am Worf, and my captain wishes to speak with you."

Did they still kill the messengers of bad news? At this point DePotter would have welcomed death. Anything was better than reporting the demise of a superior officer. What was protocol? Should he come right out and say it?

"Sir?"

Data turned from the science station. "Yes, Mr. DePotter."

Slowly . . . calmly . . . *just say it.* He'd so wanted to find them. Wanted to save them. He didn't know what to expect—he almost thought there'd be some beacon to guide him. No such ensign's luck. Or first officer's luck for that matter.

"Planetary scans complete, sir. We've pinpointed the Velexian shuttle. It's crash-landed, sir."

"Commander Riker and the counselor?"

DePotter hesitated. He didn't know how to say such a thing. He just looked down, unable to meet Commander Data's eyes.

"No life signs, sir."

There, it was said. His heart shrank and a chill washed over him.

Data stood, pulling DePotter's gaze upward as he did. "Ensign, have you scanned for corpses?"

Corpses?

DePotter looked down at the padd he carried, as if he might find the answer there. "The bodies, sir? No, sir." One too many "sirs." And two too few bodies. The thought was gruesome. He'd just assumed that with the crash . . . and he shouldn't have assumed. "I'm sorry, sir."

Data nodded, his bright gold eyes impassive to the error. "Do not be sorry, Mr. DePotter. Be thorough."

* * *

87

Barbara watched Picard intently, not knowing if she should stay or go. She wanted to stay—to hear something about Will. Was all this talk classified between Picard and his ship?

She supposed that the tight little man would tell her if so. The captain's jaw clenched so often it was a wonder he hadn't worn his teeth into nubs. And he kept playing with that damn spoon—twirling the thing back and forth between his fingers. How anyone so brusque and affected was able to keep command of hundreds was beyond her.

"Answers, Mr. Data," Picard said, annoyed. "You're not giving me answers."

"I only have theories at this point, sir."

"At this point, Commander, I'd take readings from a crystal ball."

There was silence save for some static over the communicator. Then: *"I am unfamiliar with that reference, Captain."*

Barbara smiled and rolled her eyes downward. There was a bit of gratification in knowing that someone could ruffle Picard's feathers.

The starship captain was obviously in no mood for this. "Then you have something to occupy your off hours, Commander. What's your theory?"

Data seemed unfazed. *"I have two, sir. Since Commander Riker and Counselor Troi's bodies are not with the shuttle, they may have been taken as hostages and the crashed shuttle left as disinformation."*

"By whom? For what purpose?" Picard snapped.

"I would not presume to fathom purposes while formulating such a hypothesis, sir."

One moment he demanded answers, the next he chastised Data because the answer wasn't what he wanted to hear. Barbara had never really thought about joining Starfleet . . . and she was glad.

She was going to say something, but held herself

back. Most important thing now was to hope Picard shut up so she could hear Data's theories on Riker's whereabouts. If he had any. And she had to believe—wanted to believe—he did.

Frowning, Picard rose and walked to the small window across from him.

"What would the Hidran gain by doing so?"

Data quickly answered the rhetorical question. *"The Hidran, sir? Nothing."*

Looking out across the saffron fields he began tapping the handle of the spoon on the window sill. This all made such little sense. The Hidran had no cause. The Klingons had no cause.

"What's your second theory, Mr. Data?"

"There is some inexplicable radiation residue at the site. Conclusive answers cannot be made without local investigation since the white-noise transmission is re-engaged, but indications are the area has been exposed to some form of high energy other than the explosion of the shuttle itself."

Picard cradled the spoon in his hand as if it were a Starfleet-issue hand phaser. "High energy like a weapon?"

"That is a possibility, sir."

Disgust washed over the captain. He stared at the spoon, thumbed what would be the trigger if it were a phaser, then dropped it to the sill.

The spoon hung for a moment, left a small silver mark on the ledge's stone surface, then dropped to the floor.

Chapter Six

DARKNESS.

Not the kind that came with sleep, at night, eyes resting. This darkness was without the familiar swirls of shadows, and lacked the comfort of fading memories of color.

Perhaps somewhere else there was light, but not here. Here the universe consisted of pitch blackness— chilly and sticky, a cold sweat.

It was the blindness of death, to be sure.

She reached out to grasp something. Anything. She felt nothing. There was no feeling. Was she even moving or was there nothing there to touch? All she knew was that she *wasn't* dead. And that alone was based on the fragile idea that death didn't come with headaches. If the pounding in her head was a measure of life, she wasn't in any danger of dying.

She tried to croak out a word but found she couldn't push the air from her lungs. This *was* a nightmare. It had to be.

Motion! She felt! She'd moved! A harsh shudder

vibrated through her, like the sensation of falling just before drifting off to sleep.

"Will?"

Her own voice.

Sound! Motion and sound! What more did anyone want from life?

Her eyes were open, weren't they? She felt herself blinking. They had been closed, and now she felt the cool air on her open eyes.

There *was* light here. Faint, but lovely in its own way; pencil line shafts radiating from . . . a control panel? Sickbay? No—too cold for that—too musty.

"Deanna!"

His voice choked dryly, echoing. *Not sickbay.*

"Will?"

"Yes. Where are you?"

She heard him groan and she began to rise, but her head pounded her back, dizziness washing over her, sheets of cold fog blurring her mind. She quickly lowered herself the few inches back onto the cold slab of whatever she'd been lying on.

"Deanna, stay where you are. Don't get up quickly."

"I can't feel you," she sobbed, her voice raspy. An echo. *Not sickbay.*

"I'm right here."

But he wasn't there. Not in the sense she meant. She shook her head, or imagined she did, and tried to put into words the emotions she was feeling. Her emotions—not his. His were absent, and the loss was palpable.

"No, Will," she said slowly, trying to control the quaver in her voice. "Mentally you're not here."

Riker coughed, but Deanna could have sworn it sounded more chuckle than choke. She realized just how her comment had sounded, and some of the disorientation she felt was pushed away by the humor.

Fingertips—Riker's—on her arm, brought back her empathic sense, and his discomfort mixed in with hers. But so did his high spirits, and she felt herself sigh, a bit more relaxed.

She moved her hand over Riker's and gave his fingers a squeeze. "You're here now. Mentally."

"Will wonders never cease?"

She knew he was smiling.

The air was not as stiff as a moment ago. She pushed herself up on an elbow and moved toward Riker. In the dim light she could see he was on his knees. His usually crisp blue eyes were shadowy in the dimness. He rose awkwardly, holding on to his injured leg as he pulled her up. She leaned into him, allowing him to do most of the work, her muscles weak and tired as if she'd run a marathon.

His strength, physical and mental, fortified her. She continued to hold on to his arm as they turned toward the only light they could see.

"Riker to *Enterprise.*" He tapped his comm badge and the dull tone of a closed frequency whined back at him. "Out of range maybe," he mumbled, taking a pace toward the lighted console panels.

Slowly the room seemed to brighten, the panel's lines becoming crisper, Riker's form now well defined next to her. She could see their feet. There had been light all along—it was their eyes that slowly came on.

Three walls, smooth and metallic like the floor they had pulled themselves up from gave way to the one wall of panels and lights they now stood before. Opposite was a vertical slit that went from the top of the blank wall to the bottom. A door.

Still dazed, Deanna wasn't sure of anything. Was the momentary confusion she felt Riker's or her own? She knew there was concern that was definitely his— the feeling was powerful yet comforting. His emotions were always familiar, and their mere presence bolstered her.

"Where are we?" she asked, more to herself than to him.

Riker patted her hand and pulled away to step closer to the wall of lighted panels. "I don't know, but I'd say we've been transported here from the planet . . . wherever here is." He rubbed his shoulder as if he'd been struck hard by something. "Maybe a cargo transporter, too. Or a long distance transporter. It was a rough ride."

She felt her brows draw together. "I don't understand. How do you know that?"

He moved his hand along one of the panels, avoiding any buttons or pads. "I don't. Just assuming that what we're feeling is the aftereffect of some kind of transporter—and since it was so abusive, possibly a cargo beam." He looked above at blank panels which may have been inactive computer screens. "You ever used an older transporter?"

She shook her head. "I don't think so, why?"

"They used to immobilize you first before transport. And cargo transporters even today don't have the same comforts of personnel transports. Why waste the energy on frills? A crate won't care." He made a sweeping gesture with his phaser—when had he taken the weapon from its holster?—to take in the entire wall. "This may be a transporter console. Let's make sure not to touch anything that might set off something serious. Last thing we want is to tell whoever brought us here that we're awake and kicking."

Curiosity and anxiety were suddenly his emotions of choice, Deanna realized. They covered his concern in pulsing swells and nearly blocked out the pain in his leg. She wondered if humans were aware of the fluidity of their emotional broadcasts. When excited their feelings could be torrential, when relaxed they were like slow ocean waves ebbing back and forth almost gracefully. Human emotions held a charm for Deanna, Riker's especially.

She stepped closer to him, basking in that charm. "Who would bring us here?"

He turned back, that apprehension taking over the curiosity. "I don't know. I was going to ask you the same thing."

She could feel his anger well, beginning to pepper his other emotions. His thumb hovered near his phaser's trigger. He was waiting, readying himself.

Deanna needed to turn herself away from that feeling. She needed to do her job, and let him do his.

"Well," she began, giving the console a serious once-over, "looking at the evidence we have I'd say whoever built this console is about our height, and had digits to push buttons with. Otherwise we wouldn't be able to reach a console that they obviously need."

Admiration and a twinge of surprise now mixed with all the other emotions that had been radiating from Riker.

"I *did* go to the Academy as well," she said playfully. "Reasoning 101 is a prerequisite."

Riker nodded. "I stand admonished. All right, *Commander,*" he motioned to the panel. "I'll let you open the door without pressing the button that beams us into open space."

She glanced at the panel, then looked back into Riker's eyes. "What's on the other side of the door may be as bad."

Riker pulled in a deep breath and squeezed the handle of his phaser. "Maybe. But if we're going to find out whose ship we're on, and if we're going to deal with that, we can't just sit and wait."

* * *

"Hidran justice must be satisfied!"

Grit and dust and thirsty air ground against Urosk's skin. It was not hard to maintain ferocity in an ocean full of irritants. The Hidran captain curled his wet-cloak closer around him and hissed at Picard. He was determined to wait no longer.

Picard's flat, white teeth flashed. "Is not all justice the same, Captain?"

What kind of question? "No, it is not. Klingon justice allows for the murder of innocent Hidran. Hidran justice does not."

"Does Hidran justice allow for the murder of innocent Klingons?"

"Captain," Urosk began, imitating what he thought was a human shrug, "I have yet to meet an innocent Klingon."

Picard was quick with a response. "That may have been true at one time, but surely you can see they have changed."

Urosk cocked his head toward the door. Beyond its wooden frame was the hall where his Ambassador had died. "I see death, Picard. What is it you see in Hidran blood?"

Silence ground in Urosk's point, as he intended.

Finally Picard spoke. "I see what I see in all blood. Loss."

That answer took Urosk by surprise. If any statement could be more un-Klingon in philosophy, the Hidran captain couldn't fathom it. This was a strange alliance indeed that brought the Federation and the Klingon Empire together if they were truly this different. The question was, who controlled whom? Did this peaceful Federation hold the entire Klingon population at bay with platitudes and peaceful thoughts? Urosk thought that unlikely.

A knock at the door and Picard's hazel eyes jumped away from Urosk. Curious eyes, rather dull to Urosk who was used to a planet full of bright and glossy colors that had to radiate through the natural thickness of a humid atmosphere. Human eyes seemed alive only when they moved.

Commander Kadar pushed into the room, followed by Worf. Both were unarmed. Only Picard held a weapon, and that was holstered at his side. A better opportunity to avenge Ambassador Zhad's death might never present itself.

Urosk considered that . . . but lost the moment when the woman entered, her phaser at the ready as it always was.

"I'd like to join you, Captain," Barbara said to Picard in a tone Urosk was unable to decipher.

Unsure of what part the woman played in all this, Urosk listened intently. *She* seemed to have a good idea of her position, however, as she stepped in front of Worf and Kadar and lowered herself into the seat next to the Starfleet Captain.

"Of course, Doctor." Picard nodded and gestured toward the two remaining chairs in front of table. "Gentlemen, please be seated."

"I prefer to stand." Urosk mashed his gravel voice across the room, knowing that the Klingon ego would force Kadar to remain standing as well. There was endless benefit in knowing your enemy, and Klingons were nothing if not well understood to every Hidran who had suffered the past seventy years. The Klingons had turned the Hidran into a race of people bitter and angry, and while someday that might be forgiven, it would never be forgotten. The Hidran had been a cloistered people: a united democratic government on the edge of interstellar flight. Perhaps they were quarrelsome people in a broad sense, but they were not alien hunters who snarled their way across space.

The Klingons were. And for their own defense the

Hidran had to effectively evolve into hunters themselves.

Or at least they had to act the part.

"Picard," Urosk barked, quickly yanking his arm out from his cloak long enough to shake an accusing finger in Worf's direction, "Why isn't this Klingon in custody? Do the legal charges of the Hidran government mean nothing?"

"They *are* meaningful, Captain, and I do appreciate your concerns." Picard rose, taking on a more formal stature. "I have relieved Lieutenant Worf of duty, and my chief medical officer is currently examining——"

Urosk bolted forward. His arms swung out from under his cloak and he slammed his orange palms flat against the table, leaning forward. "Relieved him of duty? That's an outrage! Is that the penalty for murder, Picard? What is the punishment for genocide? Confinement to quarters?"

Urosk felt anger heat his face as silence skewered Picard back, mentally if not physically. The Starfleet captain's mouth was open slightly, an expression that could have been surprise. Urosk wasn't sure.

"Captain," Picard began, "I cannot act until I know what to act upon. At this point Lieutenant Worf is presumed innocent."

Urosk turned, twisting a glare into Worf's eyes. *No. A Klingon face is never innocent.*

The Hidran captain jolted his tall frame upright, away from the table Picard stood behind. "Picard, bring me your evidence of his innocence now, or I will see his blood on my hands before you can kill me for the attempt."

Chapter Seven

HE STRETCHED OUT AN ARM, his fingers grasping for a nightstand that didn't seem to be there. Groaning through the fog of grogginess that came with waking from a deep sleep, he tilted up and reached a bit farther before the realization struck that he wasn't in his cabin.

The painful memory of the transporter room flooded in, as did the odor of sickbay, and he cracked out a weak call for Dr. Crusher.

"Doctor . . . *Beverly* . . ."

"Dr. Crusher is planetside, Geordi. Dr. Peiss is attending. And I am here."

The voice was unmistakable.

"Data," Geordi sighed, "what happened?"

"You are ill."

That was his friend Data, as matter-of-fact as ever. But Geordi didn't *feel* ill. What he felt was . . . blind.

He angled up, eyes open but unseeing, and turned his head toward the sound of Data's voice. "Yeah, I figured I was probably here for my health. What's wrong? Where's my VISOR?"

He heard the bio-blanket rustle at his side, and imagined Data's hand was now on the bed. The mental picture of that, even though he couldn't be sure it was realistic, was of concern. If Data was apprehensive about saying something—Data, the android of thousand-word answers to yes or no questions—then something was very wrong.

"Your VISOR is in Bioengineering. It's been tested for possible malfunction," Data said finally.

Has been. Past tense. "And?" Geordi prodded.

"No malfunction was uncovered. Dr. Crusher did find neural rejection of your visual cortex bionic implants. They have been removed."

Geordi brought one hand to his temple, and felt the smoothness of his own skin where there had been an input sensor just hours before. It had been decades since he'd felt that smoothness. Decades since . . .

"Everything is dark."

"I am sorry, my friend."

Geordi wanted to answer that Data need not be sorry . . . but didn't. Instead, the chief engineer began to listen. To the steady rhythm of the android's breath in front of him, to the hum of the medical scanner panel above him.

He remembered what it was like for the other senses to pick up the slack for a sightless man—and remembered that it wasn't the same as eyes, artificial or otherwise.

"Do you have any pain?" Data asked.

"No." Geordi answered quietly and quickly, and without thought. Then he realized it was true—he *didn't* feel any pain, and that too was a feeling he hadn't had in decades.

"Data—will I be okay?"

Somehow the android must have known what his

friend meant. "We do not know if the VISOR implants can be re-implanted. But you are otherwise physically sound." There was a slight pause as Data grasped Geordi's hand in his own, perhaps mimicking a human gesture he had seen before. "You will be fine, Geordi."

"I guess I'll have to rely on your optimism."

"It is not optimism. I base my conclusion on the evidence available."

Geordi chuckled. "Then I guess I'll have to put my faith in that." He felt himself smile, and noticed the absence of the implants again as his new skin stretched in places it hadn't a day before. "When will Dr. Crusher be back?"

"Presumably when she has proved Lieutenant Worf's guilt."

Guilt? Geordi bent himself anxiously toward Data. "What are you talking about? What's happened?"

"Much has happened. It began when our white-noise transmission was taking far more energy—"

"Give me the condensed version and save me the trouble of trying to read the book, huh, Data?"

"Of course," Data said, the small joke lost on him. "It would appear that Lieutenant Worf has murdered the Hidran ambassador, and that Commander Riker and Counselor Troi have either been abducted or are dead."

"Not necessarily." Deanna tapped her finger near the glowing pink button. "Red doesn't have to mean 'danger.' You're applying a very human cultural concept to a situation where no human may be involved."

Riker frowned and shifted his phaser from one hand to the other. His palms were moist with nervousness and delay. If they didn't hurry, whoever had brought them here might come back. "What do you suggest? Eeny-meeny-miney-moe? We have to try *something.*"

Deanna huffed. "If you're going to base your decision on poor concept formation, you might as well be arbitrary. You're just as likely to get the wrong result." Her voice held that irritating tone that patronized and lacked patience.

He nodded. "That's annoyingly logical." He shrugged consent and opened a palm toward the console. "Okay. It's your call. I'll go cower in a corner."

He turned his back to the console, assuming that the door would open up and someone would be waiting. He tapped in the highest stun setting—the painful one—and stood ready.

"Now," he ordered.

Riker heard her pull in a breath and slowly press the alien button into the wall.

Nothing. Not even a beep.

He began to turn his head toward Deanna, to rib her about the decision . . . but before him the wall opposite the panel console began to silently slide away, pulling itself apart from the slit that was the door's opening.

He turned back toward the wall and a rush of sour air rode in at him. Whoever might be waiting behind the door obviously didn't need the fresh air Riker and Deanna did.

Beyond the now open doorway was a corridor of brightness. The incoming stale air fouled the atmosphere in the "transporter room" or "holding cell" or wherever they were.

No alien presented itself to be shot. Somewhat disappointingly, Riker and Deanna seemed to be alone.

He nodded toward the new corridor that lay before them. "Good choice."

"What've you found, Doctor?"

Picard's tone, at once prodding and apprehensive, made Beverly feel as if she were back in front of a panel of medical officers at one of her final Fleet oral examinations.

Barbara, to the captain's right, with a white lab coat over what Beverly had noticed was a beautiful gown, looked especially like one of the severe physicians meant to awe and unnerve young doctors.

Now, as then, Beverly stood uneasily before a grim jury of harsh expressions. Here, however, she was not the one being judged. And the stakes were not her medical career and a prestigious post, but the life of a man who had saved her life more times than she had patients' fingers to count on.

She'd considered lying. Not just at this moment, as Picard was prompting for answers, but minutes before and deeply and seriously. But lying, like murder, had consequences, and she did still believe her friend to be innocent.

The Hidran didn't have that faith in Worf's character, and she knew that as well.

Beverly studied the Hidran captain's face, half hidden by the same type of mask that had been torn from the ambassador, causing his death. Would he give Worf the benefit of doubt? No. No mask could hide that fact.

"Ambassador Zhad died of suffocation," she began slowly, looking mainly at Picard as she stated the obvious. From the corner of her eye she could see Urosk and Worf tense, and she cleared her throat, another stalling tactic, before she pressed on.

"His breathing mask, surgically implanted, malfunctioned and was subsequently pulled out of its implanted base." She looked back down at the computer pad in her hand, and thumbed in a few commands. "There is cellular residue with DNA patterns matching the Ambassador's, as well as Lieutenant Worf's, on the surface of the mask."

Urosk straightened, sucking in a quick breath.

Picard looked immediately away from Beverly and to the Hidran. "Captain, so far that *does* support Mr. Worf's explanation of the events that took place outside the hall. Please allow us to hear the rest of Dr. Crusher's findings."

Nodding, Urosk relaxed slightly.

With a short sigh Beverly mustered her voice up again. "There is chemical evidence of recent skeletal muscular exertion, as well as the ambassador's blood and tissue under his own fingernails."

"What would 'skeletal muscular exertion' imply?" Urosk asked, his demanding voice a hammer on Beverly's ears.

She hesitated, shaking her head and shrugging. "There could be many causes. It's not—"

The Hidran captain rose. "A struggle, yes?"

Taken aback by Urosk's height, Beverly stepped backward a bit. Either Zhad was shorter than his captain or seven feet tall was only intimidating when it was alive and growling. "Not necessarily a struggle," she said.

Urosk turned away from Crusher and looked straight down at Picard. "But it could have been."

There was no question for her to answer, and she looked back at Worf who was as motionless now as he'd been when she entered. At Worf's side, Commander Kadar—had he been here all the time?—seemed to be covering a smile.

"Well, Picard." Urosk stalked toward Worf, placing

himself between the captain and his security chief. "I am convinced of the Klingon's guilt. Do I take my prisoner into custody?"

Picard pursed his lips and crimped his eyes into determined stones. "No. Mr. Worf has the right to a fair and objective trial. He will not be subjected to an unwarranted execution behind a curtain of prejudice. Since that would evidently be the case if I were to release him to your custody, this is the only choice I can make."

"I see that even you are unwilling to believe the truth." Urosk folded his arms beneath his dank, tenebrous cloak, and sat back down. Somehow, at least to Beverly, it was the most threatening motion one could imagine.

"Your *only* choice, Picard," Urosk said slowly, "was a very poor one."

"I don't believe that."

Geordi, still in his post-op pajamas as Data led him through *Enterprise*'s corridors, felt as if he'd been out of circulation for years rather than hours.

"It *is* the truth, Geordi," Data said emphatically. "Worf is not a murderer."

Data squeezed Geordi's shoulder and turned him around a person who must have just come out a doorway. The android had insisted on the escort to Geordi's cabin, displacing the orderly who would normally see to such things. A kind gesture, Geordi thought, but with the Captain gone and Riker missing, Data was in charge. It seemed not to faze him.

"If I may point out," Data said, ushering Geordi into a turbolift, "Lieutenant Worf is capable of acting to defend what he sees as his honor."

"Hey," Geordi turned toward the android out of reflex, "Worf wouldn't defy orders. Are you saying you think he did it?"

There was a dreadfully long pause. The type that meant Data was lending something considerable thought or effort. Finally the android spoke: "I do believe it is within the realm of possibility. In fact, the Klingons may also have had something to do with the away team's disappearance."

What? Did they remove my eyes, or my ears?

"You want to explain that one, Data?"

As Geordi felt the turbolift slow, Data pulled them both back to one side. Obviously not their deck. The doors opened, someone stepped in, greeted Geordi and Data, and slipped silently out of Geordi's world again.

"I think it best we discuss this later, Geordi. In private," Data said.

The obvious question was "why," but Geordi left it unasked. Instead, he just settled back against the lift's wall and took in a breath. Seemingly, the world had gone mad.

"Damn right we're going to discuss this," Geordi mumbled. "And it'll be more sooner than later."

Chapter Eight

Barbara stuffed her hands angrily into the pockets of the white lab coat tossed over the gown she'd worn to the ill-fated dinner. She continued to pace the room that had become Picard's base of failed operations. At least that was what she was calling it. In fact she was thinking of having a plaque made for the door.

"I *don't* sympathize with your diplomatic problems, Captain," she snapped, louder than she should have. "You've let this situation spiral out of control, and that's just as much my responsibility as it is yours."

That of course was a lie, more to herself than to Picard. This was all her concern, especially Will, not really her responsibility, but what was a little white lie between emotions?

Unfortunately, she knew she wasn't fooling herself, and something in Picard's unflickering eyes said she wasn't fooling him either. But at this point she was too angry for embarrassment. Too angry . . . too worried.

"Doctor, I can't accuse anyone of murder or kidnapping when I haven't any evidence." The captain was sitting for a change. She had taken his place as anxious pacer.

"I'm not asking you to. I'm asking you take Mr. Data's suggestion to search the Klingon ship. And the Hidran ship as well."

"We've scanned both ships—"

"Even I know you can hide people from scans."

"Don't presume to tell me my responsibilities, Doctor," Picard snapped.

Barbara leaned down, flattening her palms on the table top. She felt her face flush and hoped it looked more like rage than embarrassment. "Don't shirk your responsibilities, Captain, and I won't have need to remind you of them."

Picard rose, grinding her back with the coolness of his eyes. "My responsibility is my business, Doctor. I cannot and will not move without evidence. You're supposed to be a scientist, so I'll assume you understand the value of acting only on facts."

The Hidran assassin could smell the foolish arrogance of his prey. The odor wafted through the hallway, and he knew the Starfleet Klingon Worf was close at hand.

Bending his long frame over, Batok attempted stealth. The effort seemed foolishly useless—seven feet of red Hidran was just illsuited to blend in against chalk-white walls.

His last glimpse of Worf had been down this corridor, so he stalked forward, toward the room where he believed the Klingons were being kept.

The brightness of this world was an obstacle to Hidran camouflage. In fact, most things about this world were proving a burden—its air, its lack of water, its treacherous Klingon and Starfleet masters.

Batok's long fingers shifted over the human phaser

awkwardly, anxiously. The weapon had been a struggle to acquire—the humans fought better than one might think. These Terran enigmas baffled him, and all of Hidra. They were quiet, small beings, with a strange sense of when and where to show they could also be loud and large.

The Hidran tried to flatten himself along the corridor wall, with little success. He held the phaser close with one hand and pressed his empty palm flush against the chalk wall behind him. He frowned at the dry feeling against his fingers and quickly wiped the grit onto his cloak. Irritations—that's all the Klingons had ever brought.

He thought of Worf, and of the great pleasure there would be in permanently removing this one particular irritation. Pleasure, fame, reputation . . . all that and more. Killing a Klingon was at one time a rite of passage on Hidra. In his father's time the number of Klingons a man had killed was the key to elections and power.

That time was nearly past. Yes, the results of Klingon occupation remained, as did the hatred of the Klingons, but so few young Hidra had even seen a Klingon in person that the bragging of young warriors rang hollow.

Batok's boasting would be honest . . . this was his opportunity to take and shape the rest of his life. He would not only have the chance to spit in a real Klingon's face, but he would kill one and live to savor the feeling.

Peering around the corner, he spotted another Starfleet guard. How many of them were there! How many would stand in his way?

The Earther wasn't looking in Batok's direction, but supposedly they had excellent hearing. With ears that large . . .

Batok set the phaser on what appeared to be the highest stun setting. For the first time he was uncertain, not only of the weapon, but of his actions. He didn't dare kill the Terran. Had he been doing this under Captain Urosk's direct orders it might have been different. Killing the Starfleet Klingon could be explained easily, but just killing any Starfleeter? That would not be a badge of honor and would be frowned upon—severely. For reasons that had always escaped Batok, Starfleet was somewhat respected by the Hidran populace.

No, killing off-worlders arbitrarily was not politically acceptable. The act might gain him pleasure, but little else. And Batok took little risk for pleasure alone.

Yet, he also had to be sure the Starfleeter would not ruin his plans.

Quietly the Hidran lieutenant reached around the corridor, guiding and aiming the phaser. One rod of fire whined out, lancing across the hall.

The Starfleeter collapsed into a stockpile of useless muscles.

"Even your own captain knows you have acted with honor." Kadar offered Worf one of the five seats allowed the Klingons in their cell of *protective custody*. "Otherwise why would you be confined here with us." The Klingon commander motioned to the other four Klingon officers, one of whom was now standing awkwardly, his seat offered in tribute to Worf.

So this was the Klingon smugness and arrogance Worf had been accused of so often. It *was* annoying. He now wanted to somehow take back a few of the punches he'd thrown because of that insult.

"I did *not* kill the ambassador," Worf said, taking the stool, deciding to save needed strength rather than take the unneeded pride there would have been in turning down the gesture. "Captain Picard believes that, but is bound by regulations. I understand his actions and agree with them."

Kadar thundered to one of his subordinates and was quickly handed his own stool. He sat down, a chuckle rising in his throat as he spoke. "You make brave sounds, Lieutenant Worf. I like you."

Lifting his eyes from the floor, Worf seized Kadar's gaze and wrenched it into a lock. There had been a time in Worf's life when he aspired to a position such as Kadar's—the command of a Klingon battle ship.

Having served among Terrans for these years, the Klingon condescension he was so often accused of had molded itself into respect. Respect for his captain, not only because of the rank, but because of the man.

A few years ago Worf would have admired Kadar for his rank alone. No longer. In the Klingon Empire one could still attain such position more from treachery and savvy than from skill alone. There was no honor in treachery, Worf had decided. And so, he could not give Kadar respect, until he was sure it *had* been earned.

"I do not care if you like me," Worf said. "And I do not care if you believe me."

Kadar rumbled a laugh. "Are you telling me you were agreeable to the Hidran for no motive?"

The Klingon commander was anything but subtle, yet had this irritating talent for cunningly asking the most delicate of questions.

"I was under orders from my captain." It was a lie, but Worf needed to be cunning as well. If he could convince Kadar that the platitudes to Zhad were just that—platitudes, then perhaps the Klingon commander might reveal what he knew of the Hidran ambassador's death. There was a kernel of an idea that kept pushing its way into Worf's thoughts: his

Klingon brethren may well have had something to do with Zhad's murder, if it was murder.

"I believe that you drown the Hidran in banality in order to gain his trust," Kadar said.

"As I said, I do not care what you believe."

The Klingon smile that Worf felt so infrequently on his own face seemed to haunt Kadar's. "What is it that you do care about, Lieutenant Worf? Do you care about flowers and Terran kittens and other Earther pursuits? Do you have a pet tribble or a puppy dog? *Or* are you a Klingon? What is the truth about you?"

Worf bolted from his seat and had his hands wrapped around Kadar's neck before the other Klingons had a chance to contemplate moving. He pressed the Commander's throat closed with one hand, pinning Kadar's head in his other hand. Worf kept the Klingon captain balanced on the stool, not allowing bracing of any kind.

It was a gamble, and the stake was Worf's life.

"nIS wej," Kadar choked out, ordering his men not to interfere.

"Is this Klingon enough for you, Kadar?" Worf growled. "Why does the question of my blood concern you so? Why is my Klingon soul of such grave importance to you? Do you not have what you wanted?"

Worf twisted his hand round Kadar's neck again for effect, jerking the Klingon commander around.

"The wedge is back between the Empire and the Hidran Congress. They will die, as a people, as a planet, and you will only lose some warriors who will be proud to have given their lives to a disease because it served the purposes of honor. And the Empire can't even be blamed because I am a Federation citizen and not a Klingon subject."

Worf released his grip and Kadar yanked himself away. Purple marks on his neck were beginning to appear, but his voice showed no strain. "Are you suggesting that we would intentionally implicate you for a murder you did not commit, Lieutenant?"

This time Worf laughed, but only to cover his anger. Anger at Kadar . . . anger at himself. Given Doctor Crusher's inability to find any reason other than the breathing mask malfunction for Zhad's death, even he was beginning to believe his actions caused the ambassador's demise. But if there was another explanation—a *Klingon* explanation, then Kadar must be the one to reveal it to him. The Klingon commander's confidence would have to be gained.

"I am suggesting," Worf said, "that if I have not been framed, you have fallen into good fortune." Worf pushed past the other Klingons toward the one window in the small room. "I do not believe in fortune." Peering out the window and down onto the twisting saffron fields, Worf pressed his palms against the pane and wished he could press right out the window and away from such cowardly Klingons who might do such a thing. "And you do not believe in such fortune either. The universe is Klingons' to shape, and I have respect for those who mold it to their liking."

Batok twisted the light Starfleeter over like a limp puppet and grabbed for his phaser. At the same time he checked for a beating heart and a moist breath.

He felt the pounding in the Earther's chest, and was grateful. The man was alive . . . but would be unconscious for how long? With an alien weapon there was no way to tell. He rolled the unconscious guard into the corner, away from the doorway. Should he bind the guard? With what? Best not waste the time—if the Starfleeter dared to rise again, he would simply stun him back into unconsciousness.

Hastily, Batok slipped the extra phaser into a pocket in his cape. Two Federation pistols and two

Federation communicators were now in his collection. Excellent. Urosk's anger could not last long with such prizes in *addition* to Worf's death.

He looked up at the door that looked out of place—a new security hatch phaser-welded into an old stone building. The Starfleeters thought of everything. Had it been a normal door Batok could have opened it quickly, found his quarry, fired, and locked the Klingons back in. They would not have had a chance to react. Now they might.

He'd have to find Worf quickly, kill him, and close the hatch again before the others had an opportunity to make it to the door. He could not kill all of them and still retain his rank, and he could not switch settings on the phaser fast enough to stun the others. He had the other phaser, but one hand must be free to control the door.

His left hand wrapped around the Terran weapon, another on the button that activated the door, Batok readied himself. He tried to picture the layout of the room—perhaps it was the same as the one he had been kept in, yet reversed.

He took in a deep breath of the foul air the planet provided. Just adding moisture wasn't enough to kill the stench, especially the Klingon stench that was making him sick right through the door.

Worf . . . just beyond that door. The thought was full of angry exhilaration. Soon one Klingon's stench would be due more to burnt flesh than poor hygiene.

Hate stung Batok's eyes and he blinked to clear his thoughts. He *must* be lucid to do this quickly. And he must not fail. To have come this far only to have his efforts end in disgrace would mean his own death.

He glanced down at the phaser's settings again, hoping he had selected the "kill" setting that would leave a corpse. Depriving the other Klingons of actually seeing the shell of their fallen comrade would be too kind. If he accidentally chose the button that would vaporize Worf, well . . . it would be good enough, but lack the meaning he intended. What Batok really wanted was a Hidran disrupter that could cut a Klingon in half and leave him to bleed to death in agony.

Stiffly he thumbed the hatch control and slowly the door began to open. His arm tensed, his fingers tightened around the weapon.

Worf! Where was Worf?

One Klingon, another, turning slowly.

Batok saw Kadar—the rank on his armor—and moved the aim of his phaser from him to another.

That ridged head . . . turning deliberately toward him.

Worf! The murderer Worf!

Batok fired. An angry spear of energy cracked from the phaser and seared into his Klingon victim.

The boneheaded thug collapsed into a mass of charred flesh and still glowed orange as Batok jammed his fist against the door's controls.

Another Klingon rushed toward him as the hatch closed, grunting some Klingon animal curse as they always did when they had been defeated.

Rushing back down the corridor, Batok heard the muffled death scream that mystic Klingon fools would make when they had lost a comrade. He had never before heard the sound. There were stories—told by those who had heard. He—a mere Lieutenant in the Hidran Congress's grand fleet—had *caused* this scream that filled the corridor with sound . . . and Batok's heart with glee.

The bay announced that he had accomplished his task. Worf had paid for the Ambassador's death . . . with his life.

The Starfleet Klingon was dead.

Chapter Nine

A PUFF OF ACRID SMOKE drifted up from the floor, dissipating uncomfortably into Riker's face. He tried to blink the sting from his eyes as he looked down at the mark he'd made with his phaser.

"How many does that make?" he asked Deanna.

"Twenty-three."

He took two limping steps over to the wall. Bracing himself, he weakly holstered his phaser. In four hours no one had jumped out to greet *or* eat them, and he thought it unlikely anyone would come calling at this point.

If by some chance they weren't alone . . . and if someone *was* looking for them, at least the two of them would be hard to find. The ship was huge with no end to it in sight.

"Twenty-three corridors," he muttered, mopping the sweat from his brow with an already drenched sleeve. "Not one in a straight line, all turning back and twisting around. I don't know about you but this is the biggest ship *I've* ever been on. We must have traveled miles."

Deanna came up along side him, gently pushing him down toward the deck. "Sit and rest for a while. You've lost a lot of blood."

Riker nodded and lowered himself to the floor, glancing angrily at his blood-caked bandage. "What a time for a marathon, hm?"

She stooped down beside him, touching his shoulder and looking down at his leg. "You need another dressing. My uniform or yours?"

Managing a weak smile he looked up at her. "Do I get to choose what part of the uniform?"

Fingering the seam of her uniform at her shoulder, she tore down the arm of her tunic. "I don't know why I even bother asking you these things."

He smiled a bit again, and slowly stretched out his leg for her to work on. As she undid the old makeshift bandage to replace it with a new one, Riker averted his eyes up the corridor and tried to use the pain to focus his concentration.

This ship was a labyrinth—hallway after hallway, passages connecting to conduits leading to corridors that opened into other hallways. And a few doors that wouldn't open for them. *That* was suspicious.

Someone had built a giant space-maze, and was testing them. The riddle was obvious: whose ship? Where was the Minotaur? That question tugged at Riker's thoughts.

It wasn't the Hidran. He doubted they had the materials to waste on anything that wasn't a weapon or a power source.

And he didn't think the Klingons were involved either. This didn't have a Klingon feel to it—of that much he was sure. Since he had met Worf, Klingons held a certain fascination for Riker. One he indulged by taking brief assignments on Klingon vessels and by pursuing a friendship with his Klingon security chief.

That was unusual for him. Will Riker had never exactly had to seek out friends.

Until Worf.

Gaining the Klingon's respect was a given because he was Worf's superior officer. Gaining his friendship . . . his confidence . . . those only came with time. It's what Riker needed from a member of his bridge crew, to make the team run smoothly.

Pursuing that friendship was easier than Riker had first thought. He and Worf agreed on much, from tactics to politics, and Worf's loyalty to Picard and his selfless protection of the captain cemented their friendship.

A stab of pain jolted Riker from his thoughts. Deanna was tying the new bandage. This time he didn't complain of its tightness.

She rose, helping to pull Riker to his feet. "Will, you're not clotting. The wound is too deep."

He took in a long breath and hobbled-in the new bandage, making sure he could walk. "I know. Let's hope we find someone."

Deanna came up alongside him, bracing him as he limped down the hall. "I still don't sense any presence here."

"Even if there's no one here there's got to be communication equipment or something similar."

Unaccustomed to the stiffness of the new bandage, he lost his balance for a moment and gripped her arm.

"Will," she said, using his lack of balance as an excuse to turn him toward her, "What if there are beings here and they're just too alien for me to sense?"

A frightening thought, in a way. Not so much that their appearance might be alien . . . but what if their morality was. What was inside an alien mind was the real terror. Did they respect life? Even unfamiliar life? Riker had to give them the benefit of the doubt. "They're not so strange that they don't have our height, or thereabout, and breathe our atmosphere and use buttons and doors and corridors," he said.

"Well, if there *is* someone here," Deanna said, "I think I should go looking, not you. You need to rest a bit longer. You've lost too much blood and could die from dehydration or a simple infection."

"Pep talks aren't your strong suit are they?" He shook his head. "But you're right. Both of us have already been walking too long. My leg may or may not kill me, but lack of food and water certainly will." He pushed away from her and stood on his own. "Someone is here," he said. "And we're going to find them."

With a sympathetic rub of his own leg, he hobbled toward the door that just a few minutes earlier had denied them entry. He braced himself against the doorframe and dug his fingers into the gap that must have been the seam between the sliding doors.

"It's locked tight," he grunted.

Deanna peered over his shoulder. "Or it's vacuum sealed. How do we know there isn't open space beyond that door?"

Because docking bays usually had reinforced doors and backup systems, but he didn't feel up to explaining. Instead he just sighed and went for the shorter answer. "Trust me. We were in a corridor on the other side of this room. I'm sure."

"All right," she said slowly, "but what if there's a vacuum in there anyway? They may keep some rooms or corridors without life support to save on energy."

Riker lowered his head against the door, partly out of exhaustion, partly out of exasperation. She was right, of course, but it was an annoying habit. Most irritating was that he should have had the same

thought—but hadn't. Had he lost too much blood?
His mind was cloudy.

He shuffled back from the door and pulled out his
phaser. "Okay. We'll cut a small hole in the door. If we
don't hear a sucking sound or feel a pressure change,
we can blast the rest of the door. Deal?"

She smiled. "You're in charge."

He nodded as if it were true, and fired the phaser.

A thin line of light pulsed from the weapon and into
the door. A small hole sizzled open and Riker quickly
released the phaser's trigger.

No hiss. No pressure change.

Something was beyond that door . . . and it wasn't
vacuum.

"Good enough?" Riker asked.

Deanna nodded and smiled, but Riker, tired as he
was, noticed something beyond that smile. Worry,
maybe? About him or their situation? He didn't know.
Beyond the door was more important than beyond the
smile right now.

He reset the phaser and triggered it again. The door
collapsed into vapor.

After a moment the fog of destroyed metal cleared,
and they looked in.

"What is all this?" Riker took a step into the room,
Deanna following closely.

They looked up, down, left, right, and for the first
time in hours saw something other than bleak, spartan
corridor.

"Machinery," Deanna said.

Riker nodded blankly, in awe of the mastery, even
beauty: different-colored panels, not square but
rounded. They seemed alive. Not like the *Enterprise*
was alive . . . these machines seemed almost fluid, as
if there was motion . . . but there wasn't. Just the
vibration of something being done—processed or
pumped or . . . something.

These humming and thrumming machines lined the walls on all sides. The room extended as the corridor did outside—the other doors must have opened to this same room. A welcome sight from the desolate halls they had been walking for a good part of a day.

However, Riker was struck by the same feeling as in the halls. No people. No coffee cups or chairs or papers or anything that would even remotely suggest recent inhabitancy by life.

Riker trotted as fast as he could over to one of the machines. He touched its smooth, warm surface. There wasn't a button or a key pad or a screen with a graph to be found.

He turned to see Deanna stepping away from a different device that was closer to the door. "Well," he said, "busting in a locked door didn't exactly bring the palace guards down on us."

Deanna frowned.

Riker, weak though he was, took her by the shoulder. "What? What is it?"

"Frankly, you look bad, Will."

He ignored the comment about himself and instead looked at her—dark hair matted against her forehead, perspiration over her lip. "You don't look so great either," he said, noticing that the room was hot.

The machines . . . they were giving off heat.

"These are all working at something," he said, gesturing with the phaser as he returned it to his holster. "Doing what?"

She shrugged and sighed, clasping her hands anxiously in front of herself. "No way to tell. Propulsion, maybe?"

Riker bit the inside of his lip and looked around the room. Machines. Working, busy, bustling . . . "What if they break down? Someone must be here to repair them, right?"

The heat was getting to him and he shifted back toward the door way to brace himself against the wall.

He didn't wait to hear an answer from Deanna. "Someone," he repeated, "has to fix these machines if they break." He pulled the phaser from his holster. "And I'm going to break them."

"Computer."
"Ready."
"Locate and list all Federation vessels capable of warp speed, this quadrant."
"Located."
Data's desk screen filled:

U.S.S. CHARLESTON, STARFLEET REGISTRY,
    NCC-42285
U.S.S. HOOD, STARFLEET REGISTRY, NCC-42296
U.S.S. EXCALIBUR, STARFLEET REGISTRY,
    NCC-42252
S.S. EAGLE, EARTH REGISTRY, USA-3197BL-9
S.S. TAN-SHRA, TELLAR REGISTRY,
    FLN-633136052SIE

"Computer, which is the closest ship to our position?"
"The S.S. Eagle *is in sector seven."*
"Specifics on *Eagle.*"
"S.S. Eagle, *privately owned exploratory craft. Registry: Lansing, Michigan, United States of America, Earth. Crew of thirty-three. Current ownership—*"
"Discontinue. Which Starfleet vessel is the closest?"
"The U.S.S. Excalibur *is in sector four."*
"Twelve days distant at maximum warp," Data said, more to himself than to the computer.
"Correct."

The door chime to Data's quarters rang and the android quickly tapped the computer off.

"Come."

Geordi felt the door whisper open before him. He stepped through hesitantly, unsure of Data's location.

"Hope I'm not disturbing you, Data," he said, looking for a response to place the android. He probably should have just asked the man's location, but Geordi was playing the "I'm not really blind game" and that would be against the rules—like being wakened in the middle of the night and refusing to admit you were sleeping.

"Geordi," Data said, just a hint of surprise etched into his voice. "Should you be ambulatory?"

Geordi walked toward the android's voice. "I'm blind, Data, not sick." He tapped his stomach and the dark vest that lay over his uniform tunic. "Proximity detector, so I don't bang into people. And I think I should know the layout of the ship by now." Geordi used the detector to sense things—the sensor net in the vest would react on his skin, pushing his flesh as he would near an object. It *would* keep him from embarrassing himself.

There was silence.

Geordi frowned. "You're nodding again, Data." The android shouldn't have forgotten. Such things— *any* thing—didn't slip Data's mind. This was the first outward sign that something was wrong—really wrong—with Data.

"I am sorry," the android said. "Can you guide yourself to a chair?"

"Yeah." Geordi took one more step into the room. He turned toward where he believed the chair to be, felt the electrical twinge from the proximity sensor that told him he was correct, and lowered himself into the seat.

He heard Data's chair swivel toward him, and he sat back. "We have to talk about this thing with Worf."

"Bridge to Commander Data."

"Certainly," Data said to him, possibly holding an index finger up. "One moment, please."

Geordi heard the tap of the android's fingers against his comm badge and imagined he'd seen it. He'd been doing a lot of that—seeing in his mind what he fancied might be happening. He wondered if he was correct about such things, but hadn't worked up the courage to ask anyone. And who knows if they'd be honest. It was human nature to be sympathetic to those who had come upon a loss. Already three crewmen had tried to escort him "wherever he needed to go." Despite being off duty, that had prompted him to wear his uniform. He wouldn't be pitied. That was a cliche he'd promised himself he'd never indulge in because he understood the impulse—intended kindness—but it was just different when he was on the receiving end. He was having trouble pushing away the self-pity in his own thoughts . . . it didn't help to have others pushing back.

"Data here. Go ahead, Mr. DePotter."

"Sorry to disturb you, sir, but since re-engaging, there's been a fluctuation in the drain on the white noise blanket."

Restless, Geordi rose and walked toward the dresser that Data rarely used. There was a mirror there . . . of little use to either man right now.

"Ensign," Data said, "what was the percent of flux, and was it positive or negative?"

"Data," Geordi interrupted, anxiously knocking a fist on his thigh, "is this really important right now?"

"Just one more moment please, Geordi. This may indeed be important. Continue, Mr. DePotter."

DePotter chanted on with his scientific findings—a

drone of techno-babble that was irritating Geordi right now, and he wondered if that'd irritated anyone when it came from his own lips.

"A moment ago," DePotter said, *"I registered a point zero-zero-two percent decrease in the drain. It may be insignificant, sir, except that this is the first drop* or *surge since we've been monitoring."*

There was a pause, then from Data: "Intriguing. What is the status of the Klingon vessel?"

"Sir?"

"Scan the Klingon vessel for any activity, Ensign, and keep me informed of anything you find, no matter how unremarkable you believe it to be."

"Aye aye, sir."

"Data out."

Geordi heard the communicator chirp off.

"Now," Data said, "what would you like to know?"

Geordi shook his head. Something was wrong here. Different. He couldn't put his finger on what exactly, and maybe there was really nothing. Maybe he was just disoriented from his "newfound" blindness. Maybe.

Or maybe when something feels wrong, it is.

"Data, you keep saying that Commander Riker and Deanna *may* have been abducted or killed by the Klingons, and you're scanning their ship as if they're already there, but there's no evidence—"

"One need not have conclusive evidence to form a hypothesis."

They'd had this conversation three times since Geordi had awakened, and Data had indulged him each time. Unfortunately, every discussion was the same: Data with a logical argument and a shaky premise. That was the problem—since when did Data have shaky premises?

"The Klingons do have a history of such covert operations, my friend."

Geordi shot past the desk and began to pace the room. Hopefully Data hadn't moved anything since the last time he'd been here.

"This is nuts, Data," he said angrily. "There's nothing to base it on. What motive would they have to do anything like this?"

As if anticipating the question, perhaps because Geordi had asked before, Data began, "If they are hiding something on the planet, which may be the cause of the drain on our white noise blanket, then they would have motive to assure that no one finds whatever they wish to conceal. Commander Riker and Counselor Troi may have stumbled upon whatever that may be."

Geordi huffed out an angry breath. "What if they're not hiding anything?"

"Then," Data said, "they have nothing to fear by answering my questions and submitting to an inspection."

The headache that was now absent, Geordi would have gladly accepted back in exchange for this warped twist of events. "Data, none of that suggests why Worf would have anything to do with the Klingons' plans."

"He is a Klingon."

"So?" Geordi snapped angrily.

There was another pause from Data, and the silence sounded like the android's version of frustration. He was obviously searching for a way to get his point across.

"Geordi," he began, "every race has specific traits that are often unique. The Klingons do not value life in the same manner as you and I and the Hidran."

If Geordi could have gored Data with a glare he would have—and who knows, maybe he did. "The Hidran? What do they have to do with Klingon values? Or Worf's for that matter? Worf was raised on Earth, Data. About seven thousand kilometers from where I was raised." He crooked a thumb at his own chest. "Our personalities are different—our values are not. Worf would defend the philosophy of the Federation to his death."

"Or to the death of another, yes? Perhaps that is what he thought he was doing. In any case," Data said, and it sounded so detached—"he also has loyalties to the Klingons, and he is not to be trusted."

There was no other term for this . . . it was just plain insane.

"You're talking bigotry, Data, and I can't believe it. You're not being rational."

"Geordi, it is not bigotry to see the historical fact that the Klingons are not trustworthy. And it is not bigotry to see the historical fact that Worf would murder because of his nature as a Klingon. I need not remind you that Lieutenant Worf once refused to donate his ribosomes to save the life of a Romulan prisoner."

Every muscle in Geordi's back was tense with frustration and fatigue. He had awakened into a dark world where everything had changed.

"Data," Geordi said between clenched teeth, "there is a big difference between refusing to sacrifice for someone who you don't believe deserves it and murdering someone in cold blood."

"Death for any reason is permanent. The Hidran might say that Klingon neglect is murder."

Geordi pulled in a deep breath and tried to settle his emotions. If Data had said Worf was not to be trusted and had backed that up with facts that would have been one thing—but this seemed so . . . un-Data: poorly conceived, not fully thought out . . . every argument was logical, but all were built on a foundation of confused quicksand.

Data might be damaged. That would explain much

—from the absurd notions about Worf and the Klingons to forgetting that Geordi couldn't see a nod.

"Data, I think I'd like to have Engineering check you out, run a series of diagnostics."

"For what reason? I run a self-diagnostic twice daily."

Yeah, and I'll bet a month's pay that something's wrong there too.

"Just indulge me, huh, Data?"

"I am afraid I do not have the time at present."

"Why?"

"I will be leading the away team that is to board the Klingon battle cruiser."

Bolting from his seat, Geordi pressed himself against Data's desk and leaned down to the android. Maybe he couldn't see, but Data could and needed to be sure Geordi was serious.

"You can't, Data! It's unprovoked. Captain Picard would never authorize that."

"Indeed, he did. His direct order was 'do what you must to get to the bottom of the situation.'" The sigh of Data's chair cushion signaled the android had risen. "And I will do what I must."

Data had been gone a good five minutes. He'd insisted on escorting Geordi back to his quarters, but Geordi couldn't shake the feeling that it was because somehow he'd lost the android's trust—as Worf had.

Quiet thought had done nothing for that sense of paranoia.

There was something wrong with Data, he was sure, but had nothing but a subjective feeling to go on. Subjective feelings were nice to look at and consider, but only told someone how they *felt* about reality— feelings told nothing about reality itself. And that was what Geordi had to be sure about: the reality of the situation. Did something *seem* to be wrong with Data, or *was* there something wrong with him?

There was an enormous difference.

To be sure, he had to talk to someone else about what had happened while he was out of commission. At the same time he could confirm that Data was definitely doing what the captain wanted where the Klingon ship was concerned.

He found the desk communicator.

"La Forge to Captain Picard."

He was met with the dull tone of a closed frequency and furrowed his brows.

"Computer."

"Ready."

"Why can't I get an open comm-channel to the planet?"

"This station is not authorized for access."

"Override. Security access: La Forge Gamma three-four."

"Access denied."

"Denied?" Geordi pounded his fist on the table. "What do you mean denied?"

The computer began to bleep, formulating an answer.

"Belay that. Who *can* give me access?"

"Access authorization required from Lieutenant Commander Data, acting captain, U.S.S. Enterprise."

Geordi balanced his elbow on the desktop, holding his forehead in his palm.

"Well, looks like that's my objective evidence, isn't it?"

"Insufficient data."

He let out a short, bitter chuckle. "You can say that again!"

Whatever fool designed this building, Urosk thought, *should be killed.* He had not noticed before,

128

but the light was harsh and the dryness of the walls and floor were more than annoying.

But it was not a mindless architect who truly burdened the Hidran captain. It was Picard who was the real fool. And he should be treated as fools are treated: with a firm fist and little patience.

The entire Federation was made of fools, Urosk decided, from those that had offered to help to those that brought him here. Dullards all.

And he, for believing that any good might come of this, was the most foolish. Before coming here the Hidran had only been on the brink of a skirmish with their foreign foes. Now they were on the brink of war.

It was obvious. The Klingons had planned this from the beginning. They would have done anything to assure that Hidra was left helpless enough to be re-conquered. And this time the Klingons would not leave the people alive. The Hidran were a million thorns in the Klingon Empire's skin, and these pseudo-negotiations had been nothing more than a complex maneuver by the Empire and its Federation allies. It was all some scheme to force Hidra back into a war they knew she would lose.

Defeat . . . only one casualty and he was thinking of defeat! A shameful thing to think of such loss, but it was realistic and Urosk had spent too much time the last few days believing that peace was possible. He was through with such far-fetched ideas. Yet the humiliation weighed on him. Such disgrace was what the Klingons desired for the Hidran people, and they had even succeeded in dishonoring Urosk with his own thoughts.

He could not let that happen—he would not. There would not be another war if Urosk was of any worth to himself and his nation.

He straightened, smoothed his long robe, loosened his muscles.

He closed his eyes a moment, and when they blankly reopened onto the desert of the corridor, he knew what he had to do.

His heartbeat quickened at the thought—his strength both mental and physical seemed rejuvenated. There was a chance to thwart the enemy's plans, but that would take great skill and care to achieve: Every Klingon on the planet . . . and above in orbit . . . would have to die. Once more it would have to be proven that there were extreme risks to warring against the Hidran.

Urosk would have to take the mask of warrior that he wore, and transfer it to action. Perhaps for his last time.

And if Picard and his Federation interfered—

"Hold a minute, sir," the Starfleet guard said to Urosk, jolting him from his thoughts.

Aware of his surroundings and the guard again, Urosk surveyed the empty corridor—a vacant hall where there should have been another guard.

If there was to be an opportunity, this was it.

"Connors to MacKenzie."

The Starfleeter was quick to activate his communicator, and opportunity faded.

The Hidran captain turned back to face Connors.

Strange politeness to be called "sir" by him. These humans could usher someone to a cell for so-called "diplomatic protection" and yet treat their prisoner as if taking them on a garden tour.

There was no answer to the Starfleeter's call. His guard friend was either gone by his own volition or was inside the cell with Urosk's comrades. Either way, he was not around. One on one . . . the odds were better than even.

Unfortunately, there was no way of knowing if the human's call to his absent colleague would be carried to every communicator.

The comm channel would have to close before opportunity materialized again.

The Starfleet guard tapped his badge again, and Urosk thought that was his signal to move. Before he could, the Terran spoke once more.

"Connors to Picard. MacKenzie isn't at his post and I can't raise him on the comm, sir."

"Understood." Picard's voice spat from the small speaker. *"Remain there. I'm on my way."*

Blast! Picard would be on his way now. Opportunity faded once more, even as this one called Connors turned off his communicator.

"Captain Urosk," the human said, "I'll ask you to hold your position with me, sir."

Urosk nodded and quickly glanced at the Earther's phaser. Ripe for the taking . . . A phaser against all those defenseless Klingons.

That would make the statement he wanted. A statement that said something about the Hidran and the price one would pay for choosing the path of war.

There was little time in which to decide—

Urosk's muscles tensed and he waited for the Earther's eyes to drift away even slightly. He balled his fingers into a fist and paused. One good blow should be enough.

Wait . . . wait . . . the Earther still had the phaser . . .

A sound, some creak in the structure of the building somewhere, forced the Starfleeter's eyes to dart away.

Urosk's long arm reached out and struck against the Terran's head. The man was sure to be knocked unconscious.

The human stumbled back and the Hidran captain swung again, knocking the weapon across the hall.

Connors shook his head clear and twisted toward Urosk as they both tried to get a tack on the phaser that had gone sailing. Suddenly the strong thin rods of the Starfleeter's legs were around Urosk's knees. He struggled to free himself, but unbalance tossed him forward onto the hard stone floor.

Pain tried to force the Hidran's eyes closed as the two of them pinched together, limbs digging into each other.

Suddenly the human was on his feet again, looking down at Urosk, ready. How? This small being was no match! There should be no contest!

Urosk jumped up, pushing the ache from his torso as he tried to eye where the phaser had fallen. Obviously the human would seek out the weapon as well.

Urosk had to reach it first.

One more good jolt of Hidran strength should make acquiring the phaser academic. He—

Two consecutive flashes of agony exploded into Urosk—in his stomach, in his neck—From where? Why was the Earther not down? "Fall!" Urosk grunted to himself.

Urosk swung his large boom of an arm again and the Starfleeter caught it and spun him away. Another bolt of pain smashed into him. Feet! The human was jumping and kicking like some crazed monkey. *Klingons* had given up sooner.

Urosk let out an angry gasp and lashed back at the Starfleeter. Both fists clasped together into a club of bone and muscle, he swung hard against the human's shoulder.

Connors went tumbling down to the ground with a hard grunt.

Finally, he was unmoving.

Urosk stooped to reach for the phaser. Another limb—he didn't know which—whacked him in the gut and sent him sprawling onto the floor.

The Starfleeter, on his feet again, leaped at Urosk, punching and jabbing and scratching.

Urosk felt one of his eyes swelling shut and he could

feel the metallic taste of blood in his throat. Dredging his frustration into strength, he looped his arms around the Earther. If he could not beat the gangly human he would crush the breath from him!

Arms pinned at his sides, feet dangling at least a half meter off the ground, the Starfleeter struggled and grunted his breath away.

Finally Urosk felt the strength drain empty from his opponent's body. To be sure he crushed his arms together three more times. He would not be fooled again.

When he released him, the Earther crumpled into a heap, a spent log collapsing into an amber bed.

Urosk snatched for the phaser and quickly set it to stun. Unconsciousness from lack of air, if what these humans breathed could be called air, might last only a few moments. On the other hand . . . He triggered the weapon and a bright orange halo enveloped the human for a moment. The Starfleeter was surely out this time. And would stay that way for quite a while.

After plucking the comm badge from the guard's chest he pulled the man into an alcove to hide him from Picard.

The *Enterprise* captain would be walking down the corridor any minute . . . and Urosk would be waiting.

Picard . . . he had failed to see the warning signs. He *would* regret his choice.

Chapter Ten

"PICARD HERE."

The voice of young Ensign MacKenzie crackled back at the captain from the small comm badge speaker. Interference again. Picard noted the irritation and promised himself he'd be having a talk with Data.

"MacKenzie isn't at his post and I can't raise him on the comm, sir."

"Understood." Obviously Ensign Connors' voice, not MacKenzie's. When had all ensigns started blending together into a blur of youth? "Remain there," Picard ordered. "I'm on my way." He rose and shared a concerned glance with Beverly, as well as a quick look with Barbara.

"Captain," Beverly began again, slowly rising out of her seat, "this is important. I left something out of my report when the delegates were here." She cast a quick glance at Barbara. "I thought it might be best to tell you this in confidence."

Picard nodded. "Understood." He didn't mind Barbara's presence. In fact, since she had voiced her wish to do something about Riker and Troi—something that could make this entire situation worse—he was glad to know where she was. "Proceed, Doctor, but be brief."

Beverly pulled in a deep breath, held it a moment, then released it quickly. Picard had come to recognize this as her attempt to cover a sigh. He didn't have time for sighs.

"There were traces of Zhad's own skin and blood beneath his nails," she said, then paused, as if that alone should be some revelation.

The captain shrugged his response. "You'd said that earlier. Isn't that expected? Wouldn't he have tried to fix the mask?"

She shook her head and a thick strand of orange hair bobbed over her ear. "Gouges in his face and the amount of skin under his nails suggest something else."

Now Picard needed to hide a sigh. "It just gets worse and worse, doesn't it?"

Barbara unfolded her arms, gesturing to Beverly. "This is what you wanted, isn't it? This proves that your man didn't kill the Ambassador. Or at least it's some fair evidence."

Picard lowered his head, his fingers finding that pressure point on his temple. Behind there, was a thriving headache that threatened to grow before it faded. "Doctor Hollitt, I don't think Captain Urosk would accept the suggestion that his ambassador killed himself. It would look as if we were falsifying evidence for our own benefit. Hardly 'fair' at all."

"What if that's exactly what happened?" Beverly offered.

Nodding, Picard pursed his lips. "A possibility." He took another step toward the door. "I'll have more questions when I return."

Barbara shrugged, hard shoulders turning fluid for a brief moment. "Why? Why would anyone do that?"

"To make the Klingons look bad," Picard said, wanting to satisfy all her questions even if it delayed him. The last thing he desired was for her to tag along again. She had been an angry puppy at his feet since this all fell apart, and wouldn't stop nipping at his heels. "To give the Hidran a bargaining chip worth something," he continued. "Perhaps he was a shrewd ambassador to the last breath."

Barbara shook her head in disbelief. "To kill yourself is one thing. By the looks of him he suffered."

"He did," Beverly confirmed. "Not just the suffocation, but tearing it out would've been no painless task."

"It's . . . it's . . . ." Barbara seemed to be searching for the right term.

"Fanatical," Picard offered caustically.

Beverly's lips curled down into a frown. "Dim-witted is what I'd call it."

"Either way," Picard said, inching for the door again, "the fact may not help Mr. Worf one scrap."

Barbara looked as if she were on the edge of some comment as she began to rise.

Halfway out the door already, the captain quickly shook his head. "Please, Dr. Hollitt, remain here."

She raised her chin ever so slightly and ever so defiantly. "I can handle myself, Captain."

Of that he was sure. But still, his orders and instinct were to protect a civilian first, and he didn't want the regret of one more death upon his shoulders.

"Whether or not you can handle yourself is not at issue, Doctor," Picard said as he closed the door behind him. "I'm not sure *I* can handle you."

"Sir, should you be here?"

Looking down, trying to shield his eyes from the

crewman, Geordi shook his head. There was really no need to hide—a well-rounded Starfleet officer had seen things more shocking than eyes without irises. Despite knowing that, there was a self-conscious twinge that Geordi would feel if he thought someone were staring into his sightless eyes.

"I'm just working on a little project to keep me busy, Charlie." Geordi hovered diligently over his work.

"Can I help?"

Only if you want to share a court-martial with me. "Well, if you really want to do me a favor, you could check the particulate filtration sensors on deck seven. The air seemed a little stale up there."

"Aye aye, sir," Charlie said, and Geordi heard the ensign's feet pad away toward the turbolift and a busywork job in a far-off Jeffries tube.

There was silence, and Geordi still felt as if he was being watched . . . or his work was. In any case, the proximity detector said no one was close enough to get in the way, so he simply tried to ignore the feeling.

He reached over the football-sized capsule that lay open in front of him and he picked up a tool, the location of which he'd memorized. He found the place inside the exposed sensor drone where he had to make his adjustments, and set to work.

His fingertips had to be his eyes here—the proximity detector was useless on such a small scale. He fumbled inside the guts of the drone, sweat breaking on his upper lip. Sloppily, exhaustingly, he made his adjustments.

He hoped.

So damn frustrating: to go from super-sight to super-darkness was a game he'd played every night, yet to stare blankly at the prospect of never playing that game again—at staying forever in the dark . . . well, it scared him, annoyed him, filled him with uneasiness, as if he wasn't in his own body but instead in some dark cave at the edge of existence.

He refused to ask for help with the drone, of course. Not only would that be rather embarrassing, but what position would it put the crewman in? Geordi was going against Data's obvious order not to contact the planet without authorization. Perhaps it *was* Picard's order. There was too much at risk here . . . better this particular mutiny be kept to himself for a while.

He dropped the instrument, closed the door to the drone's innards, and flicked the "on" switch. Somewhere to his left, perhaps at about fifteen meters down the aft corridor, there was a chute that would launch the sensor drone outside the ship for a maintenance-pass of the starboard nacelle.

He found the sliding hatch to the chute just a few inches from where his mental picture told him it would be. The proximity detector vest—a temporary model he'd replicated, and hoped he wouldn't have to eventually have a special one made—did the rest.

With the drone down the chute, he coded in the launch coordinates. Hopefully he hadn't missed a button on the keypad. There was no way to verify such things without sight. If he was a few too many digits off the mark, he'd be sending the small robot craft off into the planet's atmosphere, out into the star system, or back into the ship itself where it would crumble against *Enterprise*'s hull plates. And that was if his jury-rigging had worked at all. The drone could blow up when activated and alert Data that something was amiss. He could see that now: Data having him confined to sickbay for psychological analysis.

The walk back to his cabin was painfully long and his mind more on the adjustments he'd have to make to his communicator than the layout of the ship. Had it not been for the proximity vest he would have slammed into bulkheads three times.

Damned if he didn't feel as if he was being watched all the time. Senselessly self-conscious maybe, but just couldn't be helped. Maybe he *was* paranoid . . . or was he just intensely aware? That thought made him chuckle. Wasn't there an old saying that if you thought you were crazy you probably weren't?

Okay, so Geordi felt embarrassed at his loss. That wasn't abnormal. Data was the one acting abnormally. It had to be some sort of damage at work there. How else could Data be so against Worf? And the Klingons? Had the Hidran found some way to tap into him? And how could the android forget—*twice*—that he shouldn't nod to Geordi? Data could remember the *names* of a thousand angels dancing on the head of a pin. For him to forget anything so simple proved there was something wrong with him.

Didn't it?

Geordi'd let the captain decide.

He skittered into his cabin, threw himself toward a table he often tinkered at, and pulled his communicator from his chest. He clutched the comm badge in one hand, and pulled a small contraption out of a drawer.

It was no easy task to change the frequency of a communicator without notifying the controlling computer of the alteration. This gadget would help—but it would have to be tricked into it.

These were the moments that Geordi fancied himself a rather dangerous gent if he wanted to be. That idea quickly cooled into a frightening thought . . .

Data could be dangerous as well.

Geordi hurried himself through the rest of his work: fingers flying untidily over the small, detailed work. Had he been able to see he would have been done in moments . . .

When finished he hastily pushed his tools to one side. Leaving the communicator on the table top, he tapped and it chirped, passing normal channels and searching for the drone that had been converted into a makeshift jumper. The signal would find the drone and jump from there to the planet and hopefully reach Picard through the white-noise transmission blanket.

Clenching his fists in anticipation, Geordi moved in toward the communicator. "La Forge to Picard. Come in."

Picard closed the door quickly behind him, a little awkwardly, not accustomed to a door that didn't follow orders. *A civilian door—like its owner.* He was already surprised Barbara hadn't followed him into the hall.

Civilians. He remembered complaining to his superior for assigning him a ship that would house civilians like some star-skipping starbase. It was dangerous, foolish . . . and yet he had coped. Riker had helped with that. Amiable, genial Will Riker who had somehow walked the line between commander and father figure to a crew of families. A line Picard didn't want to look for, let alone find. He was glad to leave that to Will.

Riker. Where were he and Troi? If they were anywhere.

One fiasco at a time, Picard reminded himself as he strode toward the corridor entrance that would lead him to Connors.

Perhaps he should try to contact MacKenzie himself. If Data had been diddling with the frequencies again . . . There was an odd happenstance. Data had been acting quite out of character. It was like him to suggest alternatives—but to act on them without authorization. Another officer might, but Data?

No large matter. Picard had endless other problems. Riker and Troi, Worf and the delegates, Zhad's death, the Klingon delegate's death ... All this had been so well planned. Or so he'd thought. The plan had shattered into a thousand shards when Zhad died and took the Klingon with him.

But was Zhad killed or did he commit suicide? That was now a valid concern.

"Why? Why would anyone do that?" Barbara's question kept tugging at him. A *good* question.

What did the Hidran gain if Worf was implicated? Perhaps the Federation would "owe" the Hidran? The politicians in the Federation Council might think so.

Maybe it had nothing to do with the Federation. What if such an act of self-sacrifice was for some internal Hidran element that Zhad disagreed with? Or agreed with? It wouldn't be the first time someone scuttled their own ship so as to paint themselves the damaged party.

There were endless possibilities.

The Hidran knew the Federation and the Klingons were allies. If a Klingon who was a Federation citizen murdered the Hidran ambassador, the Klingons themselves may have to disavow such action by supplying the Hidran with what they wanted: the Federation might apply pressure to that end because it was their citizen. Two implications in one.

But which? Did Zhad want to stop the treaty because he was against it, or did he want to assure the treaty because he thought it would be spoiled?

"I suspect you will regret your dealings with the Klingons, Picard. I know I will."

Those had been Zhad's last direct words to Picard. Did the Ambassador plot his own death at that point?

So many alternatives, the only one that seemed totally implausible, to Picard at least, was that Worf intended to murder Zhad.

But what if it was an accident? Worf admitted to striking the Hidran. What then?

Which was true?

The mind boggled.

Somehow he had to reason it all out.

Reason. Reason seemed to have evaporated as of late. He had to do something to get logic to condense again.

Without signaling, Picard's communicator suddenly spat itself to life. *"La Forge to Pic . . . —om in."* The signal broke itself with static.

Geordi? Why? What was wrong? Picard tapped at the comm badge. "Picard here. You're breaking up, Mr. La Forge."

"Little time, Captain. Jury-rigged comm. Something wrong with Data—my opinion that . . . damaged somehow. He's restricted commun— . . . —is planning to forcibly board the Klingon vessel. I believe . . . against your orders, sir. Can you confirm?"

Picard halted his gait down the corridor. "What? repeat that, La Forge," he ordered, the sharp needle of a headache promising never to fade. "I have given no order to board the Klingon ship, Commander. You are to relieve Mr. Data on my authority."

Static sputtered, filling the narrow corridor with echoing noise.

"Captain, do you read me?"

"I read you, La Forge. Carry out my order!"

"Captain? If you can hear . . . at all . . . —ease respond."

"I read you, Commander. Relieve Data of duty. Assume command and reestablish main—"

"Are you attempt— . . . to signal back? I ca— . . . no— . . . as— . . . cha— . . ."

"La Forge! You're breaking up!"

The connection withered into a blank crackle of irritating noise. The captain hit the comm badge again. "Picard to *Enterprise.*"

Nothing.

"Picard to *Enterprise!*"

"Enterprise, *Data here.*"

"Mister Data, have you released communications as I ordered?"

"Not yet, sir."

Picard didn't need to ask why. "Commander, are you preparing an away team to board the Klingon vessel?"

"Yes, sir."

"I specifically forbade that plan, didn't I, Commander?"

There was a pause. *"Specifically, sir, you said I should do whatever I must to get to the bottom of this situation."*

Picard didn't need to pause. His actions were clear. "Commander Data, you are hereby relieved of duty. Relinquish command to the duty officer and report to Bioengineering for a complete diagnostic."

Silence. No static.

"Captain, I assure you I am in perfect running order. If you would allow me to explain—"

"I haven't time for explanations, Commander. You have your orders. This time make sure you carry them out."

"Captain," Data inquired in his normal, even tone, *"are you under duress?"*

"No I'm not under duress," Picard barked.

"I believe you are, sir, and I cannot follow a coerced order."

"Mr. Data!"

There was silence over the comm. No static.

"Commander Data, beam me aboard immediately."

"I am sorry, sir. I believe you to be giving that order under threat of physical violence. I can not release the white noise transmission blanket under these circumstances."

"Commander, you are relieved of duty. Relinquish command to Mr. La Forge."

"I assure you, Captain, I shall do all in my power to achieve your rescue. Enterprise *out."*

The signal chirped closed, and Picard was alone. More alone than he had ever felt.

He jabbed at the comm badge again, twice, and was taunted, panicked by quiet.

"It couldn't possibly get any worse," Picard said to himself as he turned back the way he'd come. He'd get back to Dr. Crusher—have her call Data and beam up to the ship. Put her in temporary command. Not his first choice, but everyone else was either under arrest, missing, blind or insane.

He chuckled ironically, wondering which he would succumb to.

A pressure in his back, warm . . .

"Halt," said a muffled, gravely voice from behind him. "Do not reach for your weapon."

Urosk, a phaser pressed into the small of Picard's back, pushed the captain forward as he reached his long, orange arm around and wrested the weapon from the Starfleet captain's holster.

"You will come with me, Picard," Urosk said.

Picard turned slowly around to face the Hidran captain. "Where are my men?"

"Sleeping."

What did that mean? Unconscious? Dead?

"I want to see them."

"The time for what you want," Urosk hissed slowly, holding both phasers on Picard now, "is at an end."

Chapter Eleven

BARBARA CLENCHED THE HANDLE of her phaser close to her stomach and tried not to breathe. One overt move—one sound that gave her away—and Picard might die. She watched tacitly as Urosk forced the captain through the hatchway.

The door closed behind them. Picard had said something as Urosk shoved him in, Barbara couldn't tell what.

She anxiously chewed at her lower lip. If only Urosk's phaser hadn't been trained so closely on Picard . . . Then again, the two of them were only centimeters apart. From where she was, pressed into the alcove of a doorway, she wouldn't have been able to target Urosk if he'd had a bullseye on his back. All the training she'd had with a phaser was the two-hour class offered when she purchased one a few years ago. She knew the settings and what they could do, but even those were on a civilian hand weapon, not the sleek, military one she now held in her sweaty palm. This she had gotten from one of her lease-a-guards. It looked much more like a Starfleet weapon than her old phaser-pistol, and it was warmer to the touch, pulsing with pent-up energy.

She rose, straightened herself, then quickly shrank back against the wall. Footsteps shuffled. Heavy ones. Another Hidran—shifting down the hall toward the door. She could smell the sour mustiness of him as he passed. Unnoticed, she pushed out her breath in short, quiet bursts.

Her heart was pounding so loudly she thought that it might give her away. Not the sound—the fact that she might have a heart attack, fall on her own phaser, and vaporize herself and half the building with her.

The Hidran hesitated before joining the others beyond the hatch. He looked from side to side, seemingly apprehensive, then finally disappeared through the door.

Quickly she moved from doorway to doorway up the corridor, carefully watching that hatch for any sound or movement and pausing to hide her form behind any supporting pillar that allowed.

From behind her came a moan and she jumped. In the alcove next to her, crammed between the tight walls, were two men in Starfleet security uniforms. Picard's missing crewmen, obviously on the job.

Without a holster for her phaser she had to set the safety and tuck it under her arm as she helped one of them up. She pulled him out into the hall, guiding him to sit against the wall. He groaned a thanks and she did the same for the other. Both had lost their communicator/insignia she noticed.

"What happened?" Barbara asked.

The first one she pulled out—tall and human with brown curly hair—spoke in a raspy voice. "The Hidran captain attacked me . . . Tried to get my weapon."

"Tried?" she asked wryly.

Curly looked up indignantly. With the bruise on his jaw and an eye swelled closed he hardly looked threatening. More like a school boy who'd been in a playground scrap.

Barbara glanced at the other man, who was still dazed.

She helped the groggy one sit up straighter, cupping her hand behind his head to give it balance.

"The Hidran have your captain," she said matter-of-factly, trying to mask her building panic.

Suddenly the Starfleet men were both alert. "When?" Curly demanded, pushing himself up into a stoop.

"A few moments ago. I didn't want to try anything that'd get him killed."

Curly's eyes darted to his comrade, then to the weapon crooked into Barbara's arm. "Give me your phaser."

She grasped the weapon in her fist and shook her head. "Sorry, fellas. People weren't dying around here until Starfleet showed up. I've got mine, you get yours."

"Ma'am," Curly said, standing straight now, looking stronger every moment, "we have a situation here—"

"Is that what you call it?" Barbara snapped, gripping her phaser close. "A 'situation'? Your captain is being held by people who don't think twice about killing *themselves* for a cause let alone someone else, and you're calling it something less than a disaster?"

"Ma'am—"

"Your mother's a 'ma'am,' kid, not me. You two want to dig up some phasers and come back, that's fine—I'll stay here and watch the door, but this place is swimming with killers and I'm not giving up this weapon."

"You're not qualified—"

147

Barbara cut him off. "The way I see it, Curly, you two lost yours and I still have mine, so let's not brag about qualifications." She waved them away. "Go now, so you can get back sooner."

Curly frowned, then finally pulled his buddy up with him. "Fine," he said. "You can stay here, but don't attempt anything. You see that door open, get back to the main hall. We'll be back as soon as we can."

Barbara covered a chuckle. They'd do what she wanted so long as they could give an order making it sound as if they'd thought of it. Military types—they were all alike.

"Gentlemen . . ."

They stopped their gait down the corridor and turned back to her.

"Just a suggestion, Curly," Barbara said, "but I'd see how the Klingons are holding up. The Hidran goon who attacked your friend wasn't going out for Romulan take-out."

They both sneered at her, then were gone down the corridor—back toward the main hall. Barbara shrank into the alcove where they'd been "resting" and watched them leave. Running—they were running. A few moments ago they'd been unconscious. They *were* more qualified and she should have let them stay while she ran for help. Or the hills. Something.

Stupidity took on new definition as she realized what she was doing: guarding five Amazon fish with bad attitudes and superior training. She had one weapon and a two hour class in "how to store your phaser properly." *Wonder if they'd go for that—challenge them to properly store their phasers?*

How many phasers would they have? Picard's, the two guards' . . . so maybe three. But one of them had come back after Urosk went in with the captain. How many had he "happened" upon? She had to assume they were *all* armed. Five to one. Not exactly odds she'd play at an Argellian casino.

She should have known something like this would happen. This is what you got when you put Hidran oil and Klingon water in a Starfleet blender.

She shrank back into the alcove, her back to a door that led to some room she'd never used. This building, a grand stone hall with a maze of rooms and offices on all sides, was the only standing structure on the planet that was more or less intact. Who had built it was unknown. The tapestries that lined the walls in the main hall appeared to be of an agrarian culture, but nothing else on the planet seemed to speak to that. There were no mills, no holding silos, no overgrown farms. There were a few other structures she was sure . . . somewhere on the planet. There must have been—she remembered reading something about them in one of the articles she'd seen about Velex. She hadn't been here long enough to see for herself. Maybe Riker had found one of those. Maybe he had survived the crash. Maybe—

An electronic sound, the hatch opening, yanked her away from her thoughts. She scrambled to her feet, drawing herself up into a small crouch.

She couldn't see anything inside the door—too dark.

What was she doing here? No one called for a scientist.

She aimed the phaser, set it on heavy stun, and fired at the door.

Nothing! *Damn! The safety!*

One of the Hidran poked his head from behind the door. He looked around.

Thumbing the safety, Barbara took careful aim at the Hidran that was now stepping from behind the hatch. She fired—a bright cable of energy stabbed out toward the other end of the hall. She was watching her shaking hand and not her target, and by the time she looked up the Hidran had skittered back into the room.

She knew he'd had nothing to worry about—her shot must have flashed against the ceiling at least three meters from him, harmlessly absorbed by the sandstone. A small flutter of dust fell to the ground in the silence that followed.

A salmon-colored arm reached out, a phaser in hand. Barbara fell back into the protection of the alcove as a piece of the wall near her—where her face had been—evaporated. That wasn't the mark of a phaser on stun. They were *not* playing games.

Her hand was shaking worse. She fired blindly again, around the corner of what was left of her protection. She heard the blast—didn't know what she'd hit. Her quivering hand couldn't have helped her aim, yet there was no sound. Maybe she'd gotten lucky and stunned him.

Phaser first, at level with her nose, she peered around the corner. An orange phaser spear rushed past her and she plucked her head out of the way. The beam struck the wall behind her and turned it to dust. Choking, she crammed her eyes closed and tried to wave the sandy dust away from her nose and mouth.

Another phaser whine—another blast. This time they missed this side of the wall all together.

Still she needed more protection—they had all but destroyed the alcove with their first two shots.

The phaser squeezed between her fingers, she put her hand out and fired—once, twice, three times.

And again.

Again.

She kept pummeling the Hidran's only doorway with energy as she darted across the hall to a different alcove. She only glanced at the hatch for a moment, but saw no one there—no face looked back at her.

Safe for the moment, her protection and view of the Hidran better, she paused, caught her breath. Should she move from pillar to pillar up the corridor and away from here? Or should she stick with the more protective alcoves?

Another phaser blast—this time down the hall past her. She saw the beam cut through the air, sizzling the atmosphere and singeing her hair. She was parallel with the hatchway now—they couldn't break away at her protection without carving through the walls of the room they were in. That would prove disastrous for all, for the building was stone and would cave into rubble if its supports were shaken enough. She'd already felt the dust fall on her when the Hidran phasers sent tremors through the structure.

Phaser in her right hand, the Hidran's hatchway on her left, she crept forward, ready.

Ready for what? She was outgunned and outexperienced.

She had to get out of there—others could do this and still be alive when it was over.

Three Hidran exploded from the hatchway and three flashes of metal or plastic broke across the hall. They were all taking aim at her position at once! The fire power combined would obliterate the alcove, and her along with it.

She rolled away, stones and dust snapping at her.

Their aim was good—the alcove where she'd been hidden was no more. She froze behind a pillar, then realized that using it as protection would be her death if they phasered it rather than her. The ceiling would collapse and she'd die under an avalanche of stone and brick. She fired blindly again, at least trying to get a pause in their return, and ran—she wasn't sure toward what.

Her breath was heavy—the stone under her feet evaporated as they fired and she ran. A corridor—she took it, not knowing where it led.

Stupid—it led back to the same corridor in a big loop. She now had an even better view of the Hidran and their blasted hatch, but they also had the same vantage on her.

Aim. All she had to do was aim. Eye on target and fire. How hard could it be?

She fired, the beam *nearly* hit one of the Hidran. They moved so quickly for their bulk. She was just getting use to this shoot-and-fire thing and now they were moving the targets.

Her breath coming in long strokes, her hand shaking, she lined up the closest Hidran and thumbed the trigger. Her beam lanced past him but caught one of the others right in the face.

The Hidran soldier bounced back against the wall as if he'd been hit by a thousand fists.

"Well, what do ya know," she chuckled to herself. "Every once in a while the broad side of a barn jumps up for you."

One big red barn down—four to go.

The other two Hidran began firing more—taking broad steps toward her.

Barbara fired and ran—toward the other path of the corridor—the one that would bring her around in a loop, but at least put her farther from the Hidran and the hatch itself.

A flash of lightning and the pillar before her exploded and she pulled herself back as best she could. The ceiling cracked and crashed to the floor. Flecks of rock and sand fell on her as she fell back into another alcove. Larger stones rolled and bounced up her legs as she collapsed against the wall, crying out in frustration and pain.

She choked as the dust cleared and allowed her to

see the rubble that would become her headstone—she was now blocked from one corridor by the new crag, and the other by the Hidran.

There was no place to go.

And the Hidran were firing . . . and moving closer. She wouldn't give up without a fight. She pressed herself forward, phaser ready . . .

Suddenly the two Hidran fell forward. A table, one from the lab they'd been held in, crashed up behind them, pushing them down.

Picard exploded out the hatch and dove for the stunned Hidran's phaser. The Starfleet captain grabbed it in one hand and closed his other into a fist along the floor. He fired back through the hatch and then rolled forward toward the other two downed Hidran.

His phaser connected with one of them, and the Hidran sank back to the floor. The other Hidran spun around and knocked Picard down. The captain's left hand shot out, but not into a punch—his fist opened —he threw dust into the Hidran's face.

The alien bent forward, choking and sputtering. For a moment—just an instant—Picard's eyes locked with Barbara's. She nodded. She didn't know what he wanted, but she could go with the flow of it, and that's probably all he'd wanted anyway.

From out of the hatch came the other two Hidran. They towered over Picard as he spun around.

The captain slammed his boot into the instep of the Hidran behind him—the one that was still choking. Barbara heard a yelp of pain, and Picard went down to his knees. Instantly, the captain grabbed another handful of dust that had fallen from the ceiling and tossed it into the air. The other Hidran crumpled.

He repeated the action as he rolled away, and all the Hidran began writhing and choking, their arms flailing, trying to clear the dust.

Fantastic—horrific—as if they'd been showered with acid. Here she was, cowering in a corner with a phaser as Picard fended off all the Hidran with his bare hands and know-how.

Why wasn't she helping? That's what he needed—her help.

Barbara fired three times quickly through the small cloud of dust. She heard one Hidran fall.

She fired again, almost blindly and Picard kept tossing dust into the air as he scrambled toward her. The beam from her phaser shot forward and caught Picard in his chest, bouncing him back into the Hidran he was escaping from.

The dust was settling . . . and Picard was unconscious.

"No!"

Barbara pulled back into the alcove, wishing she could pull the beam back as well.

She heard a sound. The Hidran laughing? Her heart sinking? Both were happening. The three Hidran who remained conscious were choking and yet still moving toward her—and taking potshots with their phasers.

Picard, limp and unconscious, was tossed over the shoulder of one of them. Her fault. *Hers.* She'd gotten herself into this quicksand, he had been trying to get her out, and what did she do? Pull him down with her.

The Hidran continued to choke even thought the dust had settled. The dust—

The dust!

The Hidran, born from a water planet, *hated* dust. Dust was their enemy, a disease to them. Picard knew that and was trying to tell her. It's how he'd fought them: his knowledge of them.

Starfleet wasn't just brawn and testosterone as she'd thought. And she wished she could tell Picard that now.

She quickly set the phaser—a wide beam, thinly distributed.

They were moving closer . . . closer . . .

Not as close as she wanted them, but she panicked a bit and fired. The phaser spat energy in a thin, broad beam—a spatula of energy that she scraped not against the Hidran, but on the ceiling above them.

Clouds of dust, the sandstone ceiling turned to grit, rained down on the Hidran, and cut off their air. Gagging, they crumpled like large trees being tossed in a tornado. Barbara saw Picard pitched to the floor, a flash of red and black uniform through the chalk fog.

They tried to move forward through the dust barricade. Barbara aimed the phaser and fired again. This time the floor spat up into a gritty barrier that mushroomed into the Hidran. Beyond the patchy thickness she saw them choking, but they refused to retreat back through the hatch.

She choked as the dust found its way forward and reset her phaser back to stun. Stun—if she'd left this to the professionals Picard wouldn't have been stunned. Then again, at least she had only stunned him. A phaser setting more and he might have died.

Her mouth was dry and she licked her lips, suddenly frightened by the thought that he still might. The Hidran were trapped and who knew what they'd do now?

They did.

The Hidran moved forward, despite the dust, and continued to fire.

She was trapped, and knew she had to make a run for it—to get help—

Taking a deep breath, Barbara leapt forward and began a sprint down the hall—toward the Hidran.

The falling dust half cloaking her, she turned away from them as soon as she could and ran toward the main hall, her muscles screaming and feet barely able to balance on the line of fear she felt.

Relief melted through her as she saw three new Starfleet security guards running toward her.

The calvary had come, and just in ti—

Beside her the wall exploded into large chunks of rock and—

She felt her head snap . . . and consciousness evaporated.

Saxon was glad he was only the transporter chief. That seemed almost a cowardly thought, but he knew how many security teams were down on the planet, and wasn't really sure what Commander Data hoped to gain by making a personal rescue attempt.

The commander, holding his phaser rifle and tricorder, waited near the transporter platform.

"Lieutenant Wyckoff just signaled that the team is on its way, sir," Saxon told the android.

Data nodded. "Very well. I will want to beam down outside the main hall."

"Aye, sir." A wise move—sensors said no one was on the streets.

The transporter room doors parted, and acting security chief Wyckoff entered, flanked by six other security officers.

"Reporting as ordered, Commander," Wyckoff said, nodding his men onto the dais before them.

Each man, Saxon noticed, was also carrying a heavy-duty phaser rifle and a few power-pack replacements.

Data nodded to the men who'd taken their places on the transporter platform, then spoke to Wyckoff. "The captain is being held, presumably by the Klingons. I will not discontinue the white-noise blanket for fear that the Klingons would attempt to beam the captain off the planet. However, keeping the transmission jammer active means that our sensors cannot pinpoint his specific location. We are aware that all the life-forms in question are either in the main hall or in other buildings, however, and for that reason we will transport down outside the main hall."

Wyckoff nodded and stepped onto the transporter dais, as did Data.

The android nodded to Saxon.

"Energizing," the transporter chief said, running his hand along the controls. Suddenly the console turned dark. He jabbed at the panel, then looked up to Data. "We've lost power, sir."

Data handed his phaser rifle to the guard behind him, who, with both rifles and a utility bag hanging off him, took on the posture of a bandito out of an old Western movie.

"What is the cause?" Data asked, stepping down, leaving the seven security men to hold their positions.

The chief shook his head and shrugged. "I don't know, sir. Just no power to the console."

Data quickly tapped at his comm badge. "Data to Engineering."

"Engineering. Lieutenant Cheng here."

"Transporter Room Four has lost power. Are we experiencing difficulties?"

"One moment, sir." There was a pause. *"I show your null activity, sir, but it's not coming from any engineering console. There may be a problem on site."*

Data looked up at Saxon, who dabbed at his console, then shook his head.

"The problem does not appear to be down here," Data said.

"We'll get right on it, Commander. In the meantime I can put Transporter Room Five on priority."

"Very well. Data out." The android waved the

security men off the transporter dais and nodded a "carry on" to the chief.

Smoke was filling the room, billowing from phaser-punched holes, forming black clouds near the high ceiling. Riker shifted his weight onto his bad leg for only an instant, then quickly switched back, wincing in pain.

Five lovely machines, seven lovely craters burned into their sides. Riker pulled Deanna into the corridor, then lowered himself to the floor and admired his handiwork through the open door. Unfortunately, five minutes had passed and no one had rushed in to stop the damage. An automatic fire-suppression had begun to work its magic, but a phaser blast had quickly terminated that operation as well. The thought struck Riker that all this could be for nothing. What if no one was on this ship? What if they had just done something to hamper life-support?

Deanna stooped down next to him. "Your leg needs treatment, Will. You can't lose any more blood."

He nodded lethargically. "I know. I'm open to suggestions."

Grasping his hand in hers, she said, "I have an idea, but it will be painful."

"More painful than death?"

She smiled weakly and brushed away the hair that had fallen over his brow. "Probably."

He tried to return the smile. "Deanna, my strength," he said mock-seriously. "What's your idea?"

"Give me your phaser," she said. "I'll cauterize the wound."

Eyes bulging, he edged away from her. "Have you lost your mind? Even at the lowest heat setting you'd burn my leg off!"

"You haven't heard the whole idea—"

"I don't think I want to."

She rose, and gestured into the room, toward one of the broken machines. "Look at the wealth of metal. All we must do is cut a piece off, heat *it* sufficiently, then use it to close your wound."

He looked from her to a bent piece of the metal panel on one of the damaged machines. "You're not kidding when you say painful."

"I'd rather you were in pain than dead," she said.

"Why are those always my only two choices?" He smiled. They did this to each other in times of stress—each tried to be the one that lightened the mood a little more. It didn't seem to be working today. Under each smile, Riker knew, was worry and trepidation.

She held out her hand. "Your phaser."

Nodding, he handed the weapon to her. "Be careful."

"I'm going to stun you first, on the lightest setting," she said, playing with the phaser's settings. "It should daze you dull the pain. I don't want to use anything stronger because your system is already weak."

"Understood." Riker didn't want all the details. "I've agreed. Just do it."

She let out a long breath, then silently aimed the weapon and fired at the large section of metal that Riker had been looking at a moment earlier. The beam of the phaser sliced easily through the strip of paneling and sent a metal wedge clattering to the deck.

What hit the floor was a triangular edge of some alien ore, still sizzling and spitting sparks.

Balancing on the balls of her feet, she lowered herself to Riker's injured leg. Slowly she unwrapped the bloody bandage, revealing a deep angled wound that was as painful as it looked.

Riker was not exactly the squeamish type—he could bear the sight of his own blood, just didn't prefer it.

Deanna wrapped the thick end of the strip of cloth she'd torn from her uniform around her right hand. Her uniform was now sleeveless, having sacrificed both arms to Riker's wound. With the phaser in her left hand, she picked up the sharper, cooler edge of the metal wedge. A line of energy linked the wedge and the phaser when she thumbed the trigger. They could see the orange heat creeping up from the edge of the metal toward Deanna's fingers. When the red glow was halfway up the strip of metal, and perhaps she was beginning to feel the burn on her fingertips, she clicked off the phaser and reset it.

"I'm going to stun you now."

He smiled back weakly. "I've always found you stunning."

She couldn't seem to return the smile, and instead just looked at him anxiously. She aimed the phaser at his chest . . . and fired.

Darkness blotted his consciousness in parts as the surge of energy jolted him, then sent him falling into waking sleep where pain was just a shadow.

He thought he saw Deanna stooped over his leg. He could sort of feel her holding his knee firmly in her free hand. Brighter than the rest of his view—in fact, the only thing he could make out clearly—was the hand that held the wedge of hot metal.

He slipped into complete darkness for a moment, then awoke to a strange feeling . . . He scratched at his beard as a line of sweat from his temple drizzled down his cheek.

He heard himself moan, and tried to focus. He could make out Deanna's eyes—they seemed large, and he could also see her hand shaking over his leg. Was it over?

She lowered the searing shard of metal toward the gash that was trickling blood. The wound hadn't even tried to clot.

Pain smacked him wide awake and he had to cram his eyes shut. A spike of agony shot through his leg and up his back. A heat so hot it felt cold, he flinched and Deanna's grip on his knee tightened. Where had she gotten such strength? He heard the sizzle of his own blood against the hot wedge of metal. He could feel the heat on his skin—it mixed with the heat of the blood until he couldn't tell the difference.

He grunted—couldn't help it—the burning—the odor of his own flesh being scorched. He opened his eyes. Deanna yanked the angry torch away from his leg and grabbed her own hand off. His breath pounded in his chest, whistling through his teeth. The blood on his leg was dried and cracked and there was a red patch where the gash had been. It would blister soon, but the bleeding was stopped.

Deanna was talking, saying something about leaving the bandage off to let the leg breathe. Riker was exhausted and couldn't really listen. The pain in his leg was pulsing—waves of heat that radiated up his leg and gave him a headache. Water . . . He was suddenly thirsty and wanted to be immersed in a pool of cool water.

"Are you all right?" Deanna asked.

"Water . . ." Riker groaned. "I'd like water . . ."

"I know," she said softly. "Relax a moment."

And he did. The room seemed to darken and brighten as he slipped in and out of light sleep. The pain became a steady thudding in his leg and was manageable like that. After a few moments, perhaps it was longer, he opened his eyes wide and thanked her.

"I'm better," he said, and noticed the smoke was so thick in the machinery room that it was beginning to glide out into the hall. "No one's shown up, huh?"

Deanna shook her head. "And I still don't feel anyone."

Riker sighed. "We have to get off this ship. We—"

He turned his head left, trying to hear down the corridor. The sound of the still sizzling machinery got in the way. "You hear that?" He asked, suddenly feeling stronger, as if he'd had a good meal and a long night's sleep. He licked his lips, his mouth still dry. "What is that?"

"I don't hear it."

He held up an index finger. "Listen."

She cocked her head in the direction he was looking. "I hear it. Someone's coming!"

Riker grabbed at his phaser. At some point Deanna must've returned it to his holster. "Help me up. I don't want to meet our generous hosts sitting on my butt." He tested the weight on his bad leg and decided he could live with the pain. "You feeling anything?"

"Not a thing," she said, gripping his arm. "Whoever or whatever . . . it's too alien for me."

"I'm sorry, sir, we've lost power again."

Geordi imagined Data's brow wrinkling at that one.

"Explain," Data said, static etching his voice. Geordi tried to tune the hand communicator a bit better. He laid it on a level place in a crevice of the Jefferies tube, thanked his lucky stars that he'd found it—knowing the old-issue comm wouldn't be missed—and set about his work as he listened.

"Same power loss as before, sir," the Transporter chief said, probably struggling with his controls.

"Data to Engineering. Transporter Room Five is now experiencing a power loss."

Geordi stifled a chuckle. This was all too serious and dangerous for that, but he had to admit a little pleasure at being such a good mutineer. His father had always told him to do his work as best he could.

And even blind, quarreling with the darkness and fumbling with his tools and the circuits before him, he was doing just that.

"Cheng here, sir. I still see you as reading full power."

Geordi shook his head. He was really going to have to spend a little more time showing Cheng the ins and outs of Engineering. Of course, the tampering *was* being well hidden.

Quite the decision Geordi had made here. He hoped he was right. He'd heard a word or two of Picard's response to him. It wasn't enough to know what the captain had said, but it *was* enough to know that Picard hadn't been under duress. If so, why did he have his communicator? And why did he contact Data right away, as Data himself had admitted? Chances were the captain had heard most of Geordi's message and when he contacted Data to see what the problem was, the android had slipped further into . . . well, whatever his problem was.

Geordi's problem was more obvious: he couldn't allow Data to beam down and start accusing Klingons —or, in his absurd state, do something worse. Geordi was taking a gamble. He might lose, but knew that if he didn't try, the Klingons on the planet surely would.

"Stand by." Data's voice again. *"Computer, locate Lieutenant Commander Geordi La Forge."*

"Locating my communicator will be easy, Data. I'm smarter than that," Geordi said to himself.

"Lieutenant Commander Geordi La Forge is in cabin 2471, deck two."

"Don't do it, Data," Geordi grumbled, his hands fiddling faster with the controls at the end of the Jefferies tube. "Don't force me to up the ante."

There was silence from the comm, and for a moment Geordi thought he'd lost his link or had been found out. Finally, though, he heard Data's order: *"Scan cabin 2471, deck two, for life-form readings."*

"Scanning. No life-form readings."

Geordi heard the opening of the transporter room door, and then Data again. *"Lieutenant Wyckoff, I have reason to believe that Commander La Forge is either ill, or under the influence of a Klingon agent. Security is to locate Mr. La Forge and confine him."*

"A Klingon agent, sir?"

Well, at least someone was questioning all this . . . garbage.

"It is a possibility," Data said, too damn convincingly. He sounded as if he knew something they didn't.

"Aye aye, sir."

Damn. They were going to trust him. The reluctant, questioning tones were there—just not strong enough.

"Also, signal General Quarters. I will be on the bridge. Please contact me when you have located Commander La Forge."

Geordi heard an "aye, sir" and the swishing of the transporter room door again.

What now? If security backed Data, eventually Geordi would be found and . . . he'd be powerless to do anything.

And he would be found. Unless . . . unless he found them first. But only when he was ready.

He stuffed his tools back into his small bag, covered the access plate, grabbed the hand communicator, and scurried back down the tube. There was no way to tell where security was going to look for him first, but it might be a Jefferies tube that had something to do with transporters, so best to get out of that one.

"General Quarters. All hands, General Quarters . . ."

The alarms began to sound and Geordi could hear

the rush of people scrambling to their quarters or duty stations. He decided to duck into a rec room bathroom.

He flipped open the hand-comm and fingered a few dials. "Computer, tie in to communicator, authorization La Forge."

"Ready."

"Now *that's* more like it." He sat down on the head's seat, allowing his tool kit to drop to his feet. He held the communicator intently before him, and started to map out the orders he'd need to use.

"Computer, locate Lieutenant Wyckoff."

"Lieutenant Wyckoff is in turbolift twelve."

"Computer, what is the heading of turbolift twelve?"

"Turbolift twelve's destination is deck two."

Geordi yanked himself up so quickly that had the commode not been attached to the deck it would have fallen back. "Okay. My cabin. Good place to start."

By the time Geordi reached deck two—and he was sure to take the access ladders rather than the turbolifts—he knew Wyckoff would already be at the cabin. That was fine. Geordi didn't want to walk into his cabin when Security was there—that would make it seem as if they were catching him by surprise. He needed to catch *them* by surprise.

And he did. When Wyckoff and his two men came out from Geordi's cabin, the engineer made sure he was standing in front of that door.

"Commander La Forge—"

"Lieutenant Wyckoff, I presume?" Geordi asked. He could feel the tingling from his proximity vest that said they were only a few feet from him. "I'd heard you were here. We need to talk."

"Sir," Wyckoff said apologetically, "I'm to take you into custody. Commander Data's orders."

"I know." Geordi gestured toward his cabin door. "Let's talk."

"My orders, sir—"

"Lieutenant," Geordi said, opening his eyes wide, allowing them to see his blank, white, sightless eyes, "I'm blind. I'm not going to try to overpower you. I'm not going to phaser you. I'm going to *talk* to you. And if you don't like what I have to say, I'm going to go with you quietly. All I want is five minutes of your time. If I were trying to avoid you, it would have taken you more than two minutes to find me, right? Instead, *I* came to you."

There was silence for a moment. Perhaps they were all exchanging glances. For all Geordi knew, a crowd had gathered, including Data.

"Okay, sir," Wyckoff finally said. "Five minutes."

Geordi nodded, and walked forward, through them, and into his cabin.

As soon as the door swished closed behind them, Geordi turned and began.

"Data isn't himself," Geordi said. "Jim," he said to Wyckoff, "you know me. Am I a Klingon agent? Worf is your superior—your friend. Is *he?*"

Geordi didn't allow an answer.

"Look at Data's warped facts," he continued. "No one is allowed to contact the planet. Supposedly Commander Riker and the counselor are missing, and that's the Klingons' fault. Worf is *maybe* accused of murder, but it hasn't been proven—even by Data's admission—and yet Data pronounces him guilty. Captain Picard is apparently under duress, but then why did he have his communicator? And why won't Data let me talk to the captain as I requested? Why am *I* assumed to be a Klingon agent just because I've questioned Data's orders?"

Geordi paused, and let all sink in. No one spoke and

he could only imagine the expressions passing their faces. If only he could see—to get a tack on what they were thinking.

"Sir," Wyckoff began, "did you have something to do with the transporter malfunctions?"

Geordi nodded. "Yes. I did. I can't let him go beaming down into what could be such a touchy situation. You didn't hear him when he talked about boarding the Klingon cruiser and searching for Riker. He's not being rational, Wyckoff."

"With all due respect, sir," Wyckoff said, "this is what I'd assume a Klingon agent would say."

Sweat broke out across Geordi's forehead. He could feel it, and hoped it wasn't seen. He avoided scratching his head nervously. He didn't want to give Wyckoff any body-language cues that might compromise what he was saying.

The security lieutenant hesitated a moment, then continued. "Commander, I *do* know Lieutenant Worf, and I do know you. But I also know Commander Data, and he *is* in command. It isn't within my purview to decide that he should be replaced by you."

"I'm not fit to take command. You *can* see that. I won't ask you to make that decision." Geordi stepped forward, pointing to his chest. "Arrest me, Lieutenant. I wouldn't ask you not to. But arrest Data too. Put us *both* in the brig and sort it out later. Let the captain do it. Let anyone else do it but us." The engineer pressed himself forward again, until the proximity vest told him he was right in front of one of them. He hoped it was Wyckoff, or his flair for the dramatic would look farcical. "Lieutenant, if nothing else, *ask* Data why he thinks the captain is under duress. Ask him why he thinks Worf is a murderer. *Ask,* Lieutenant . . . and base your decision on what you hear." Geordi stepped back and gestured his hands in a surrendering motion. "I'll put my trust in your reason. I sure can't trust Data's."

"What kind of coward are you, Batok?" Urosk hissed at one of his men. They were both still choking. Picard himself was choking some, but noticed the Hidran looked especially depleted. They had changed filters in their masks and were breathing steadily, but Picard would have bet anything that this wasn't what they'd expected at all. There weren't many sandstone buildings on Hidra, to be sure.

"I am inferior, sir," Batok said, slumped over, coughing. The man was obviously exhausted. "I am sorry."

"Sorry?" Urosk muffled a gag with his ranting. "We were being held at bay by a *woman*—a very *small* woman—and all you have to say is you are sorry?"

"I did stun her, sir. Had the other humans not appeared—"

"I do not want your apologies, Batok, I want your perfection!"

Removing his jacket, Picard snorted, "Is that all want? Perfection? You'll need it, Urosk. You've assaulted Starfleet officers and managed to abduct the captain of a starship. The Federation will not play at this situation lightly."

"Silence from you, Picard!" Urosk growled, pointing his phaser. "You are the reason we are here. You—who would not listen to the truth."

"Truth?" Picard scoffed. "What truth? Your truth? All you seem to need to define truth is that you speak it."

"Silence!" Urosk exploded, then turned back to Batok.

Urosk needed to be pushed—but not so hard that Picard would get himself killed in the pushing. Just hard enough so that he might give up whatever foolish plan he had. It was on this end that such work had to be done: there would be no help from the *Enterprise.* If La Forge couldn't hear him, Picard was on his own in all this. Worf was weaponless, Crusher didn't know what was going on . . . She would soon enough, though. On his way down the corridor Picard took notice of the two security guards. They had moved a bit—alive. They were obviously found by Barbara, and would—do what? Contact the ship? Unlikely that would prove fruitful. Something had obviously happened to Data—something that had caused him to cease thinking rationally. Or stop listening.

Picard knew he should have seen this all coming. He'd thought something seemed strange about Data, and should have acted on that suspicion.

He looked at his plush red jacket, now filthy with tan and yellow grit, and tossed it on the bench behind him. He mopped his brow and pulled on the collar of his turtleneck. Disappointed in himself, angry at the situation, Picard tried to focus his thoughts on what the Hidran were saying. Any information he could gain would be helpful.

"I don't expect my soldiers to act like fools!" Urosk barked.

"She *did* have a phaser, sir, and—" Batok cut the end off his own sentence.

Urosk backhanded him and the clapping sound of flesh against the plastic-like construct of the breathing mask echoed in the small room.

Picard cleared his throat. Batok's mask was intact and seemed to be functioning well. Obviously well manufactured. Could Worf's blow to Zhad have been much harder than Urosk's just now? Picard doubted it. Perhaps Zhad *had* killed himself.

Wanting to blend away into the background for now, to see if he could get a fix on the attitudes he'd be dealing with, Picard lowered himself silently onto the bench along the wall. He looked about the room. Some of the dust from outside had settled on the floors and tables. Before its history as a base of operations/holding pen for the Hidran, it must have been a lab of some type. Nondescript computers stood along one wall and a great many tools and trays and jars of dirt were scattered on the tables. At one time they'd probably been neatly stacked. The Hidran were obviously not known for their housekeeping.

Batok's head was down. He slouched yet spoke loudly and clearly as possible through his mask. "Sir, if I may speak . . ."

Stomping away—then back again, Urosk took on the posturing of an angry bull. If he had nostrils somewhere under that mask, they were flaring. "Shall you speak? I'm not even sure if you shall continue to live! *There* is the heart of my lunacy—indecision as to whether I *should* kill you rather than *how* I should!"

Well, at least all captains were alike in some respects. Picard had never actually said anything like that to a member of his crew, but he could sympathize with the feeling.

"I would only speak to please my captain," Batok said.

Urosk laughed. "Not possible, Batok. The sound of your voice is as grating as the dust in the air."

"Sir, I have been to the Klingons' holding cell. I did not leave here solely to supply us with two weapons."

Urosk turned toward the younger, shorter Hidran who still had his eyes focused tightly on his own boots. Despite wishing to remain seated, something in the Hidran's tone pulled Picard up. Thankfully they had not taken his Universal Translator, or all this talk might just have been a series of hisses and clicks.

"Tell me what you must, Batok," Urosk said intensely.

The Hidran lieutenant looked up at his superior, returning the intensity with his eyes. "I have killed the ambassador's murderer. The Klingon—Worf—I have watched him die at my own hand."

Picard rose forward slowly, but didn't move any closer than that. He couldn't if he'd wanted to—his spine, his legs, his jaw—all locked with the tightness of anger and fume.

All that had happened until now suddenly seemed trivial. Worf was dead—tried and convicted by a jury of one.

Chest tight, Picard balled his fists at his sides. He had let this entire predicament swing wildly out of hand . . .

Time to bring it back in check.

Urosk's eyes became slivers. He was obviously smiling behind that blasted mask. "You have done well, Batok. How many of the others did you kill?"

"Others?" Batok battled with himself—he obviously wanted to look away from his captain, but couldn't.

"Surely you didn't only kill the Starfleet Klingon!" Urosk snapped.

"Sir—I . . ."

Picard watched Urosk stifle Batok with a glare. "Speak no more, Batok. You killed only *one* Klingon when you had the chance to kill them all." He wheeled away toward the table behind him. On it he dropped the two communicators he'd collected. Together with Batok's there were four. "You will redeem yourself, Batok, by joining these into a communicator that will reach our ship."

Batok said nothing, but slithered toward the table, obsequiously silent.

Two steps forward and Picard was nearly on top of Urosk. He felt an urge to wrap his hands around the Hidran's throat.

Worf . . .

"And what then, Captain?" Picard snapped. "What happens when you return to your ship?"

Urosk towered over Picard. "We destroy the Klingons—in orbit, then on the planet," he said frankly.

"Why?" Picard spat bitterly. "What will this do? Why must hundreds die for your revenge?"

There was a choking sound from Urosk that must have been a laugh. "Revenge? You know nothing of me, Picard. Batok acted on revenge. He is a young fool. I might have done the same for justice, but there is a grander plan at work here." The Hidran captain still kept his phaser in his palm, pointed toward the floor. Picard glanced down at the weapon. Urosk noticed, and once again aimed up toward Picard's chest. Had it been reset to stun?

"What's your grand plan?" Picard asked. "Killing me? Would full Federation intervention really meet your end?"

Another Hidran chortle. "Is that how precious you are? How many Federation Starships would be deployed to hunt me down if I killed you now? Two? Three? Five? A hundred?"

Jaw hardened, Picard held his anger in check. "There *will* be political implications if you kill me, Urosk. More if you attempt to attack the Klingon ship. And the *Enterprise* will stop you."

"I will allow nothing to stop me, Picard. Not you, not your ship. The Klingons want war and I will prove to them such a move would be much more unhealthy for them than any virus."

Picard's hands flinched. He wanted to grab the Hidran, shake him. It was unfortunate that logic couldn't be beaten into people. "My people will stop you, Urosk."

With his gravel voice grinding into every ear, the

Hidran captain gestured to Picard's chest with the phaser that was once his own. "If your *people* do stop me, you may never live to see it. I would not mourn if you went the way of your Klingon lieutenant."

Bleeeeeeeep.

Both Picard and Urosk turned to Batok.

The young Hidran spun around. "Captain, one of their communicators signals."

"Bring it here."

Batok rushed over. He held the comm badge in the palm of his right hand. The gold tips were wet where he'd touched it.

Bleeeeeeeep.

"Activate it," Urosk ordered, then turned to Picard. "Answer, but take care in what you say. You will tell your people to disengage your communications jammer."

Tentatively, Batok tapped the face of the comm badge.

It chirped to the open frequency.

Picard opened his mouth to speak, and Urosk thrust the phaser into his gut as a reminder.

"Picard here."

"Lieutenant Worf here, sir. We have a situation in the Klingon delegates' chamber. There has been another murder."

Chapter Twelve

"TAKE COVER!"

Riker fired again but Deanna still hesitated. She stood there, motionless, as the roving machine grew closer. He upped the phaser another level and fired. A thick orange rod of fire spread over the machine— then dissipated, not fazing it.

A wicked bolt of white plasma launched from the robot's middle.

Deanna shrank behind one of the machines that *wasn't* trying to kill them, as Riker rolled in the other direction. He hurled himself into an alcove of equipment, and fired again as the robot sailed ominously closer.

It was a meter high and hovered off the deck, bobbing and weaving as Riker fired. The first ones weren't like that—they had taken their phaser hits squarely and crumpled into debris. And the potshots they'd fired—some sort of pulse beam that felt like a mild electric shock—had been harmless.

Had been.

Now the machines were getting stronger with every generation. Riker would destroy one, and another would appear within minutes—bigger, or more adept at avoiding the phaser, or sometimes just able to take stronger and longer hits before finally succumbing.

The robot in front of them spat energy that sizzled over Riker's head and sparked against the wall behind him. Riker fired again—connecting for a moment—bouncing the machine back. The steel monster swung quickly out of the way and recovered its floating course toward them.

Riker glanced hastily toward Deanna. "Stay down!" He didn't know if it would go after her—she didn't have a weapon and wasn't a threat to the other machines as he was. No way to be sure, though. Nothing about this ship was right. No people—just machines guarding machines. Not unheard of, but what'd it have to do with Velex? Were they even still in orbit. Or in the star system.

A prickling charge skittered across Riker's skin as another bolt of energy carved out a dark blotch on the bulkhead behind him.

He chewed his lip and considered whether or not he should raise the phaser to its maximum level. One quick clean shot and the rover would be turned to dust . . . but what would come in its place?

Rover. That's what this devil machine was: a snarling, angry dog. Every neighborhood had a mongrel like that—some barking, spitting, gnarled mutt that lived to swipe baseballs and chew the pockets off kids' butts. Riker's neighborhood especially—Alaska and dogs still went hand in hand.

This dog was a new breed of Rover, though. It didn't want his pockets—it wanted *him*.

Riker raised his head and fired. The beam plunged forward and caught Rover in its middle.

The robot tried to move out from behind the beam.

"Uh uh," Riker grunted. "Bad dog!"

He stood and aimed the phaser as Rover moved, making sure to keep the beam straight into its middle.

Finally a bright flash and a crashing sound: Rover the Fifth fell to the deck, disintegrating into chunks of smoldering, crackling debris.

Slowly Deanna lifted herself up. "Are you all right?"

Riker stepped out from his alcove, nodding. He moved toward the debris, looking it over.

Deanna followed. "How's your leg?"

"Fine," he said shortly. The bleeding *had* stopped and he hadn't noticed the pain much until she mentioned it. Suddenly the leg throbbed with pain and the inner heat of the burn.

Riker knelt down to inspect Rover's carcass. He pushed the charred remains back and forth with his phaser, sifting for something, he wasn't sure what. Some clue as to how it was made.

"It doesn't appear to have a simple 'off' switch," he said tiredly, pushing himself up with a grunt.

Deanna grabbed his arm, helped to steady him. "Where are we?"

Riker shook his head. "I lost track three dogs back."

Deanna's brows shot up. "Dogs?"

The slightest smile shadowed Riker's face. "Rovers." When her face still expressed perplexion he added, "Never mind."

He looked around, keeping his phaser at hip level, and put his arm around her shoulder for support.

"Let's try to find our way back to one of our floor marks. I want to know where we're going. Especially if another of Rover's brothers shows up." He motioned with the phaser toward the shards of computer and robot left on the deck.

"They're getting harder to destroy," he added. "It

took setting twelve this time. That's five higher than the first one—five Rovers, five settings."

She pulled him forward. "Wonderful. Let's get out of here before we end up with more of them than there are phaser settings."

He chuckled nervously. That was a very real concern. There might be endless litters of little Rovers—the ship was big, and whatever its purpose was, there appeared to be a wealth of material. Who knew? Maybe that was the ship's full-time function: Rover fabrication.

He limped, she walked, and together they trod down the corridor, over the debris of the robot that had forced them off their marked trail.

"There's something odd going on here. All these machines . . ." he said, testing his right leg with more and more strength every other step. He needed to be able to run again if chased. He couldn't lean on Deanna, that would drag both of them down.

"Odd how?" She looped her fingers around his hand as it came over her shoulder. "It makes sense to me: an automated ship with automated machines and automated robots to protect them. And an automated transporter that brought us here."

"Maybe," Riker said, trying to cover his fatigue with a strong voice, "but I don't remember seeing another ship when we entered this system. And if we were somehow beamed right off the planet and out of the star system as well, that still doesn't explain what all this is—or how the sensor readings back on Velex fit in."

She nodded, her soft hair pressing against his arm as she did. "Will, where do we go from here?"

He almost lied—made up some tale about a plan he had in the back of his mind . . . but he was too tired, and she was too smart. No food—no water—they were trapped.

"I don't know," he said. "Survive for now——" He stopped, pulling her back. "Listen . . ."

A flurry of sound rumbled up the corridor from behind them. The unmistakable vibration of metal and circuits: Rover number six. There was no place to take cover, and no strong legs to run on. Riker set his phaser on the next level and turned toward the sound, waiting.

Did he send Deanna to hide somewhere, behind a door maybe? Or would that put her in more danger? She had no weapon. If a Rover came up behind her . . .

He looked up the corridor toward the sound, then down the other way.

"Let's go." He motioned toward the far corner where one hall forked into two. "We'll get a little cover from the bulkhead."

Once there he pulled Deanna behind him.

"Crouch low," he said. "Make yourself as small a target as possible."

The roving machine turned down the hall toward them, hovering, and about the size of the last five, Riker noticed this one was . . . smoother in appearance, like a giant tool—something for utility, not protection. Then again, Riker thought, a phaser looked just as benevolent.

Slowly Rover VI moved toward them. A ring around its middle was where the charges would come from. Something told him they'd be even stronger than the last time.

He thought the Rover moved stalkingly, as if there was something personal in this battle. The robot didn't just want him to stop destroying the other machinery—that sentiment had been lost four Rovers back.

He was the goal: revenge for its roving brothers.

Okay, maybe he was reading more into the machine's motive than was there. Maybe there was nothing personal and it was just programming—"defend ship until threat is suppressed." Something like that.

One thing was certain: the machines wouldn't stop until their prey was dead.

He fired and a flashing spike leaped from his weapon to the Rover. The blast was absorbed fully. The smooth metal casing glowed white, then orange, then dissipated, leaving the Rover still heading toward him.

A bolt spat forward from the rover—and from farther than the other ones had been able to fire.

No time—

Powerful fingers of energy, luckily only the tendrils of the bolt rather than the full brunt, gripped Riker and tossed him back and into Deanna as it passed close to them. They crunched together in a fluster of limbs. Riker rolled off her, reset his phaser to its highest, took careful aim . . . and fired above Rover's head.

The ceiling over the robot exploded into a shower of spark and rubble. Riker kept the beam steady, and finally a heavy chunk of bulk slammed into the floor.

Crushed under the wreckage, Rover VI abdicated the throne.

Choking on the smoke drifting up from the debris, Riker pulled himself up with Deanna's help. They nodded their "okays" to each other and stood a moment, gripping one another.

"Well, I have to commend their ability," Riker grumbled. "They change designs like Starfleet changes uniforms. And all theirs work."

He turned and glared at the debris, then back to Deanna. "Why don't *you* have a phaser?"

"I'm a psychologist," she said. "I just *question* people into submission."

He waved away the comment. "From now on I want you to carry a palm phaser on away missions."

Nodding, her arm around his waist to lend him support, she asked, "You all right?"

"I'll live if I can get a good steak and a cold drink within the next five minutes."

"Must you *always* make light of your own health?" she huffed.

"Making light of anyone else's is rude."

She shook her head and they continued around the corner.

"Any idea where we're headed?" she asked.

"Away from those damn robots. They all seem to be coming from the same direction."

"You think there will be others?"

"I'd bet credits. I'm assuming there's some central store room or manufacturing room or something. Maybe we can get as far away from that as possible, and at the same time . . ."

Looking up, she cocked her head, probably sensing what he was feeling. "What?"

"We've still got to find some way off this ship. Maybe there's a communications room or deck. Some way to try to contact the *Enterprise.*" He looked down at her, no longer masking his thoughts, because he knew she was aware of his feelings. "We haven't got much time. We're either going to run out of phaser settings or phaser power . . . or life. We can only last a few days without water."

And which of them would go first? He was weak, had lost a lot of blood. If he gave in to that weakness, she would be left alone. If lack of water was to be their undoing, he would go first, but what if one of the Rovers got her before that? Which was worse? His being without her, or she without him? And with one phaser, they couldn't even safely split up to lure the

Rovers away from the other. Especially since the pack of Rovers got stronger and better with every litter.

All these things ran through Riker's mind, and so quite possibly through Deanna's. He tried to stop thinking that way.

He gripped her arm and turned her toward him. *Don't worry yet.* "We'll be fine."

"I know," she said. "And I won't . . . yet."

They turned down the fresh corridor and made a few steps headway before Riker stopped them. "Not again!" He cocked his head forward. "Another one. Hear it?"

She nodded brusquely. "Yes. What now?"

He pulled her down and behind him as he shrank down to one knee. "We drop and fight."

Another Rover, similar to the first six, came floating around the corner. As soon as Riker made visual contact he aimed and fired. The shot went past, Rover dodging and bobbing as it came down the corridor in a zigzag pattern, swiftly making its way toward them.

"Here, puppy . . . here, boy." Riker fired again, and the phaser beam crackled the air, making a fire bridge between them. Rover was struck in his middle and whimpered as the energy engulfed him.

Suddenly the robot spun away out of the beam, then around, avoiding a second shot.

Riker fired again and missed.

He aimed for the ceiling again, bringing it down in an avalanche of hot metal and burning cinder.

Rover flew back away from the cloud of debris as it dumped harmlessly to the deck. Through the rising dust and smoke, the robot began again to make its way toward Riker and Deanna.

As it sped closer, Riker jumped up and started to run.

Toward it. As fast as his throbbing leg would allow.

"Will!" Deanna shrieked. "Will! What are you doing!"

Rover closed in, the band around its middle starting to glow with the pulse of a deathly charge.

Riker dove forward, head first, twisting onto his back. He slammed into the deck just under the robot and fired. A brilliant trunk of energy pounded out of his phaser and into Rover.

The robot tried to move away, but Riker kept the beam locked on its underside.

He stuck up his arm, as if he could pound the beam through Rover's heart. The beast glowed red then white, and finally shattered from inside and outside simultaneously. Riker pushed himself away and rolled halfway up the ceiling debris, burning his back as the robot crashed to the deck in a thousand pieces.

Riker pulled himself out of the wreckage and shakily got to his feet. He looked to see Deanna was all right, then glanced at the twisted and melted workings of the late Rover.

He nodded approvingly at his handiwork. "Good dog."

Deanna stood and rushed over to help steady him. A strand of her thick curly hair had fallen over her eyes and she blew it out of the way. "You scared the daylights out of me."

He put his arm around her shoulders again. "Didn't have time to explain. I—"

Hummmmmm.

They turned . . . and there he was—Rover the Eighth, larger, and looking determined.

"Enough of this!" Riker moved Deanna back and yanked up his phaser again. "I've had it!"

He reset the phaser to its highest level and fired.

The beam bounced off into small sparkles of fire. Bounced! Riker fired again connecting longer, letting

the beam pound into the robot. The machine stag-
gered back a moment, then began to move forward,
into the phaser beam—through it—

Riker rested the phaser, holstering it, and spun
around. "Let's get the hell out of here. Now!"

They began to run. Toward a far door. If they could
get through—lock the door behind them—

Riker stumbled, pulling Deanna down. They collapsed hard against the floor. "Go," Riker barked.
"Leave me. You have a chance."

She ignored him, pulled him up.

No.

They ran again, Rover following, humming, and,
eerily, not firing. What was it waiting for?

Moving faster, Riker ground out the pain with
clenched teeth, as they limped toward the door. *We'll
make it.* He wasn't sure if that was his voice or
Deanna's in his head, but he pushed on.

As they approached the door, Riker turned and let
Deanna go forward. He aimed at the Rover again and
fired a last time. The shot sizzled off its hide like water
on a skillet.

"Come on!" Deanna called from the door way, as
Riker spun around and leaped through, the door
closing behind him.

He stumbled forward, unable to stop himself—

And nearly fell off the ship.

He grasped the handrail that pressed into his stomach and struggled to keep his balance. He heard
Deanna gasp—turned to look back at her—but his
gaze caught itself on the horizon.

The horizon.

Before him, extending forward as far as the eye
could see, was group after group of machines, tube
after tube of conduits, pump after pump, after machine after . . .

Riker looked through a haze of warm air at the ocean of machines, and at the far, far distance, where the ceiling met the floor.

"Worf to Captain Picard. Come in." Worf tapped at the comm badge again. "Worf to Picard. Come in."

Kadar grabbed at Worf and pulled him around. "Your plan has failed, Worf. Your captain has abandoned you."

Worf yanked himself free of the Klingon commander's grip. He felt his muscles knot and turned away before he released that tension with a blow to Kadar's face. "You are delusionary," Worf said. "Communications are merely down."

"Again?" Kadar growled. "Or is it an excuse to ignore you? Did you not adjust your communicator frequency?" Kadar gestured to the form of his fallen comrade as he wrenched Worf around again. "We are falling one by one! Your captain has left us here to die! I gave you the time you wanted and you have failed. Now I say we will act."

Face hot, jaw tight, Worf narrowed his eyes and glanced at the deflated shell of the Klingon that had died at the Hidran's hand. He then turned back to Kadar and spoke slowly, evening his angry tone with forced composure. "The death of your crewman was not random. *I* was the target of the attack."

Kadar jerked his grip from Worf as if he'd been touching some infected leper. "You do not know that, *Earther*. You speak the lies of a Terran—you do not know the truth and you do not know the Hidran."

His scowl still grinding into Kadar, Worf tapped his comm badge again. "Worf to Connors."

"Connors here, sir."

"There has been a murder in the Klingon security cell. Please notify the captain. I am unable to reach him."

"We're on our way to you, sir. The captain is being held by the Hidran."

Worf and Kadar shared a gaze, less mutually antagonistic than before, but more annoyed and angry. "Understood," Worf said, and jabbed his comm badge off. Questions, demands, flooded his thoughts. With communications what they were, however, it would have been foolish to ramble off those thoughts. He'd have to wait until his men showed up, and if they knew what was good for them, that would be quickly.

"Do you see now?" Kadar began in a low growl. "Will Picard see? The Hidran are insane. There is no honor with them. They will destroy us here, and then they will move to destroy the Empire."

"They could *not* destroy the Empire."

Kadar looked at his remaining men a moment, then stepped closer and lowered his voice. "Do not be so sure, Worf. They could wreck such havoc that the Empire would not be able to defend many of its worlds." The Klingon commander shook his head and gnashed his teeth together in disgust. "Don't underestimate them. Don't trust them. They have been building their military strength while claiming these economic troubles and power failures. Five hundred war ships have been built! They have planetary defense bases now that can knock a starship from orbit! Their economy is market—its recessions small—its productivity too high. They are liars—they have no troubles save for those in their minds. And, as you can now see, they strike without reason."

"There *was* a reason," Worf said, his voice its normal pitch. He refused to play Kadar's game of secrecy. "I believe he meant to kill me. Did you not hear him call my name?"

Eyes cold and dark, Kadar croaked his answer: "All I heard was the death of another of my men." He took Worf by the arm and pointed him to the body. "There is the second Klingon who has died under the guise of trying to avenge one Hidran death. How much would you wager that if the Hidran had their way, you would be the very last Klingon killed . . . because you'd be the last left alive? It is you they will end with, Worf—it is the Empire they wish to destroy first." Kadar's grip on Worf's arm tightened. "We *must* act now—to preserve the Empire!"

The hatch hissed open, and both Worf and Kadar turned, tense.

Connors and Mackenzie entered, nodding their salutes to Worf.

"Report," Worf ordered habitually. Off duty or on, under arrest or not, to them he was in charge, and he knew that.

Connors stepped forward. "Sir, the captain was taken by Urosk. We were caught off guard—"

"Excuses will be discussed later," Worf snapped, and got the flinch he wanted from his men. They'd been sloppy. "Report the situation."

"Yes, sir," Connors continued. "Stalemate for now, Lieutenant. Phaser fire was exchanged. The captain was stunned, as was Doctor Hollitt. They retreated back into their chambers, with the captain as a hostage, when security reinforcements arrived. We have three of our team and two of Doctor Hollitt's for-hires guarding to assure no movement."

Worf nodded. "I see." Perhaps Kadar was right—perhaps the Hidran were fools without reason. What did they hope to gain by abducting the captain. It would merely anger their only allies: the Federation. "Has Commander Riker been found?"

"No, sir."

Worf nodded. "What command officer is left on the planet?"

Connors shook his head. "Just Dr. Crusher, sir."

The captain was being held hostage. The first officer

was missing. The second officer could not be reached. The chief engineer could not be reached—nor any one else on the *Enterprise*. The ship's doctor . . . was a ship's doctor. "I will need a phaser," Worf said. "I am returning to duty."

"Aye, sir," Connors said, handing Worf a phaser.

"Possibly the ship has been attacked if it is no longer responding to hails." Worf glanced at Kadar, torn. Part of him needed to work for the captain's release . . . and part wanted to keep an eye on Kadar. His threat to take action was not idle.

Finally, Worf turned back to Connors and MacKenzie. "How many teams are still searching for Commander Riker and the Counselor?"

"Two, sir," Connors said.

"Call one back. I want two guards stationed outside this door at all times."

"Worf!" Kadar protested angrily.

"For your protection, Captain," Worf said, taking just a bit of delight in the moment.

"Arm us for our protection!" Kadar barked.

"No," Worf said simply. "You will remain here in protective custody. I will see to the safety of Captain Picard, and we will remedy this situation per his orders."

"You, Worf," Kadar spat, "are a Terran fool."

"Perhaps," Worf said as he nodded Connors and MacKenzie out the hatch. "But for now I am the fool in charge."

Data *was* in charge, and DePotter had to follow the commander's orders.

"Ensign, are the defense systems energized?"

"Yes, sir."

"Then please plot a course within phaser range of the Klingon vessel."

Okay, maybe he was just a know-nothing ensign

who could count his hours of bridge duty on two hands and a foot, yet . . . all this seemed wrong.

But DePotter couldn't disobey such an order. If he did, there would be no more bridge duty. No more duty ever.

DePotter tapped at his console. "Course plotted and on the board, sir."

"Hail the Klingon vessel and lock phasers on target, Ensign."

"Hold, Ensign. Belay that order."

Swiveling around, his hands still on his board, DePotter saw Lieutenant Wyckoff enter from the fore turbolift, flanked by three security guards. Their phasers were drawn.

Data stood and confronted them. "That is not within your purview, Lieutenant. Your actions constitute mutiny. You are relieved of duty."

Wyckoff shook his head.

What the hell was he doing? What should DePotter do? Sit back—wait? Follow his order? Which order? Why was this happening on his shift?

"Commander," Wyckoff said, "you can't relieve me of duty. Your actions lead me to believe you're either ill or under an alien influence. In accordance with Starfleet regulations, I'm turning command of this vessel to the duty officer until Captain Picard returns."

Data nodded, almost sympathetically, or knowingly, or something. DePotter couldn't be sure if anything was really there. He seemed so calm. Anyone else would be livid.

"Lieutenant," the android said, "this *is* mutiny. I seriously doubt your interpretation of that regulation would be upheld."

"Maybe, sir. I'll let the captain and Starfleet decide. You can, of course, file a complaint when we reach the nearest Starbase. Until then, I'll have to confine you to quarters. If you don't come with me now, I'll have to make that confinement to the brig."

Silence reigned as Data seemed to consider the weight of the threat. DePotter didn't know if he should defend the Commander or what. Sit. Wait. See what happens. He knew there *was* such a regulation. He could always lean on that. Somehow that didn't comfort him though—his palms were sweaty and his heart thumped loudly in the absence of speech.

Finally, though, Data answered. "Very well, Lieutenant," he said, and quickly stepped past them to the turbolift.

Wyckoff turned, nodded his guards to stay behind, and followed the android into the lift.

"It's been a long time," Geordi said to himself. Then he looked up at where he thought the guard still was. If the security man didn't move often enough, the impulse from the proximity vest would just blend in to the background of the wall. "Why don't we check on him?"

Perhaps the man nodded—Geordi wished people'd stop doing that. In any case, the man agreed—his comm badge chirped. "Computer, locate Lieutenant Wyckoff." The guard *was* still near the cabin door.

"Lieutenant Wyckoff is in turbolift five."

"Computer," Geordi chimed in, "heading of turbolift five?"

"Turbolift five's heading is deck two."

"He's headed back here," Geordi said.

"Yes, sir. He decided that confinement to quarters would be enough."

Geordi leapt up. "Damn! We're talking about *Data* here—not some skinny ensign. You can lock me in my quarters and you *might* be able to keep me there. You'd have no chance with Data."

The man probably nodded again. "Let's meet them at the lift."

Swoosh. The lift doors opened—Geordi could feel the rush of air.

The guard gasped.

"What?" Geordi snapped. "What's wrong?" To his proximity detector, the lift felt empty. "Where are they?"

"Lieutenant? Are you okay?" The guard's voice now came from Geordi's feet.

"What's happened?"

"Sir, Mr. Data is gone, and Lieutenant Wyckoff is unconscious."

Damn! Geordi pulled the old hand comm out of his pocket, glad he'd remembered to keep it. He snapped the grid up. "Computer, locate Commander Data."

"Commander Data is on the Battle Bridge."

The rustle before Geordi was the guard's uniform as he rose. "Emergency medical team to deck two section 31-A!"

Geordi reached out, grabbing the guard and pulling him forward. "I need my freedom. I think my case is proven."

"Yes, sir. You sure have."

"Good." Geordi yanked back the communicator and barked, "La Forge to Engineering! Priority one! Disengage power to Battle Bridge. Now!"

"Sir?"

With Wyckoff in the turbolift, Geordi had no choice but to head for the next one. Using the proximity vest as his only guide, he began a blind rush down the corridor—literally. And he didn't have time to explain his actions to Engineering. "That's a direct order, Mr. Cheng. Follow it!"

"Aye aye, sir."

Geordi bounced into three people on the way to the turbolift. "Report, Cheng."

"I'm trying, sir. Someone's overridden with manual control."

"Damn!" Where was the turbolift when he needed it? The doors wouldn't open for him. Unless . . . Data sealed off the lifts! "Cheng, make sure all civilian personnel report to the saucer section on the double if they're not already there. And override any initiation of saucer-sep, you got that?"

"Aye, sir. Will do!"

Geordi slammed his fist against his thigh and spun away from the closed lift door. There was a ladder around the corner with his name on it. Whatever Data was doing wouldn't go down this flawlessly. Not on a bet. As he ran faster than the proximity detector could handle, he bumped into a wall or two, but pushed off and kept on going.

Gracelessness under pressure.

"Computer," Geordi barked, beginning to pant, "unlock all secondary hatch pathways deck seven to deck twenty-seven."

"Access denied."

No, no, no, Data . . . It's not that *easy.* "Override on authority of Chief Engineer Geordi La Forge, access La Forge: Theta two-nine-nine-seven."

"Secondary hatch pathways now available."

Geordi couldn't help but laugh. "Now that's the computer we all know and love." Before lifting the hatch on the secondary path he closed the communicator and—where was his tool kit?

Left behind somewhere. *Damn.* Three "damns" in as many minutes. It had been that kind of day.

Geordi scurried down the Jeffries tube. Deck eight by now? He'd go down one more to make sure—if he'd lost count he could be left behind. That wouldn't do.

Hand under hand . . . foot under foot . . . he had done this quickly a million times without looking—why couldn't he do it blind?

"Red alert. General Quarters. Saucer separation in 'T' minus one minute." The computer droned on, klaxons sounding. At least Data was making sure the civs and the non-essential personnel were off the battle section. That was the odd part—something was wrong with his best friend—he was obviously damaged, yet he seemed to still care what happened in most respects. *He actually sounded concerned when he ordered security to find me,* Geordi thought.

He jumped down to the deck, stumbled a bit, then straightened himself. He pulled out the hand communicator and flipped it open. "La Forge to Engineering. Cheng, report."

"Commander Data has overridden all Engineering access, sir. I can't stop the saucer sep."

"Status of the sep?"

"Lift, umbilical, and SIF interconnects are separated. Docking latch servo seals are counting down to sep."

"Do what you can, Cheng. Force the warp core output to less than ninety percent! Make him override *everything* to get what he wants. Buy me some time. See if you can't stall some turbolifts between the two sections. La Forge out." He rushed toward the nearest door, banged into the jam, and cursed himself for rushing to the point where he actually was beginning to slow himself down. He composed himself, tried to get his bearings, and spoke into the comm again. He nearly collided with the next door and grumbled an insult at it. "Computer, relinquish all control of engineering subsystems to Engineering. Authorization: La Forge."

"Access denied."

"Override! Personal authority, La Forge: Theta two-nine-nine-seven!"

"Access denied."

"Dammit!" The communicator clenched in his fist, Geordi reached out to pound the wall, missed, and stumbled. He fell to his knees, then yanked himself up and steadied himself. He was getting too worked up—funneling his adrenaline into anger rather than action.

"Computer, pinpoint location of this communicator. What deck is this?"

"Deck Eight, section five."

Battle bridge on this deck—weapons conduits not far. Data could control the computers—he couldn't control the crew. He'll need automation to fire any weapons . . . and those systems would have to fail.

"One way or another, Data," Geordi said to himself, "I'm going to have control of this ship."

Ships were big, but not this big. Riker had never seen one like this—there wasn't one.

"We're not on a ship," Riker said breathlessly, losing himself in the distance. He gripped the handrail and slowly turned back to Deanna.

"I don't understand. What is all this?"

"Look," Riker said, pointing to the clean lines of machines and bins . . . somethings doing something. They pumped and hummed and grunted in effort. At what? There was no way to know without interrupting them, and he wasn't going to play that game again. "We didn't beam *up* . . . we beamed *down!*

"Will—" Deanna said as she stepped forward and grabbed his shoulder with one hand and the rail with her other. "Of course! I've had the same lack of empathy here as on Velex."

"Because this *is* Velex. You were right, Deanna.

Nothing on this planet is alive. Nothing! It's all machinery." Riker turned from the amazing view, strength somehow filling his legs again. "This changes everything." He gripped his arms, almost smiling, for there was hope now, where there had been none. "We must be kilometers underground . . . and we have to get back. Find the room we arrived in—if that's a transporter room then we don't have to worry about beaming ourselves into space. If we're lucky."

He looked into her eyes, those dark and tired wide orbs.

She nodded. "Why? Who—"

Boooom!

Behind them, the wall exploded, a bubble of white heat spreading over the corridor. They were tossed against the railing and Riker dropped to his knees. He looped his arm through one of the rail bars and gripped on to Deanna as the wall behind them vaporized into metal dust.

As Rover the Eighth pushed through the downpour of debris, Riker forced Deanna away and fired. Again his beam was reflected off to one side, and the Rover moved forward, unharmed.

Riker turned to run down the corridor. Deanna was well ahead of him. His leg was bellowing agony to his brain. He pushed it out of the way. Don't think about the pain—it doesn't exist. Pain is a myth—an evil fantasy someone once had.

The corridor extended up against the rail for at least a city block, curving around at an angle. Riker fired, hoping to blast Rover off balance at least—maybe knock the robot into a wall or into the handrail. He missed once, twice, and again . . . there was just no way to get a clear connecting shot between the curve of the corridor and bobbing of the Rover.

"Move, move!" Riker barked at Deanna. Speed would be their only advantage . . . if Riker could keep his up. And he couldn't forever. They'd run out of phaser settings, and out of options. If they couldn't find a way to the surface . . . well, there was no place else to go. They might avoid the Rover for a while, but without defense, without a way to destroy the robot, they were as dead as the planet they were on.

Damn, he'd been stupid. He hadn't rethought, hadn't reconsidered his first assumptions, and it could mean their deaths. Had he even considered the idea that they were in the planet rather than on a ship, his entire course of action would have been different. Had he not started to destroy the machines, he and Deanna probably could have roamed peacefully until they found a way to the surface.

Could have . . . but there was no going back.

What was it Deanna had said about poor concept-formation? He'd never let that happen again.

Up the next corridor, leaving the Rover trailing behind, Riker caught up with Deanna and they ran together evenly.

"The old dog's learned all my tricks. *And* it's immune to the phaser," he puffed out. "Try to put some distance between us and him. As soon as we have a corridor between us—"

He coughed and stumbled, and she reached back to draw him along. "We can't run forever, Will."

"I know," he choked out. "I know." His leg knew too. "We have to find that transporter room—or one like it! You run ahead—come back when you have one. I have an idea that might buy some time. If you don't find it, just keep running."

"Will—"

"I don't want to hear it! That's an order and I expect you carry it out, Commander!" He motioned up the corridor. "Now go!"

She looked back a moment, then took off, and Riker realized just how slow a snail he'd become. He was dragging her down—she'd stay alive—find a way to the surface and inform the captain, if he didn't become deadweight for both of them.

As Deanna disappeared around the corner, Riker hobbled on and felt like that steak he'd wanted a few minutes earlier—raw and lifeless. Sweat dripped from his hair onto his cheeks and he smeared it away with an already soaked wrist. He looked back, listened, and heard the Rover still coming.

And it would keep coming, and even if destroyed—there would be others.

"There's got to be a way to the surface," Riker grunted, looking up the corridor to the corner Deanna'd turned. "She'll make it even if I don't," he assured himself as he slowed even more. The pain in his leg wasn't buying the "mythical" story anymore, and his gallop had become a deadly trot.

He turned up the corridor, his limp showing. She was no where to be seen. The Rover could be heard behind him—a constant reminder.

Hope had again become the myth, pain the reality. He had no more ideas to slow it down, as he'd assured Deanna. It would be on him in moments. He was tired, and wanted to sit and wait.

"Will!"

Her voice came from behind him—he'd passed her. How had he missed seeing a door? He spun around, pushing himself off balance as he stumbled toward the sound. She poked her head out a door that was nothing more than a slit in the wall.

"Over here!"

"Coming," he grunted, and tried to push the pain away again.

When he was close enough she pulled him in and the door closed behind them.

She pushed the hair from her eyes and motioned around. "Recognize it?"

He looked around, squinting at each corner, at the wall that was lights and panels. "We started from here," he gasped, trying to catch his breath.

Deanna nodded. "Either this room or one just like it."

He took in one long breath and straightened. "Here." He pressed the phaser into her hand. "You take this. You're going to buy us some time. Weld the door shut. If Rover breaks through, melt the ceiling and make it a wall."

"I'm not the best with a phaser," she admitted.

"Just aim and fire. Hit the wall and we'll be fine!" Riker nodded toward the door. She aimed at the split between the doors, hesitated, then fired. As he worked over the console, trying to determine which way these people had invented the modern-day wheel that was teleportation, he felt the sparks from Deanna's work fly. Alien metal was bubbling up, welding solid—he could hear it. He concentrated on his task, trying to ignore the orange nodules that spat forward before they fell to the ground cold.

The air was getting hot as he ran his hand over the many different buttons and lights, unwilling to touch them. For now he was just trying to get a feel for the board. Intelligent beings tended to pattern things. The eye will look for structure in randomness . . . from constellations to buttons . . . and perhaps Riker could find a pattern here.

To his left were a series of switches and what looked like a numeric keypad with symbols. Above that was a screen with what might have been a graph. It was unmoving, and had more symbols. He mopped his brow—the heat from the door was adding to his basic misery. After being gouged, bled, skewered, dehydrated, chased and exhausted . . . well, he should have realized that boiling was next.

Booooom!

A shudder jostled Riker against the console and he gripped the panel as best he could. The makeshift wall where the door had been glowed red, then cooled to silver-black.

"Rover again!" Riker called to Deanna. "Melt more of the ceiling if you have to—keep 'em out!"

The whine of her phaser was the only response. He spun back to the console and looked hard. No manual. No 'help' key. No Starfleet touch-pads—just old fashioned buttons that seemed to be laughing at him as they kept their meanings hidden.

He looked up at the graph. *If that's a zero . . . and that's a zero as well . . .* He looked from the graph to the keypad. A coordinate selector maybe?

Maybes were damn risky where transporters were concerned. Accidents happened even when people knew what they were doing . . . guessing was . . .

Boooom!

Their only hope.

Another bolt against the door. Rover was knocking —loudly. Riker could feel the heat from the blast, and then a wave of hot air and the scream of the phaser filled the room again.

"Keep it up, Deanna!"

He didn't turn—his work was here, hers there. His only problem: where was "here"?

Enter coordinate here, he thought, *and activate here.* He moved his hand from one place to another—there were only two main key sets—the rest of the panel was lights and indicators. *What coordinate, though?*

It was getting hotter—the air savaged his skin and eyes. Deanna was melting more of the ceiling into a barrier and she was backed up against him.

Focus! Focus! None of that mattered! Rover was scratching down the wall between them and there was no place left to run.

This is zero he decided, touching the keys as if that

confirmed his guess. But zero meant what? The planet's surface? The planet's core? The transporter room itself? Could be smack-dab into the middle of Rover's dog house for all he knew. The coordinate could be for wherever they were taken from—which was two hundred meters in the air.

Booooom! Booooom!

Riker cringed instinctively and looked at the wall— Deanna was running out of ceiling.

If they tried to escape they might die. If they stayed they surely would. The temperature of the room, the walls, the air . . . Riker was ready to lose consciousness. Breath now painful to his lungs, he held his chest with one hand, and the console with his other.

"Get over here," he yelled. "Stand by!"

He hit the "zero" key three times and then jammed his fist onto the other key pad.

BOOOOOM!

The wall ruptured. Orange and red slivers hurled forward in a ball of flame. Riker felt the heat on his face—turned to Deanna, tried to cover her with his body—

The world became molten—the explosion engulfed them—

Pain was no myth. They were wrenched to the deck, and the universe closed dark around him.

Riker's agony was finally gone.

Chapter Thirteen

AT FIRST IT WAS NIGHT—the blackness, the cool dryness of the air . . . A river of cold wind washed over him. A good feeling. Riker had thought he would never feel so cool again. Then he remembered the effect of the alien transporter . . . brightness returned to his world, and paralysis lost its grip on him.

I made it.

Pain returned as well, and he almost welcomed the continuity—he had all his limbs, he could feel them.

"Deanna . . ." He called out, probably more mentally than physically. He couldn't be sure. "Are you all right?"

Silence, and the distant howling of the wind, frightened him. He was in an eerie world of half-substance and half-feeling, of half-light and half-sound.

He tried to flex his muscles and clear his throat. How frustrating—to be uncertain of that which was always so absolute—the control of his own body.

"De-anna?" His voice cracked dryly.

She groaned in response. She'd made it too.

His eyes fluttered open and light pounded against him, too brightly. He yanked his arm up to shield his eyes, then rolled onto his stomach, allowing his eyes to open in the shade of his own frame.

The rock was cool against his palms—grit and cold stone. He shuddered, chilled, and relished the feeling after so many hours of sweaty exhaustion.

"Deanna—" He looked to his right and saw her lying a few feet away.

"Give me a moment . . . I'm fine."

He nodded and lifted himself to his feet, using the incline of the rock face as a brace. This was where they'd found the sensor beacon—the same clump of rock and stone. Somewhere around here was a crushed flitter.

Squinting into the bright day, Riker recognized the flowing Velexian fields in the distance. He tapped his combadge, then shook his arm awake. "Riker to *Enterprise.*"

A hollow, empty frequency beeped back at him. He tapped it again.

"Riker to . . . anyone."

Looking down, he saw Deanna was now shielding her eyes. He stretched his arm down to lift her up, give her balance. He was the weaker, yet had come around first . . . the effect must have to do with something other than just a physical paralysis.

The communicator suddenly cracked with static, then came alive with a woman's voice. *"Halford here, sir! You just appeared on our scope!"* The beautiful sound of another being.

"Where are you?"

"Looking for you, sir. In a shuttle. ETA to your location is three minutes."

Deanna pulled herself toward Riker and spoke into the communicator. "Good . . . have a medi-kit ready. Commander Riker is hurt."

"Acknowledged. Sir, mind if I ask where in hell you two've been?"

Riker chuckled with the irony of that, and, still dizzy with adrenaline and blood loss, steadied himself against Deanna. "Lieutenant," he said, looking from Deanna to the sky, "you're awfully close. Except it was a bit hotter than hell."

The small combadge crackled, sputtered, then died under the weight of Urosk's boot. Picard, both pleased and disgusted at the illogic of it, nearly smiled.

Worf was alive. Alive and well and talking. But someone had died for him . . . another Klingon was dead, and only trouble could come of that.

Suddenly, rather than turning to Batok and taking his anger out on him, Urosk twisted toward Picard. "He will not live forever! *I* will see to that."

Picard held his ground, neither pressing forward nor retreating from Urosk's tirade. "Is that your only goal, Captain? Would you give up your entire planet's life to avenge the death of one?"

Urosk crunched his heel into the damaged communicator as he stepped closer to Picard. Towering over the Starfleet captain, he ground angry words through his breathing mask. "I *am* acting for the preservation of my planet! You are too blind to see it, Picard, but this entire string of events was meant to destroy us. The Klingons want war—and it is war I will avert!"

"How? By beginning one? None of this is any help, Urosk," Picard said. "You can't stop a war by waging one. Not when the odds are against you."

"No, Picard, you are wrong." The Hidran captain turned away and walked toward the table in the center of the room. "The Klingons can be stopped. They have forgotten what a war with the Hidran means." He pressed a button on the tabletop and a spigot rose from the center as a sink opened into the counter. Water began to pour from the tap and Urosk ran his hands and arms under the flow. He shuddered, perhaps with pleasure, and then turned back to Picard. "They will be reminded what a war with us would mean."

"That's a gamble, Urosk. Perhaps they will be reminded of a need to eradicate your threat rather than avoid it."

"Silence, Picard! Unlike you I am not riddled with indecision! I know what I will do, and what it will mean. I may die in the process, but the Klingons' heartless empire will know that killing me wasn't worth the price. We will destroy them here, and in orbit, and perhaps one will live to actually tell the tale." Urosk stomped back to Batok at the head of the counter. "Not only have you dishonored yourself by killing but one Klingon, you have embarrassed yourself by killing the *wrong* one! You will take the remainder of the Federation communicators, as well as our own, and find a way to break through this transmission jammer of Picard's. This *may* begin to make up for your errors of the past, Lieutenant . . . but fail me again and I'll have your life."

Stepping forward now, voice firm, Picard hoped to still find some way to talk the Hidran out of such a reckless plan. "The *Enterprise* will not allow you to destroy the Klingons, Urosk." That, of course, was just a wild hope. He didn't know what the *Enterprise* would do. If Data had been damaged, and if La Forge was unable to relieve the android, then perhaps the *Enterprise* was now acting not to stand in the Hidran's way, but to further their cause.

Urosk yanked his Starfleet phaser up and aimed at Picard. "I do not want to kill you, Picard. I do not need the wrath of the Federation to complicate things for Hidra . . . but be assured—interfere with me and I will shatter your limbs to dust, and leave you to live in undying pain."

There was no difficulty in reading Urosk's expression or tone. He was quite serious, but no threat could stand in Picard's way. The Hidran had to be stopped, and if that meant pain or death, then that is what it meant.

Subtlety would have to be his weapon, Picard decided, as the Hidran collected all their communications devices on the center lab table. Every few moments one of them would go to the sink and douse their hands in the tap water. Then they would drink, with difficulty due to the awkwardness of their breathing masks, and return to work.

The dust trick would not work again. Too obvious, and too dangerous now.

Picard watched as they pried the delta-shield covers off the three remaining Starfleet communicators. At least this was delaying them—the white-noise transmission blanket was still intact. How long could he count on that?

Time to act.

"You use a lot of water, Urosk," Picard said, making his way slowly around the far end of the table.

Urosk looked up from his survey of the work. "You no longer have concerns, Picard, except the preservation of your own life."

"Water is a scarce commodity on this planet, Captain," Picard continued, edging closer to the tap. "You'd be wise to conserve it."

The Hidran captain's phaser came up and he stepped toward Picard. "Move back, Captain. I care more for comfort than conservation right now. You are dangerously close to interfering with me, Picard."

Picard shook his head. "Actually, I was only going to suggest you turn the water up. That red button is hot water—run that and the room will fill with steam after a while. I believe that is what you want. It will save you from constantly having to drink and soak."

"Why?" Urosk asked, squinting at Picard. "Why attempt to help us? Why make us comfortable?"

Picard pressed the red button and the tap spat a thick bar of hot water into the sink. Steam rose to the ceiling and slowly worked to fill the small room. "You have much to learn about my people, Urosk," he said, and hoped that would suffice as an answer.

The Hidran captain jabbed his phaser in Picard's direction. "That's no answer." Urosk was no fool.

"Let's just say," Picard said, thinking quickly, "that your comfort seems to be in my best interests right now . . . wouldn't you agree?"

"Will!" Beverly Crusher ran toward the hall's main doors and scooped the first officer out from under the guard who was helping him in. "What's happened to you?"

"Where's the captain?" Riker demanded.

With Deanna's help, Beverly lowered him into a chair near one of the tables that had been forgotten in the storm that followed dinner. She knelt down in front of him and flipped open her medical case. She was a sight for sore . . . legs.

"The captain is still with the Hidran," she said, distracted by his injuries. She flipped open a plasma-concentrate hypo and injected it straight into his calf. "How did you manage to mangle your leg like this?"

"Luck. Tell me what's going on. Halford here filled us in up to the captain being taken," Riker said tiredly, but with anger in his voice. "How the hell did all this happen?"

Beverly looked up to Deanna. "You all right?"

Nodding, but obviously exhausted, Deanna mumbled, "Fine."

"Doctor . . ." Riker prodded. She injected him with another hypospray and he flinched. "Hey!"

"Electrolytes. You need them. That and a good two day rest."

"What I need, Doctor, is answers."

Crusher flipped open her tricorder and mumbled into the readings. "Worf is on his way."

"Is there anything to eat or drink?" Deanna asked.

Halford nodded her auburn-haired head. "I think so," she said. "Permission to find some food, sir?"

Riker nodded quickly. "Granted—double time!"

Her medical tricorder chirping, Crusher took a moment to run the scanner over Deanna. Riker knew what she would find: dehydration, fatigue. They were a mess. Riker didn't have a sleeve or pant leg left, and Deanna was sleeveless as well.

"Where have you two been?" Beverly demanded.

Riker sighed. "There's an entire underground planet to Velex. Kilometer after kilometer of machines and rooms . . . all self-animated. Maybe. We didn't see anyone."

"Who did all this to you then?" Beverly was now back working on the tangle of flesh that was Riker's calf.

"Some machines were *very* self-animated." Riker glanced to Deanna. "But they did have help." He smiled weakly. "Dr. Troi here played arc-welder with my leg."

With a plate of bread and a pitcher of water in hand, Halford strutted back to the table. She set the plate down, found two glasses, and even poured for Riker and Deanna. "I'm afraid this is all that's left," she said.

Riker nodded a salute. "Thank you, Lieutenant. Secure the shuttle and report back for security duty."

"Aye aye, sir," the woman said, and walked back toward the hall's main doors.

Both Deanna and Riker tore large chunks of bread from the loaf. Riker took a long swig of the cool water. He'd never tasted anything better. There was something to drink on the shuttle back, but nothing so cold and natural and thirst quenching. He gulped down the bread, barely chewing, and was already feeling like a new man before he began his second piece.

"Lieutenant Worf, reporting, sir."

Riker looked up, crumbs dropping from the corners of his mouth. "Fill me in," Riker mumbled, stuffing his mouth again.

"We have not yet contacted the Hidran regarding the captain," Worf said. "As soon as I released myself from protective custody, your rescue was reported and I decided you might handle the situation better in the Hidran's eyes. If you'd like me to return to custody—"

"No, Mr. Worf," Riker said, taking a gulp of water and another chunk of the bread. "I'll need your help." He would have risen but Beverly had hold of his leg. "We couldn't reach the ship. Halford said that's been a problem."

"Communications have inexplicably failed intermittently throughout the day. We believe it is because of the white-noise blanket."

"Wait a minute!" Beverly rose, rechecking her tricorder and taking another reading. "This can't be . . ."

"What?" Riker demanded. Why did doctors do that—keep their patients in the dark to wonder which limb would be falling off unexpectedly? "What's wrong?"

"You're healing very quickly all of a sudden."

Shrugging, Riker said, "So you're good. We knew that—"

"No . . ." Beverly began, mystified, running her scanner over Riker, then Deanna. "Deanna checks out normal—her problems were minimal, fatigue . . . but you shouldn't be doing this well."

"Sorry."

Beverly's brow wrinkled. "No, Will, I mean I haven't done enough yet. I didn't give you anything to accelerate healing."

Crusher ran her scanner over them each again, then she reached up and snatched the chunk of bread from Riker's hand. "Give me that a minute."

"Hey—"

Worf stepped closer to Riker. "The Velexian grain *is* supposed to have some mystical health-enhancing effects."

His bread now the center of attention, Riker looked longingly at Deanna's slice as Crusher ran her tricorder over his a second time.

"I don't believe in magic," Beverly said.

"Do you believe in feeding the hungry?" Riker said dryly.

"Oh," the doctor pulled out her hypospray again. "Here," she said, pushing the spray into his neck. "This is a nutritional substitute."

Riker frowned. "Mmmm. Delicious." Strength returning to him nonetheless, he turned back to Worf. "I want all available security to report here. I want the Hidran's area surrounded, both inside and outside the building."

"If they were to break through the outer wall," Worf began, "the structure would crumble, perhaps on top of them. This hall is the only standing native Velexian building, and is estimated to be more than twenty thousand years old. It is not sound enough for such a rupture."

Riker nodded and stood. "That doesn't mean they won't try it. I want the bases covered." He looked down at his tattered uniform and grimaced, but knew his appearance was the least of his problems. "Also, there should be a subspace communications center around here. Find it, try to reach the ship. It should have the strength to break through the white-noise jammer."

"Aye, sir," Worf said.

Riker looked back to Deanna. "You okay?"

She nodded.

"Find anything interesting, Doctor?" Riker asked.

"Very," Beverly mumbled. "I can't scan through this bread. I can't get past the individual grains."

"Neither could Dr. Hollitt's equipment," Riker offered.

Beverly stood and turned toward them. "No, I wouldn't think so."

"If you have a conclusion, Doctor, spit it out," Riker said. "We don't have time . . ."

"I don't have one yet. I have a guess. Where is Dr. Hollitt? With her help and the scanning equipment I brought earlier we might be able to prove something." She held up the chunk of bread. "This is *not* magic."

"Do you believe in nothing mystical, Doctor?" Worf asked.

Beverly flashed her eyes at Riker, then at Worf. "I do—when I can see the proof, and the equipment it was tested on."

Chapter Fourteen

"SAUCER SEPARATION *in five . . . four . . . three . . . two . . . one.*"

Only Data could have stopped the separation . . . and he was the one who wanted it.

So did Geordi, really . . . he just didn't want to be trapped on the saucer where he'd be helpless to act. And he *had* to act.

He moved his hand over the wall and found the control panel that would open the door. On that door there was a sign—he couldn't see the letters, but knew what they said: "DECK 8 PHASER AUTOMATION: RESTRICTED ACCESS."

His fist tight, he punched the door's control panel, loosening it so he could snap off the cover and get its guts. His fingers fumbled inside—too long. Everything took too long. A minor accomplishment: to be able to navigate around the ship blind. But if he didn't put that skill to use more quickly, in a manner that would change the situation, then it was just a meaningless achievement. What value was there in a skill if it met no end?

A rumble vibrated through the ship. Geordi knew the feeling: the saucer unlocking itself from the battle-section and pulling away. Someone was on the main bridge . . . Ro or someone, and would take care of the saucer and its civilians. He imagined the lie that person was told by Data, how they probably didn't doubt his veracity for a moment. Data certainly wasn't above lying—any intelligent being understood that a lie could be a wise course of action from time to time—perhaps even moral. Who, when asked by a murderer, would describe the location of their family? Who would tell an enemy the entire truth? Only a fool.

While Data was most certainly not himself—he was no fool.

Finally, sweat dripping down his neck, he fingered the override control and the doors swished open.

He ventured into the alcove and jumped through the doors quickly, then stopped himself, trying to get a bead on where he was standing and where the controls he wanted would be.

Counting off paces to the main console, he was abruptly stopped by a wall that shouldn't have been there. He leapt back, bumped into something—a table, and grabbed on to it before he lost his balance.

Geordi straightened and put his hand out to touch the wall. He felt the cool plastic-like smoothness of a computer touch-pad. "Computer, what room is this?"

"Deck eight, section twelve: Recreation room four."

Angry, Geordi sent the chair that had been at his side flying across the room. It crashed, clattering against other chairs and perhaps a table. The feeling was a good one, a release, but was fleeting. He needed help—had to get to Engineering. Cheng would help.

Pulling in a deep breath, he retraced his steps through the doors and back into the corridor. Left? Right? He'd forgotten. *Deck eight . . . section twelve . . .* Where was everyone? *General quarters—that's right.* He'd let his frustration get the best of him and was now paying the price: a muddled mind.

Think!

He turned left and rushed up the empty corridor, his open arm outstretched, fingertips gliding along the inner wall for guidance. When his fingers didn't scrape the wall he knew there was the alcove for a doorway, and he counted those . . .

Five . . . six . . . seven . . . eight—a corridor . . . nine . . . ten . . .

Dropping his arm, he stopped. "Ten" was a Jefferies tube. Of course, he also knew the rec room back there was supposed to be phaser automation control. All he needed to be was off by one step, one pace, one count, and he could do more harm than good. Or he could slow himself down into uselessness.

He reached out, felt the cold, metal rungs of the Jefferies ladder, and knew there was no miscalculation this time.

Slowly he made his way down the tube, one rung after another, flipping a hatch when necessary, counting his steps as he went. There was no way he'd allow Data to trap him in a turbolift, and the Jefferies tubes would allow him access to the guts of the ship if he needed to hide. Even without a communicator, Geordi was traceable if Data wanted to make the effort . . .

This was no way to function, though—he couldn't keep his career as engineer of this ship if he were to remain blind. He wouldn't be drummed out of the service, but he would be given some desk job, or a teaching job . . . And that wasn't what he'd signed up for.

Not until then had the thought occurred to Geordi: What would become of Data? What if his damage was so severe that *his* Starfleet career was over? And what would that mean? Data wouldn't be relegated to a desk. What would become of a sick android that couldn't be repaired? Imprisonment . . . or worse— dismantlement.

Geordi tried to shake that thought from his mind. Such a consequence could be considered later—there were lives at stake now, and that was the most pressing situation.

The thrumming of the ship—he knew every sound —told him the saucer was totally detached and that the battle-section was probably maneuvering free and clear.

He reached Engineering deck and tried to get his bearings again.

Turning on his heel as he jumped off the ladder and onto the deck, he heard what sounded like—yelling!

Straining to listen as he moved toward the door, suddenly he heard hissing.

Gas.

Data was flooding the ship with an anesthizine. Had to be. *He must've found out Cheng was helping me. Knew he couldn't rely on the crew to help him any longer—knew I would be here—*

Geordi let out a dry cough, covered his mouth, and tried to think of an escape as the smell of the gas began to overtake him. It burned his sightless eyes and scraped against this nose and throat.

Where? Where could he escape?

How could he escape his own breath?

"If you do not mind me saying so, sir, I believe you are wasting your breath." Worf nodded down the corridor toward the hatch. "They will not come through there as long as we are here, and they will not give up the captain as long as they don't have me."

Riker glanced at Deanna, then shook his head. He wouldn't consider that option. Some things were *never* alternatives. "Sorry, Worf. I'm not sacrificing you. And, it's not a waste of breath so long as I'm buying time." He tapped his comm badge. "Riker to Captain Urosk."

There was a delay, then the gravel voice of the Hidran captain: *"You are annoying me, Riker."*

"My intention isn't to annoy you, Captain." *Although it's a respectable side effect.* "My intention is only for a peaceful outcome to this situation."

"Give me the Klingon."

Riker and Worf exchanged a glance. The tall Klingon was tense, and Riker knew why. It wasn't because Worf thought he may be forfeit—it was because he *wanted* the honor of being forfeit for his captain, and knew Riker wouldn't allow it.

"Captain Urosk—"

"That's my only demand, Riker. Give me the Klingon within thirty minutes, or your captain dies."

The frequency closed.

Thirty minutes. Why? They were stalling for some purpose. In most hostage situations Riker had dealt with he'd had to beg for time. It was being *given* here.

Riker considered his options. *Enterprise* couldn't be reached—and no one knew why. That meant the security complement on the planet, a total of twenty including Barbara's guards, was all he had. It should be enough . . . would have been if there weren't such an important hostage being held. This type of danger was why Riker objected to Picard leading Away missions. Unfortunately, there were still certain things that only Picard could handle, and he *was* the captain —if he told Riker to belay his protective attitude, Riker would have to do so.

"Deanna?" Riker nudged her. She looked better than she had an hour ago—more rested. Maybe it was the grain, but Riker doubted it. Deanna was quite the trouper. She'd even given him a reassuring smile when he and Barbara had embraced.

"I'm not sure if Urosk means what he says," Deanna said, her eyes etched with the pain of feeling such anger and hate. "I don't have to tell you they're furious enough to kill. They always have been."

Riker nodded. "Suggestions, Mr. Worf?" he asked, absently smoothing a tattered uniform that needed sewing rather than primping. "Aside, of course, from serving you up to the Hidran with an apple in your mouth."

"That *would* ensure the captain's safety, sir," Worf said.

"Maybe, maybe not."

"It is our only alternative," Worf said gravely.

Riker's eyes narrowed and he glared at the hatch across the corridor. Beyond that door was the captain. He knew Picard well. "Ours maybe . . . but not the captain's. He may have something to say about his own fate."

"We cannot assume that," Worf said.

"We can," Riker countered, "for at least the next thirty minutes."

"Will!"

Riker swung around toward Beverly's voice as she jogged up the corridor from the main hall. Barbara was with her, and Riker smiled a bit, then looked back to Deanna, who smiled in return.

"We've found something," Beverly said, joining Riker and Worf. Barbara came up alongside and stood opposite Deanna. "Dr. Hollitt's grain here is very special."

With thirty minutes ticking quickly by, Riker grew irritated and let them all know it. "What's so special,

Doctor?" he snapped. "Tell me something I *don't* know."

Barbara, her eyes dazzling with . . . well, what looked like cheer, spoke up. "We'd never tried anything as sophisticated as your medical equipment on the grain. We didn't think it necessary—*and* we didn't have it. We would use a simple tricorder on those who had eaten it, but didn't treat the grain itself with anything other than bio-agricultural scanners."

Another case of not rethinking assumptions. At least Riker wasn't the only one who made that mistake. "I understand," he said shortly, if only a bit sympathetically. "But *what did you find?*"

Pulling her hand from her pocket, Barbara held out a palm filled with the small kernels of wheat. "This isn't grain," she said, almost giddy.

"Then what is it?" Riker demanded.

"It's the best inorganic molecular representation of an organic construct I've ever seen," Beverly said.

"I do not understand," Worf huffed.

"I do," Riker said, sharing a look with Deanna and holding his stomach with one hand. "It means I just ate a lot of Rover's cousins."

"Computer."

"Ready."

Data tapped a command into the battle-bridge Ops console. "Estimated duration of unconsciousness provided by anesthizine gas?"

"Twenty-three hours, seventeen minutes."

He nodded approval. It was a drastic matter, but there appeared no one left to trust. It was difficult to fathom that Geordi may be a Klingon collaborator. But he was also friends with Worf. And once before Geordi had unwittingly become a pawn in a Romulan plot. Perhaps something similar was happening here.

There was nothing that could be done about that

now, however. Ending the captain's duress was more pressing.

Of course, without a security team he could hardly beam aboard the Klingon vessel to search for Commander Riker and Counselor Troi, and he could hardly beam down to free the captain when the Klingon vessel needed to be watched. Data would have to deal with the Klingon vessel first—threaten to damage their vessel unless they released their captives.

He hoped the destruction of their vessel would not be necessary. Such a waste was terrible—so illogical. However, the illogic was on their part, and if they did not comply, there was little choice. The Klingon threat had to be stopped now. If not, the Federation would be as weakened as the Hidran. How many other peaceful cultures had fallen to the Klingon threat? That was perhaps something to investigate if he could get control of their memory banks.

Data tapped another command into his console, opening a channel to the Klingon vessel. They had been hailing since *Enterprise* separated, and now they would be answered.

"Enterprise to Klingon vessel *hIV SuH."*

The main viewer flashed on. The obviously angry face of the Klingon in command of the enemy vessel appeared. *"This is Lieutenant Chakba. What is the meaning of not answering our hails? Why have you prepared your ship for battle?"*

"Commander Data, in command of the *Enterprise—"*

"Where is your captain?" demanded the Klingon.

Such subterfuge. "I believe you know the answer to that," Data said. "I am formally demanding that you return to us your captives, or risk retaliation."

"Have you gone insane? We are allies, not enemies! We have no captives!"

"I have evidence to the contrary. Surrender your vessel."

"You are *insane!"*

"May I take that as a confirmation that you do not wish to comply with my request?"

The Klingon motioned to someone off screen, then said, *"You may take that as your epitaph!"*

"Very well," Data said as he closed the channel and moved the *Enterprise* into a higher orbit. "I regret it has come to this."

Chapter Fifteen

PICARD MOPPED HIS BROW with a sleeve and tried to breathe through his mouth. The room had filled with warm, stifling steam. The Hidran, of course, enjoyed the moist air, basked in it, and went about their work quickly. Too quickly.

On the lab table was a line of communicators—the Starfleet comm badges as well as the Hidran hand units. They were all open and exposed, yet still functioning since Riker was able to get through.

Riker—alive, just as Worf was. Fortune was being favorable. Would Data know all this? Could they get through to him? Perhaps no one could. If Data was as damaged as La Forge said, Riker's obvious safety might not even register with the android. If Data had lost his rational faculty . . . well, no fact would matter. The dank air now carried the Hidran's musty odor straight to Picard's nose and eyes, and made them burn. Perhaps this hadn't been the best of ideas.

Glancing up to the ceiling, he watched small beads of water condense and shimmer in the light. The moisture darkened the cold stone, spreading until the rock was saturated. He looked down at the Hidran's work—small and delicate . . . and quite ill-suited to their long, sticky fingers.

They needed tools, had few, but were making do disturbingly well. So far three communicators had been linked together, soldered with bits of wire and thin phaser beams. Their own disrupter-phasers were of little use here—those were for killing. Starfleet phasers could kill when necessary, but were also tools, and the Hidran took advantage of such utility. Razor thin phaser beams and microwire were their only real instruments, that and the few microscopes left in the lab.

Picard needed a distraction . . . something to slow them down until his plan could stop them cold. Cold and wet.

"Urosk," he called. "What if Commander Riker refuses to give you what you want?"

The Hidran leader looked up. "You know he will. And you know that your Klingon is no longer all I want."

"Yes," Picard said gravely. "You also want to destroy every other Klingon."

His weapon still in hand, Urosk stalked toward him. "Not every Klingon. That would be too much to hope for. At this point I wish only to kill enough of them that *Qo'noS* will think twice before breaching war again."

"How can you know that is what they want?"

Urosk shook his head and his tone took on a pitying quality. "I know it, as surely as I know my own soul. It is in their nature."

"No!" Picard snapped. "It is not in their nature."

The Hidran tensed, but did not bring his weapon up. Instead he spoke in a rather calm voice. "The Klingons themselves admit it's bred into them."

Captain Jean-Luc Picard, who had traveled the known galaxy, met life-form after life-form, intelligent being after intelligent being, who had himself taken in part in Klingon politics, and who perhaps knew Lieutenant Worf better than anyone, knew what a lie that was.

"No," he insisted. "It may be their culture, ingrained into their society, but those are decisions—*acts* . . . of volition—which any Klingon, any conscious being, may choose to embrace or deny. *Your* society and culture had been ravaged by what their society once was—"

"Still is."

Picard pressed on. "The *point* is that your culture changed because of an influence, the influence of *their* culture, and now you both hold similar customs."

Urosk's cheeks grew ruddy with anger and he took a step back. "No! You are twisting and distorting—"

"Listen to me, Urosk. Listen to yourself. This," Picard said motioning around him, indicating the situation as it now stood, "it is all because of the Klingons?"

"Yes!" Urosk hissed.

Picard stepped closer, his eyes intent, backing the Hidran away. "The Klingons have turned your people into what they did not want to become, yes?"

Anger contorting his expression, the Hidran captain nodded sharply.

Picard took only a moment to glance up at the other Hidran. They were listening too now, ignoring their work. "And," he continued, "your culture has been totally disrupted by values you never held, and by a morality you once disagreed with."

"What is your point, Picard?" Urosk yelled, taking another step back as Picard closed in.

"What has happened to your nature, Captain? Has it changed?" he asked. "Or are you ignoring it in favor of a philosophy that has gripped you as it did the Klingons? Has your reaction been to fight them using your nature—that which is every intelligent being's nature—your minds, your capacity to reason, your ability to think—or have you been fighting them with the very tools even they are coming to reject—anger, hatred and—"

Ftsssiiittssss.

They both spun as the row of communicators crackled with the electrical whine of overload, then flashed into flame.

Silence followed for a moment, as Urosk looked incredulously at the sizzling mess. A drop of water fell from the ceiling into one of the communicators, making the smoldering circuit hiss and sputter.

The Hidran captain looked again, and watched the rain—drop after drop of water that had condensed on the ceiling, only to fall back onto the Hidran's work.

The line of Urosk's spine tensed and sank, not in defeat, but in action. He hissed something to his men, then swung toward Picard.

Picard felt his own muscles tense, and he readied himself for a fight—not soon enough.

The Hidran captain grabbed him by the neck, then lifted him off the floor. They struggled—Picard forcing a knee into the Hidran's chest—but without leverage he had no force.

With his free hand, Urosk seized Picard's right arm and twisted until they both heard the crack of bone and a grunt of agony.

Dropped back onto the bench against the wall, Picard cupped his left hand under his right elbow as his side filled with heat and pain. His hand throbbed and moving his fingers was white-hot misery.

"Next time," Urosk spat, "it will be your neck!"

* * *

"You were attacked by dogs?" Worf glowered, and his question sounded a lot more serious than the words implied.

Riker shook his head and Deanna chuckled.

"They're roving machines, Worf," Riker said. "And I'm going to guess the industry we saw down there is busy pumping out this grain." He turned to Barbara. "Sound like everything's beginning to fall into place?"

Barbara shook her head. "I should have seen this coming . . . should have put it all together . . ."

"Oh, come on," Riker said, thinking of his own bout of jumping to conclusions. "Who doesn't miss something once in a while?"

"You just didn't have the equipment," Beverly added.

"Even if I had, I wouldn't have thought that the grain was inorganic. I just assumed—"

"You did what we all do from time to time," Riker said softly.

Stuffing her hands into her lab coat, Barbara shook her head again. "It's my job not to."

Mine too, Riker thought.

"I think you're all missing something," Beverly said. "Don't you know what this might mean?"

Riker waited only a moment. "Obviously not, Doctor. Tell us."

Holding up her tricorder, she pointed to a graph on the small screen. Riker could barely read it from where he was, but it looked like his own bio-scan.

"The grain isn't magic," Beverly said, "but it does seem to have the properties Barbara claims. Someone designed this—it has programing and structure, all on the molecular level. A lot like the nanites we use in certain medical procedures, but much more advanced in design and programming."

"I can probably still market it," Barbara added.

Worf sighed and shifted his phaser from one hand to another. "This is all very interesting, but does not help us in our current situation."

"Agreed," Riker said, impatient. None of this would help rescue the captain.

"It might," Beverly said. "It has *programming,* Will, just like my tricorder does. It enters the body and that programming takes over. I'm not sure how, but it obviously scans the body and takes some action to balance any system *out* of balance."

"How does it know," Deanna asked, "what that balance is?"

"We don't know," Beverly said. "I assume it scans the DNA of whoever ingests it, and then is programmed to restructure the body, or repair it, based on the genetic model it has to go on."

Now Riker sighed. "This is all fascinating, but—"

"Hush and listen," Beverly snapped. "Geordi and the Hidran Ambassador both ate the grain and *both* had bio-neural implants. Prosthetics aren't written into DNA, so the grain probably thought they were foreign bodies. I've already scanned the Ambassador's body. The grain-machines are still active within him. Idle, having nothing to do, but they are still 'living,' for lack of a better term." All at once she took Riker's arm and gasped. "Jean-Luc didn't have any of the grain, did he?"

Riker shrugged and turned to Worf.

"He did not," Worf said.

Beverly released her breath in relief. "Good. The time it takes for the grain to activate seems to vary depending on the person, but if he had . . . he'd be dead by now. The grain would have recognized his artificial heart as foreign and responded the same way it did with Geordi and the ambassador . . . rejection."

"This is proof I did not kill Zhad," Worf said.

"Yes," Beverly said. "I can prove it. The pain of the rejection, the same pain Geordi felt, was too great for Zhad, and he most likely tore out his mask in an effort to stop it."

Riker smiled. "This is good."

"I do not understand," Worf said. "Why then did the grain not give Geordi his sight and allow the ambassador to breath?"

"Because," Beverly began, "that wasn't a condition the grain read in their DNA. Geordi never *had* sight—it is not a malady, but a condition he has genetically. I think we can safely say the grain would heal a cut faster than the normal, but it won't rewrite DNA code or grow you a new arm. Or—maybe it will grow you new a new arm. I don't know. But it wouldn't grow you one with a different number of fingers than you had before. It's only a sophisticated antibody as far as I can see. So, the ambassador, by definition of his genetics, couldn't breathe this atmosphere, and all the grain on this planet wouldn't have helped him to. Location and needs weren't listed in his DNA—only his basic physical structure was."

Perhaps already writing the marketing proposal to her company, Barbara added, "And any being with DNA and without synthetic parts could probably eat this quite safely."

Pushing out a breath, Riker glanced down the hall toward the Hidran's hatch again. He was interested, thought he may use this information, but wasn't sure how. That irritated him, made him anxious as if he were wasting time.

"Why would anyone construct this?" Deanna asked. "Why disguise a machine to look so natural and biological? The machines underground didn't look that way."

"No way to know," Barbara said. "Maybe if we can access any computers underground . . . right now we're just guessing they found it easier to ingest in this form, or maybe they wanted to keep secret the planet was industrial rather than agrarian."

"That would make sense," Beverly said. "The grain is nearly impervious to sensor scans. You can't imagine the backflips we had to go through with my medical equipment to get past the illusion that it's just an uninteresting new grain. In any case, there's no way to tell what their motive was for hiding it. What we need is access to the computers below the surface."

"We *do* have a more immediate problem," Riker said, his neck tight with tension. "The Hidran are not going to lay down their arms and release the captain just because we say Zhad *wasn't* killed by Worf. They believed he was *without* evidence. Proof to the contrary isn't going to matter."

"They'd have to listen to reason, though," Barbara said.

Riker smiled. Perhaps a bit more patronizing that he'd wanted to. "No," he said. "They don't."

"What if we could demonstrate to them how it worked and exactly what happened," Barbara offered.

Shaking his head, Worf grunted a laugh. "You'd be dead before you spoke your first sentence. You can physically force someone to take almost any action, except changing his mind. *That* they must do of their own accord."

"Computer, engage all auto systems. Accelerate to one-quarter impulse power and prepare to apply set course out of standard orbit." Data quickly tapped commands into Ops console.

"Acknowledged," replied the computer.

Data nodded. "Bring main phasers on line, and transfer full power to all offensive and defensive systems."

Another acknowledgment from the computer, and Data nodded again.

"Engage course and display tactical on main screen." Unlike humans, Data did not need the view of the actual scene as it would appear if the naked eye would view it. He preferred the tactical display with its grid and specifics.

"Course engaged. Leaving orbit and coming about to course three-one-zero mark five."

On the display, Data watched the Klingon vessel's attitude change as it prepared for an obvious maneuver out of orbit.

Data typed quickly, moving the *Enterprise* to a new course. "Lock phasers on primary targets of engineering and weapons centers. Stand-by to lock phasers on secondary targets of life support and bridge operations."

"Phasers lock achieved."

Data nodded again.

"Fire."

227

Chapter Sixteen

ORANGE THREADS CONNECTED the *Enterprise* Battle Section with the Klingon Cruiser. Data's tactical board sparkled. Each filament represented an *Enterprise* phaser blast that had hit and caused damage.

"Computer, estimate damage to Klingon vessel."

"Damage to forward and rear shields, seventy-two and sixty-one percent respectively. Warp engines of Klingon vessel are overloading and being taken off line."

A series of beeps brought Data's eyes off his console and back to the tactical screen. The Hidran ship had entered the fray, and was firing on the Klingon vessel as well. This was, of course, not truly within their purview, but Data could hardly fire on them in return. They were only seeking to protect themselves from the Klingon threat.

His hands flying across the controls, Data opened a channel to the Klingon vessel *and* continued to fire. "Klingon cruiser—you are out-gunned and out-maneuvered. Surrender your vessel."

There was no response. Klingons tended not to surrender, and to Data that was a pity: they would lose. Yes, they were experienced and clever, but Data was equally experienced, and he knew that what he lacked in creativity he made up for in speed and foresight. His only limitation was the automation of ship's systems: if something broke down, or was damaged, he could hardly go repair it himself without leaving the battle.

Surprising . . . that no Klingon infiltrators had sabotaged the automation or weapons systems to destroy the ship when engaged. Were there limits to the Klingon's influence? Or, more likely, they wanted to capture the *Enterprise* intact.

Data assumed there was some type of mind-control taking place—perhaps that was what interfered with scans of Velex and also accounted for the drain of the white-noise broadcast.

"Klingon Battle Cruiser is now attacking Hidran vessel," announced the computer. *"Hidran vessel is damaged on port nacelle—weapons systems down."*

"Target Klingon cruiser's offensive system conduit and fire repetitive photon burst," Data ordered.

Red globes lit up across the tactical display, connecting the *Enterprise* and the Klingon ship.

"Direct hit," the computer said. *"Null power reading from Klingon weapons systems."*

Data nodded and re-hailed the vessel. "Klingon cruiser, this is the *Enterprise*. Surrender your vessel."

Silence.

"Computer, scan shield strength of Klingon cruiser."

"Scanning . . . overall shield strength is at forty-three per cent."

"Achieve phaser lock at shield generation points."

"Phasers: locked."

"Fire."

A pause . . . a series of tones . . . *"Unable to fire."*

Data looked up from his console. "State problem with phaser controls."

"There is no problem with the phaser controls."

Tapping at his board quickly, Data took the Battle Section into a high orbit. "Computer, run diagnostic on all offensive systems."

"That function is not available from this station."

"That is not possible."

"That statement is incorrect."

Something was wrong. Had someone escaped the anesthetic gas?

"Computer, assure all command functions are routed to this station."

There was a much longer pause and a longer series of bleeps.

"Computer, acknowledge," Data ordered, keeping an eye on the Klingon and Hidran vessels that were unmoving on his scope.

Another series of beeps was the computer's only reply.

Data's tactical display suddenly went blank, then his phaser controls.

He tapped in a manual override code.

"Computer, transfer all command functions to manual control."

Silence—this time not from the Klingons, but from his own ship.

"Computer, acknowledge."

Suddenly what was happening became clear, and Data stood.

"Geordi."

Picard felt Urosk's cold fingers around his neck again. The Hidran captain wrenched hard and brought Picard to his feet.

Holding his broken arm lightly with his good hand, Picard refused to make a sound in pain.

Urosk's grasp tightened.

"Are you going to kill me now?" Picard asked tightly through his closing airway. "Is this Hidran justice? The murder of an innocent man?"

The Hidran's face was a twist of angry flesh. Green eyes blazed as he yanked his phaser up to rest on Picard's left cheek.

The heat of it—the throbbing energy . . . Picard needed to slip his one good arm up, get that phaser. Maybe he'd die in the action, but even if there was the slightest chance—it had to be taken. If it was within his power, this conflict could not leave the plant.

As the muscles in his left arm strained, Picard brought a fist up to Urosk's arm and slapped the phaser away.

The Hidran's fingers tightened around Picard's throat and Urosk dragged him toward the back of the room.

"I will wait no longer," Urosk hissed, releasing Picard with a shove toward the back wall.

Picard recovered his balance as Urosk played with the settings on his Starfleet phaser, and tried to find some means of escape. There were two Hidran soldiers on either side. He saw Urosk thumb the phaser setting higher—heard it hum as it built up the surge of power, ready to be fired.

Urosk wouldn't get the satisfaction of fear from the captain's eyes. Picard would stand tall and earn a grudging respect for the Federation by dying without a flinch.

The Hidran captain aimed—and fired.

Orange flame spat forward and singed Picard's face. The beam enveloped the wall behind. The stone disintegrated, collapsing into vapor and dust and rubble. Shards of gravel snapped against his back and arms, and he crouched to protect himself as the wall came down around him.

Another rumble shook the room—the ceiling cracked and threatened to fall in on them and the side walls lost their form as they toppled in.

"Move! Everyone move! The Earther first!" Urosk choked over the dust, but endured and pushed Picard through the hole that had been wall. Beyond was cool air and an open alley between two buildings.

Picard stumbled through the dust, his arm hot with pain. He saw his moment for escape, and took it. He crouched low—rolled to the left through the rising dust he knew the Hidran would not venture into.

He choked, coughed through the pain and over the stone, as he tried to push toward fresh air. Before he could press further, long fingers coiled around his limp arm and pulled him up. He gasped in bitter pain, but covered any outcry with a grunt.

He twisted angrily, saw he was in the grip of some Hidran soldier—Batok—and tried to wrench his broken arm free of the alien's massive grip.

Thwock—thwock-thwock—thwock.

Suddenly the Hidran began to convulse. First a small shudder, then a series of trembles as pockets of moist blood opened on the Hidran's tunic. The sound of wet flesh slapping against itself filled the air.

Thwock-thwock. Thwock.

The Hidran fell forward, dragging Picard to the rubble with him.

Dead—the Hidran was *dead*.

"No one move!"

The voice—deep and angry.

With great pain Picard managed to pull his arm free. He rolled away and looked up . . .

Captain Kadar stood, some kind of metal hand weapon aimed out toward the Hidran behind Picard.

"Where is Urosk?" demanded Kadar. "And where is the animal that killed my warrior!"

"What the hell was that!" Riker spun toward the rumbling sound—toward the room where the Hidran were.

Worf turned an instant after him. "They must have broken through the back wall!"

"Get back to the main hall!" Riker ordered Beverly and Barbara. "Deanna, you're with us." He aimed toward the main hall and began to run, Worf and Deanna at his side. "I thought you said they wouldn't try that," he grumbled to Worf.

As they ran, Worf shrugged. "I believe I said *I* would not try it."

"Okay," Riker huffed, suddenly realizing he was *running* on his supposedly bad leg. "We assume they're outside rather than crushed under the rubble. Deanna and I'll take to the roof. How many people do we have up there?"

"Five," Worf said.

They all stopped at the entrance to the main hall. Riker looked into the hall, saw a few of Barbara's security, then turned back to Worf. "I want five more waiting inside, in case the Hidran decide to fall back. Give Halford five and have her come around the eastside of the building, and you take five and come 'round the westside."

Worf nodded. "Understood."

"This is our chance to get the captain back," Riker said as he turned toward the stairway that led to the roof. "Let's not blow it."

"Stop this!" Picard stood, blocking Kadar's direct view of Urosk. "No more!"

Kadar, and the three other Klingons who had taken positions a few meters behind him, were all carrying sophisticated projectile-firing chemical combustion rifles. Each of them had a Hidran target, and each of the Hidran, Picard assumed, had a Klingon one.

Everyone had some sort of cover as well, behind a wall corner or the rubble from the fallen wall.

Stand-off.

The Klingon weapons—with no active power source—were difficult to scan for. Firearms of this type were still used by some, for sport usually.

There was no sport here.

Obviously the Klingons had planned ahead and hidden the weapons. Amazing—that Kadar had been kept in his make-shift cell for so long. Picard knew they couldn't be kept there forever . . . now the timing might be used to his advantage.

"Stay out of this, Picard!" Kadar stomped forward aggressively.

With the four remaining Hidran loosely around him, and the dead one at his feet, Picard took a step toward the Klingons. "Lay down your weapons! All of you!"

Glancing back Picard saw only the tops of three Hidran. Urosk came up behind Picard, guarding himself from the Klingons with Picard's small frame.

"Yes," Urosk called, his voice rough from the dust, "lay down your weapons or Picard dies."

"No!" Picard spun around and faced Urosk. Despite his arm throbbing with blood, swollen and numb, anger nearly clenched his right fist. "I will not be used as an ongoing excuse for murder! End this —now! You have each encountered loss needlessly. Talk to each other—settle differences as *civilized* beings."

Urosk aimed deliberately at him and called to Kadar. "I do not care what he says! Do as I say or he d—"

A meter behind Urosk the ground exploded into dust and clods of dirt. The whine of a phaser snapped the air and Picard looked up just long enough to see Riker firing from the roof of the main hall building.

Seizing the moment of distraction, Picard swung his good arm around and knocked the phaser from Urosk's grasp. The weapon went flying and Urosk belted Picard out of the way as they both scrambled to retrieve it.

Kadar took aim at Urosk and fired. Shells ricocheted off the ground. Picard jumped forward and forced the Hidran captain down, out of the line of fire. They rolled onto his bad arm but continued to grapple for the phaser.

Wincing relief as he tilted off his broken bones, Picard gripped the weapon and kicked Urosk in the stomach, then the face.

The Hidran captain crumpled away, grunting in fierce pain.

With effort, Picard pulled himself up. He could feel a trickle of blood run down his right arm. He made the break worse with every move, but had to ignore that for now as best he could. He aimed the phaser at Urosk and took a step back, making sure he was out of assault range by the Hidran's long arms.

"Excellent, Picard!" Kadar laughed. "Now, the Hidran will lower their weapons—"

"If we die, we die in battle!" Urosk dragged himself off the ground and into a crouched position. "Not helpless at the hands of executioners!"

"As you executed two of our men?" Kadar bellowed.

Picard glanced up at Riker again and nodded sharply. Another bolt of phaser-lightening sizzled into the ground—this time in front of Kadar.

"No more!" Picard shouted. "It's over!"

"Because you say it is over, Picard?" Urosk bel-lowed. "Will you kill us if we choose to exercise our right to kill one another?"

"You have no such right!" Phaser in hand, Picard managed to keep pivoting between Urosk and Kadar, letting both know neither had an ally right now. "You cannot have the right to take away someone else's right to life."

Tall frame shaking with fury, Urosk rose to his full height. "Do you not believe in justice? Does a mass-murderer have the right to his own life?"

"No," Picard snapped, "there is an obvious differ-ence between the blatant initiation of violence and the use of defensive force—"

"Retaliation is defense!" Urosk roared.

"Retaliation for what?" Picard shot bitterly. "A crime you cannot prove? Upon individuals who did not commit it? Is that your justice, Urosk?" He spun around to face Kadar. "Or yours? Your cultures may suggest that a son pays for the sins of his father, but who are you to force that upon others without their consent? How can you assign to all Hidran the punish-ment only one should receive?" He turned again, backed up, and faced both as best he could. "Both of you are guilty of *that* crime—acting outside your purview because of some misplaced indignation."

"They killed our ambassador!" Urosk shouted, pointing at Kadar.

"There is no 'they'!" Picard thundered. "'They's' do not exist! Groups neither have rights nor shared responsibility upon which judgments can be meted out! There is insufficient proof to suggest *one* Klingon killed your ambassador, let alone the entire race."

"There is more than enough," Urosk growled, "to see that you act to protect your Starfleet Klingon!"

Stepping into the circle of angry combatants—from where Picard had not noticed—Worf answered for himself as he stepped toward the center. "I need no protection. I've done nothing wrong."

Worf's timing was impeccable, but Picard noticed he only held a knife, no phaser, and that might add to the tension rather than quell it.

"So says every murderer, Klingon," Urosk spat.

Picard could see the Hidran's muscles tense and knew Urosk was in want of a weapon.

One of the Hidran moved toward Worf from behind his barrier of rubble. Picard noticed and gestured to Riker.

Another phaser shot from above, this time just centimeters in front of the Hidran aggressor. The ground plumed up, mushrooming into a cloud of stone and grit, and the Hidran collapsed forward, choking and sputtering. His weapon fell and he quickly scrambled for it before retreating back behind the collapsed wall.

"You will hear me out," Worf said evenly. "Ambassador Zhad was not murdered. His death was a twist of fate—"

"It is not fate that is twisted—" Urosk barked.

Picard brought up his phaser. "Hear him out."

"There is a human saying," Worf said, and drew his knife. "Actions speak louder than words."

The blade sparkled in the setting sun . . . as Worf thrust it into his gut and twisted.

"Worf!" Picard leapt forward, astonished, as Worf pulled out the knife and let it drop to his feet. What was he doing? What kind of impulsive act of honor had motivated this?

"Riker," Picard called up the side of the building, "I want Crusher here on the double!" He turned back to Worf and demanded, "Why?"

"No doctor—no help!" Worf grunted, crushing the wound with his hand as blood began to soak his uniform tunic. "The knife even the Hidran will recognize as Klingon—the blade specially made to bring slow and certain death."

"You have a Klingon fool for an officer, Picard," Urosk laughed. "His enemies need only wait for him to kill *himself.*"

Worf shook his head. "No, I have not," he said, obviously pained as blood soaked between the fingers of his hand. "I have eaten a loaf of the bread that killed your ambassador. That shall save my life."

Ignoring Kadar and Urosk, Picard pressed closer to his security chief. "Explain," he ordered.

"This planet's flora is artificial," Worf said. He shifted his weight, but had trouble keeping his balance. "The grain is machinery—on the molecular level, with a purpose . . . healing the host's body."

"And yet it killed Zhad," Urosk spat. "With your reprogramming, no doubt!"

Warily, Worf shook his head. "No," he said softly. "Zhad died because the grain treated his implanted mask as foreign. It was trying to heal him—" He stumbled forward, fell to his knees.

Beverly rushed up from wherever Worf had come, her medical case in hand.

"Doctor . . ." Picard pointed to Worf, then glanced quickly at Kadar and Urosk and their respective soldiers again. "If anyone takes aggressive action, Riker has my orders to fire at will."

The captain looked up and got a nod to the affirmative from Riker.

"Dammit, Worf," Beverly Crusher said as she dropped to a kneel beside the Klingon, "what are you trying to prove?"

"The grain . . ." Worf said weakly, "it will restore me as called for in my DNA."

"Is this true?" Picard asked in a hushed tone.

"We're not at all certain of all our facts," Beverly said, her voice edged with anger and anxiety. "We determined it was the cause of Zhad's death and Geordi's blindness, and it helped repair Riker's injured leg, but we don't know how long it lasts or just what it can and can't do."

Urosk kept his position, but folded his arms and growled, "Spare us this charade, Picard. An elaborate act for our benefit, but your doctor will now cure the Klingon and he will claim it is this bread—"

"No!" Worf yelled, lifting up the knife from his feet. "The doctor will not tend me," he rumbled and shoved her off.

"Worf!" Beverly stumbled but wouldn't back away. "You could die!"

Picard pulled her back. "Let him, Doctor."

Beverly twisted toward him. Outrage arched her brows. "Captain—"

"No," Picard said. "It's what he wants. Death is what they all want." He released Beverly and pushed himself toward the Hidran, toward Urosk. "You want death, don't you, Captain? You want to die."

"If I must, for my people," Urosk said gravely.

Picard nodded bitterly and shook his phaser in front of the Hidran. "And I know you think this will help your people. You're certain of it, in fact. As certain as Kadar is that all Hidran are insane with murderous rage. As certain as Worf is that his life will be saved by a loaf of bread!"

"Nothing can save his life, so long as I am alive," Urosk growled.

"Ah," Picard snapped back, "but if he *is* saved by that grain, then your entire premise fails, doesn't it? Doesn't it! And you have killed for no reason. How many of your people have died because of such erroneous rationalizations? How many will continue to die?"

Anger pounding in his heart, he pivoted to Kadar. "How many of *your* people have been killed for the same reason? And how many," he finished slowly, "have you both killed yourselves?"

Worf grunted again in pain, fell onto his side, propped himself up with the hand that had been covering his gut, then held up his knife as Beverly tried to approach. "Stay back, Doctor."

"Shall I stun him?" Picard asked of Kadar. "Shall I force Lieutenant Worf to submit to treatment and save his life for him?" He spun around and paced toward Urosk. "Should I hand you the phaser and let you kill him, even though your entire reason for hating him may be totally false?"

Visibly shaken and surprised, Urosk looked from Worf to Picard. "I do not care what you do, and if the Klingons wish to engage us, why should *you* care?"

"Because," Picard said as he angrily marched toward the Hidran, "you're better than all of this. You're better than wavering uncertain on a precipice of illogical un-thought. You're better than some animal who acts on instinct. You're better than you drive yourselves to be, and I, for one, detest seeing people wallow in the muck of their own subjective whim." He held up his phaser to Urosk. "If *this* is what you want—if death is what you covet—then tell me! Tell me you don't care about the sustenance of your people's lives, and I will leave this planet . . . Tell me! And I will leave you with the tool of your own destruction—your irrational hate."

"I care for the sustenance of my people—" Urosk said.

"No, you don't," Picard said, almost chuckling in irony. "You don't care whether you were right or wrong—whether anything you believe is right or wrong. You act on what you *feel* is right, and don't care to compare that with reality. And if your feeling is opposed to reality, it's reality that gives way."

"That is a lie!" Urosk thundered.

"Here," Picard said, closing the final steps between himself and the Hidran captain. "Take my phaser." He set the level and stretched out his hand to Urosk. "Take it. Murder me—an innocent man—because you *feel* I might have ordered Worf to kill your ambassador."

Awestruck, Urosk just stood there.

"Take it!"

"I . . . I don't think that," Urosk said.

"Take it! Kill me!" Picard pressed his phaser into Urosk's chest, handle first. "What you *think* is irrelevant—there was no reasoning involved when you accused Worf—why do you need a reason to accuse me?"

"You are not Klingon—"

"There are no Klingons!" Picard shouted. "There are only individuals, with biases, yes—with values, yes—but there is no such thing as collective volition! A being—any sentient being—is not some mass of genetic characteristics, all interchangeable and acting under one racial mind. People form their own opinions, right or wrong, and act on those opinions—right or wrong. You've been forming yours improperly, Urosk, so why stop now?" He pressed the phaser harder into the Hidran captain's breast-bone. "Kill me, or kill Worf before he proves you wrong. Act on your emotion if it's all that matters."

Picard lifted Urosk's palm and pressed the phaser into it until the Hidran's fingers closed around it.

"Kill him, Captain," Picard said. "Fulfill your adopted Klingon heritage and embrace the irrational hate that the Klingon Empire itself is coming to reject!" He turned to the Klingon commander. "And then, Kadar, you can kill Urosk for Zhad's actions, and for Batok's."

Kadar remained silent.

Picard shook his head. "No? Why not?"

His hand now free, he gripped Beverly's arm and pushed her toward the Hidran captain.

"Kill *her*, Urosk! Surely someone with red hair once murdered a Hidran. Or is it only Klingons that are all alike in their thoughts and motivations. Perhaps I can find a Hidran that once murdered a Terran, and that will give me cause to murder *you*."

"No," Worf said, his voice stronger.

Picard twisted around—Worf was standing.

Weakly, the Klingon—*Worf*—took a step forward and dropped the knife into the dirt. "No one here is going to die."

His hand fell from his wound. Blood trickled where moments ago it had gushed.

"Kill me now if you must," Worf said, "but do not delude yourself into thinking it is justice."

Phaser in hand, Urosk extended his long arm. He aimed at Worf—glanced to Picard a moment . . . then dropped the weapon from his grasp.

The phaser bounced once on the ground, and came to rest at his feet.

Chapter Seventeen

"COMPUTER, OVERWRITE-CODE THIRTY, access level seven."

Geordi slid to the deck and quietly set down his phaser. The weapon was the first thing he'd searched for after the gas was blown clear. It was absurd, really—what was he going to do? Ask Data to announce his position so a blind man could take aim? Somehow, though, the weapon was a comfort. And, if worse came to worse, Geordi would just use the weapon to destroy a few key systems. That was his goal—keep the ship not totally defenseless, but weak enough that Data wouldn't try anything drastic.

Unfortunately, without his vision, he really couldn't go yanking wires and switching chips. One wrong pull and life support might go—or warp core containment, for that matter. It was amazing enough that he was able to find the Jefferies tube cubbyhole that allowed him an escape from the gas. He wasn't about to test his luck again.

The computer would be his eyes, through his hand

communicator. He knew as much as Data did about the *Enterprise*—the capabilities, the possibilities . . . the computer programing.

Data had reprogrammed the computer by taking control of certain functions and lock-outs. He was telling the computer what to do. Geordi was taking a different tack.

"Overwrite-code thirty enabled," replied the computer. *"Level seven, available."*

"Good!" Geordi nodded approvingly. Data hadn't thought of any of this. "Computer, command functions are no longer accessible through any station or terminal on the Battle Drive."

"Command functions switched to saucer access only."

Despite the super-speed of nanoprocessors and the complexity of modern computers, they were all still, like their electronic-abacus ancestors, basically stupid. Computers could only do what they were programed to. Data, either damaged or . . . Geordi couldn't guess what, had told the computer to do certain things—had activated certain aspects of the computer's emergency programming. Geordi decided to trump Data by going a step further—rewriting the computer's actual program. If Data was going to take over phaser controls, Geordi was going to make sure that Data could only control them if he were . . . say, doing so from Starfleet Command on Earth. If he wanted to use the tractor beams, perhaps he'd have to be in New Chicago on Mars.

"Computer, transfer to level eight, overwrite-code thirty-A."

"Transfer complete."

The only flaw in this plan was that Data knew the computer just as well as Geordi. He would find out what was happening, as soon as the command functions disappeared, and a battle of reprogramming would ensue. Unless, of course, Geordi took certain steps to protect his changes. He couldn't lock Data out completely, but he could screen his path in a manner that would take Data time to find.

Geordi wagered that Data was, despite his recent fit of illogical conclusions, still a creature of systematic habit. If told to look for a needle in a haystack he'd start at one end and sort through the straw until he found what he was looking for or reached the other end.

So where would Geordi hide his needle? Dead center of a computer haystack—no matter which end Data began looking from, it would take him the longest amount of time to reach the middle. The android wouldn't dive into the task randomly—he'd pick one end and work toward the other. Of that much Geordi was sure.

"Computer, access tenth nested command table."

"Tenth nested command table available."

"Disallow further changes to command pathways from any level but this one."

"Working . . . acknowledged."

"Restrict access to nested command tables, levels one through twenty, with vocal password protection."

"Working . . . acknowledged. State password."

Geordi smiled. "Five-seven-three-six-one dash two-nine-two-three-eight-three dash nine-six dash five-three-six-four." He took in a deep breath, then continued. "Dash seven-three-two dash seven-three-one-two-five dash nine-nine-six-five-two-three-eight dash alpha-six-two dash gamma-eight-three."

There was a series of beeps, then, *"Password entered. Restate for verification."*

He wrinkled his brows. "Oh, right," he mumbled. "Guess I got carried away." He blew out a breath. "Computer, override verification function and accept password as entered."

"Acknowledged."

A chuckle pressed its way out—Geordi couldn't help himself. This was pretty good even if he did say so himself. "Computer," he began, grinning from ear to ear, "now restrict ability to request access to the password *with another* password."

"Working . . . acknowledged. State password."

"Mares eat oats and does eat oats . . . and little lambs drink coffee." He laughed. "Figure *that* one out, Data."

"Password entered. Restate for verification."

"Mares eat oats and does eat oats and little lambs drink coffee."

"Incomplete."

"What? Oh." Geordi smiled. "Figure that one out, Data."

Another series of bleeps from the computer. *"Acknowledged."*

This was going too well. As any engineer could attest, as anyone who worked on *anything* could attest, when things went off without a hitch for too long, it meant something bad was coming. Either what was being fixed wasn't really broken, or a part was wrong, or something . . . No job hadn't at least *one* problem lurking somewhere.

Geordi thought for a moment. What was next? What needed to be done? Assume Data found a way to the command pathways . . . real possible. What would he do?

"Computer, switch to Warp Propulsion Sub-system. WPS factor initiator control."

"Switching . . . ready."

"Restrict access to warp factor one acceleration. Use password in encrypted file: La Forge twenty-three."

"Complete."

"Restrict access to warp factors two through nine

246

respectively, using passwords in the following encrypted files: La Forge twenty-four through La Forge thirty-one."

"Working . . . complete."

"Computer, you're beautiful."

The computer chirped in confusion.

"Delete files La Forge twenty-three through La Forge thirty-one. Overwrite current file allocations with life support commands located in nested area fifty-five and mark entire block as unmovable." Even if Data wanted to recreate the erased files, he wouldn't be able to: they were being overwritten with files that couldn't be transferred. Geordi didn't need a password for that—some things you could just never recover from a computer.

"Function complete."

"Okay—" Geordi turned his head—thought he heard something . . . a change in the ship . . . a creak somewhere, a thrumming that shouldn't have been there.

He was getting paranoid. *Keep calm, go about your business.* "Computer, are we still broadcasting a white-noise transmission from the deflector array?"

"Affirmative."

"Disengage. Attempt to contact planet."

"Channel open."

"La Forge to Picard, come in."

Static snapped back, then: "Picard here."

"Captain . . ."

From behind: "Geordi, please put the communicator down."

"Data—"

Geordi reached down and spun around.

"I have the phaser, Geordi."

There was no anger in that voice—no animosity. It was . . . spooky.

"Why, Data?" Geordi asked, carefully setting the

communicator down, making sure the antenna grid was open and sending. He pushed himself away, taking Data's attention with him.

"I would ask you the same question," Data said. "Are you doing this of your own volition?"

The voice was from another part of the room now—Data was moving about—keeping Geordi disoriented.

"Data, what's happened to you?"

"Nothing has happened to *me*. It would seem I am the only one who has *not* been affected by whatever is coercing you."

"Well . . ." Geordi shifted left along the wall, hoping that Data's constant movement had led him away from the door. "I don't think I'm being coerced . . . instead, I think something's wrong with you."

"I have run several diagnostics on myself. There is no evidence of any abnormality." That casual voice— now from the left—so unmalevolent, so reasonable.

"You don't see mutiny as abnormal?" Geordi said, moving right now.

"Please stop moving, Geordi. I have the phaser set on stun and aimed at you." Matter-of-factly—as if describing a chess move.

Geordi stopped his shuffle and stood facing where he'd last heard Data's voice. "Are you going to stun me, Data?"

"I would rather not," Data said, "but that does depend on your actions. Please detail what you have done to the computer."

"Why?" Stall stall stall. Data was a talker—keep him talking.

"It is necessary for my mission."

"What mission?"

Data paused, obviously considering whether it was in his interests to tell Geordi. "I intend," he began, perhaps thinking he could convince Geordi, "to take this vessel to *Qo'noS*. A course is set and we are already underway."

"What?" Geordi gasped. "You can't!"

"I can," the android said coldly. "The Klingons must be stopped. It is my hypothesis that your mind, and the minds of most *Enterprise* personnel have been corrupted, perhaps coerced, into actions against your respective wills. This is farther reaching than I thought earlier. Captain Picard is also under their control."

"Talk to Starfleet, Data—how could *everyone* be under a Klingon influence? How is it that only you are immune?"

"That you suggest I talk to Starfleet is evidence enough the Klingon influence is indeed pervasive. And I am evidently immune because I am an android."

He's not paranoid. Everyone is *against him.*

"So you're going to do *what* at the Klingon homeworld, Data? Destroy an entire planet?"

"I sincerely hope not," Data said evenly. "One can use the threat of violence as easily as violence itself."

"And if they don't comply with any demand you make?"

"Then," Data said, from the area of the door now, "force must be used. A threat without intent and ability is no threat."

"Then you'll have to stun me, Data. Because you're not getting my help. A threat not only has to be real—but the person you're threatening has to care. I care more about stopping you than whether or not I'm stunned . . . or even killed."

"Geordi," Data said slowly, still near the door, "I am very sorry. I do hope you can be rehabilitated."

Data's voice fell quiet . . . his phaser whined . . . then silence dominated.

Chapter Eighteen

"Geordi . . . I am very sorry. I do hope you can be rehabilitated."

They heard the phaser whine, then silence.

Picard jabbed at the communicator he'd grabbed from Beverly's jacket. "Picard to Data! Return to orbit and beam me aboard. We have found Commander Riker. He's injured and needs medical care."

He could still hear the open frequency—heard Geordi fall to the deck—then a footfall, and then the static crunch of a closing frequency.

He punched at the comm badge again. "Data!"

A closed frequency argued back. He should have spoken up sooner—while Geordi was talking. Perhaps he'd have had a chance to argue with the android himself . . . convince him somehow.

Kadar stepped forward. "I have confirmed the attack on my vessel. We have sustained damage and casualties." The Klingon Captain was somber, his tone almost sympathetic. There was no accusation in his voice. Part of this was his fault—Kadar too had let the situation escalate, and perhaps he felt the regret Picard saw in Urosk's eyes as well.

They stood together, Urosk and Kadar, Picard noticed. An almost surreal sight—for two people who'd been trying to kill each other fifteen minutes before, they were practically cuddling.

Quietly, Urosk pulled Picard's attention with low voice. "My ship . . . We participated in the battle and have both caused and sustained damage."

His wound still very sore, Worf shakily stepped forward. Picard realized now just how close to death his officer had come. Had the wound been a little worse, Worf might not be standing.

"Data must be stopped," Worf said gravely.

Picard nodded and looked down at Beverly who worked on his arm. He wasn't sure when she had begun or what she had done, but from his shoulder to his fingers, his arm was numb and he was glad of it. Worf probably could have used the same, but no mention was made of it. To do so would be an insult, and both Picard and Beverly knew that.

"Doctor—could Data have taken this grain? Might *he* be affected by it?" Picard asked.

Barbara, following Riker to the core of the little group Picard and his fellow captains had formed, spoke up. "Yes! I gave him some. I didn't think it—"

"When?" Picard snapped.

She paused, taken aback, then said, "When I was with him on the ship. I was running tests and he was . . ."

Picard glanced to Urosk who remained silent. "He was reading the Hidran history of the war with the Klingons."

Will Riker, appearing very much like a shipwreck survivor with his tattered uniform and rather rancid smell, pressed his way through to Picard. Deanna followed, her uniform looking no better. In contrast, physically they both looked rested and refreshed.

"I overheard," Riker said. "I've made contact with the saucer section. We have a very confused ensign in command. He wasn't been able to use communications until just a few minutes ago."

"Our subspace communications are down," Kadar said. "If you have access, we must alert our homeworld to protect itself. The *Enterprise* will go unchallenged—Worf's ship would not be questioned. His brother sits on the High Council—Worf himself is respected."

Worf straightened proudly. He looked stronger. No grain there—just ego.

"I know," Picard grumbled. "But they'll destroy the *Enterprise,* Captain. I can't let that happen."

"You can't let *Qo'noS* be destroyed either," Kadar said.

"I know that as well," Picard said. "But if we can catch up to Data . . . reason with him . . . or trick him. I need your ship, Kadar."

Kadar looked from Worf to Urosk, then back to Picard. There was no way to know what the Klingon commander thought, but Picard wagered there was some regret in there. "My ship is yours. But the damage is extensive—we are lacking materials and manpower. Five deaths, twenty-three injuries . . ."

Deaths . . . injuries . . . No sooner had Picard convinced these two warring parties to lay down their arms than they found the *Enterprise* itself had led an unwarranted attack.

"We'll help effect repairs," Picard said. "If we can overtake him before he reaches Klingon space . . ."

"We must, at any cost," Kadar said tightly. "If not, the Klingon fleet will have to disable or destroy your ship."

The ship . . . the lives . . . Picard pulled away from Beverly, who'd been fussing with his numb arm, and faced Kadar, grabbing the Klingon commander's shoulder with his left hand. "I understand that, Captain," Picard said, making sure the Klingon knew Picard wouldn't assign blame to those who were guiltless. "But if there is a way to avoid that," he added, "I *must* try."

Kadar said nothing, just nodded, but there was that flicker in his eyes. The flicker of a captain who knew what a ship was, what it meant to its master's soul.

Picard nodded his gratitude then swung toward Riker. "Coordinate the Saucer with the Klingon vessel. I want their ship up and running within the hour. Data said Geordi had used the computer to lame the ship. Knowing Data, that's temporary. We've been given knight's odds, Number One—let's not waste the advantage."

"Aye, sir," Riker acknowledged, moving away, already shelling out orders into his comm badge.

Beverly snatched Picard's arm again and tried to wriggle it into a make-shift sling. The pain gone, he pulled away, but she struggled and he finally gave in and turned to Deanna.

"What can you tell me about Data's condition?" he asked. "I assume you heard the broadcast."

She nodded. "Data is difficult to read. Most people when they act irrationally have an emotional reason —Data can't, yet from the sound of it, I'd say he regrets his action with Geordi."

"Regret is an emotion," Barbara said.

Deanna turned to her. "Confusion can manifest itself as regret in Data. He doesn't really have emotions. He does have likes and dislikes, opinions, but . . . there's conviction, not passion."

"We don't have time for a seminar, Counselor," Picard said. "Give me something I can use."

She hesitated, looked down a moment, then sighed. "I don't know, Captain. Data is different. If the grain is somehow affecting him it has more to do with biology than psychology."

"I realize that." Pulling his arm from Beverly for the last time as she closed her medical case, Picard tugged at the sling and cast her an appreciative glance.

"Your arm needs more than I can do for it here," Beverly said. "The bone is set and mending but sensitive. No more rabble-rousing."

Picard nodded, caring less about the condition of his arm and more about the condition of his ship. He returned his attention to Deanna. "What I need to know, Counselor, is if there's anything I can use when dealing with him."

Deep brown eyes looking distant, then intently at Picard, Deanna finally said, "Work *with* his insanity, rather than against."

Twisting toward the opening lift doors, Picard bumped his still tender elbow on the Klingon's high command chair. He winced in pain and sucked in a breath of the stale bridge air that still reeked of smoke and burnt circuits.

Riker stepped off the lift, followed by Kadar.

"Nearly ready to get underway. Warp speed should be available in a few minutes," Riker said. "We'll only be able to manage about warp four—there's too much structural damage."

Picard knitted his brows. "Let's hope it's enough. Sensors indicate *Enterprise* Battle Section is nearing warp three. We can catch up *if* she maintains speed."

"It's only a matter of time before Data fixes whatever Geordi did in the computer," Riker pointed out. "And once we get there, what can we do? Kadar's engineer is injured, and even if he wasn't, the disrupter core is fused."

"Torpedoes?" Picard asked.

"They are operational but damaged," Kadar said, lowering himself into the command chair. "The entire system could short out any moment. I have contacted *Qo'noS*. They will be ready for the *Enterprise* with ten cruisers. If we fail to stop the android . . ."

Kadar let the sentence trail off, but it hammered into Picard nonetheless. The Klingon captain obviously understood the sensitivity and perhaps had also gained some respect for the Federation and its Starfleet.

"Vessels in this sector?" Picard asked Riker.

"Nothing within range. The *Excalibur* is Ambassador class, but it's twelve days away at maximum warp. They're the closest."

"We have nothing, Picard," Kadar said. "Not even the element of surprise. Our cloak is destroyed, your android will see us coming, and in a ship he believes is the enemy's."

"Us" and "we." It was the closest Kadar could come to an apology . . . and it meant a great deal. Picard nodded his acceptance.

"We have *one* thing in our favor," Picard said. "Where is Urosk?"

Surprised, Riker looked from Kadar to Picard. "He and his men beamed up. They're also making repairs."

"Get him on the comm."

Riker nodded, mumbled permission from the Klingon communications officer as he walked over to the console, and pecked at the controls.

"On screen," he said.

Turning toward the main viewer, Picard cleared his throat. "Captain Urosk."

Urosk, on the bridge of his own vessel, appeared as the screen flickered to life. "Captain."

Picard stepped forward. "I'm in need of your help—"

Cutting Picard off, Urosk stood and stepped closer to his viewer. His now unmasked face filled the screen. "We are prepared to leave orbit at a course of your choosing. Give us your coordinates and we will beam you aboard."

A slight smile curling his lips, Picard nodded his thanks.

"You have a plan, sir?" Riker asked.

"Indeed I do, Number One," Picard said. "Though I can't say you'll enjoy it. And I know I won't."

The Hidran bridge was cool and dreadfully humid. Uncomfortable, but breathable. Urosk's face, perhaps because the breathing mask was gone, was less harsh than it appeared on the planet, his expression was calmer.

Few words had been spoken between the two captains since Picard had beamed aboard. Perhaps Urosk felt somewhat responsible—Data had been reading their version of shared Hidran/Klingon history when he'd eaten the grain. They all assumed the same thing—the android was in some sort of a logic-loop. The conclusions he'd been reading had become his own, all because of the grain's impact on his organic components.

At least that was the hope. If not, then Data *was* insane, or damaged, or had malfunctioned. In any case, he had to be stopped. Picard wanted to do that himself, with the help of these two vessels. Otherwise Data, Geordi, and everyone else on Battle Drive might die when the ship met the Klingon fleet.

Through the haze that was the Hidran's normal breathing environment, Picard squinted at the main viewer. The Klingon vessel was a dot at the center of a bland starscape as it struggled to match the Hidran's pace.

Riker had stayed with the Klingons to repair as

many systems as possible, as Picard and the Hidran took the lead, in hopes of masking the Klingon ship from *Enterprise*'s sensors.

"I need a current sensor scan," Picard said to Urosk.

The Hidran captain rose and gestured to a console near what appeared to be the helm. The control panel was higher off the deck than Picard was used to, but amazingly like a Klingon access board.

Pecking at the console, Picard brought up a display of the sector, then tapped the coded-frequency comm badge he'd requested sent from the Saucer. "Picard to Riker."

"Riker here."

"*Enterprise* is approaching warp four," Picard said, following the flash that represented the Battle Section with his finger.

"We can't push this ship, Captain," Riker said. "She'll tear apart."

"Damn," Picard huffed, pounding his fist on the console. What good was any of this? He twisted toward Urosk. "What's your maximum?"

"Coolant leaks are causing overheating," Urosk said, his voice more fluid and smooth without the muffling mask. "We can manage warp six. Slightly more if we are lucky."

"Got that, Riker?" Picard asked.

"Aye, sir. But if we speed ahead to slow them down, that ruins any chance of surprise. Right now surprise is all we've got going."

Tension filling every muscle, Picard stared at the blip that was *Enterprise*.

"Commander, stand by for further orders."

Picard closed the frequency and turned fully toward the Hidran Captain. "I need to risk your ship."

His head tilted a moment and Urosk glanced from Picard's arm to his eyes. Maybe he regretted his earlier action, or maybe he understood something about commanding a mission.

When the Hidran captain finally spoke, it was for the bridge crew to hear as well as Picard. "I will belay any action I believe an indiscretion. Other than that . . . I give you my ship."

Light was a turtle, *Enterprise* the hare.

Picard shifted his weight from one foot to the other on the lower deck of the Hidran bridge. The deck plates were humming, rattling in a way he knew they should not.

The *Enterprise* battle drive was a dot on the forward viewer—a foreboding dot. A goal Picard needed to reach. Didn't want to, but that made it no less an imperative.

They could fire on her from here, but without much effect. Torpedoes could be maneuvered around, disrupters or phasers would lose their bite. He needed to be close to her. Close enough to . . . fire on his own ship. To tear apart what he was sworn to protect. To rip at his own soul in the hopes no one else would have to.

Slowly the *Enterprise* grew on the screen. Too slowly. All this speed underneath him—physics warping, bolts pulling, energy gripping the ship to hold it all together—and yet all too sluggish. And all for naught if she couldn't be reached.

Data refused to answer any hail.

"Klingon ship firing, sir!"

White-hot globes of power slapped into the Hidran ship.

"Aft disrupters, fire," Urosk ordered.

"Clean miss, sir."

"Again, fire!"

The ship buffeted as another volley crunched against her shields.

"Shields down sixty percent, sir."

"Vent coolant from decks twelve and thirteen."

"Send out a frantic SOS," Picard added, pivoting back to the main viewer. "Aft view."

Angry orange bolts came screaming from the darkness of space. They almost enveloped the screen before exploding into flame, glaring Picard's view.

Picard gripped the helmsman's chair. "Drop aft shields now!"

Shock from the salvos razed the unshielded hull.

"Power down all weapons," Urosk ordered. "Resend distress call on all Starfleet frequencies."

Come on, Data . . . a friend in need is a friend indeed. I know your morality is still there, even if misplaced.

The Hidran Picard remembered as Meliosh twisted from the helm. "Captain," he said to Urosk, *"Enterprise* is slowing. She reverses her course!"

"On screen," Urosk ordered. "Stand by."

"Standing by, sir."

Picard tensed. His ship out there, ready to be scuttled at his own order. He stepped back down to the lower command deck. "Captain," he said, pointing at a tactical display of the quickly approaching *Enterprise,* "Here, here, and there—main shield generators."

Urosk shook his head. "Computer locks are not functioning."

Pulling in a deep breath, Picard turned back toward the main viewer.

Gracefully *Enterprise* strutted toward them, growing larger as they likewise sped toward her.

"Speed?"

"Half impulse. He is requesting communications."

"Range?"

"Three hundred thousand kilometers—closing."

Urosk glanced up to Picard. "You have command, Captain."

Chest tight, his right arm tensing itself into pain again, Picard stared at his ship, perhaps for the last time—

His ship. *His.*

"Stand by, everyone," Picard said, and felt the tension of the Hidran who'd been told to obey his commands. How far could he push them? He could not ask them to give their lives for his ship. Data could be stopped, with some loss to the Klingon fleet, but was that risk the Hidran's to take? Did they have a duty to sacrifice themselves because Data believed their rhetoric?

How could he ask for their lives merely because they had written their history with a jaundiced eye?

"Captain Picard?" Urosk prodded. *"Enterprise* is within range."

"The Starfleet vessel is locking phasers on the Klingon ship."

Again the Hidran craft shook as torpedoes sped passed her, glancing the shields.

Enterprise ascended as it took an evasive course toward the Klingons.

"One hundred thousand kilometers."

Picard nodded and narrowed his eyes. "Full shields —power to weapons. Fire!"

The Hidran ship gathered itself and fired. Orange bulbs of energy punched point blank into *Enterprise,* spreading out over the shields and wrenching the marrow from Picard's own bones.

"Fire!"

Red snarls of disrupter fire spiraled around *Enterprise* as she twisted away and volleyed a few torpedoes in defense.

The Hidran vessel shook, pummeled by the shots.

"Bolster the shields!" Urosk called out. "Come about to aft course."

"Target engineering," Picard ordered, gripping the edge of the helm console with tense fingers. "Fire!"

Another salvo of torpedoes engulfed her. Picard couldn't breathe.

The Klingon ship swooped down out of warp and its phasers sliced into *Enterprise's* hull.

It burned, by god it *burned*—as surely if it were his own skin.

"Status!" he barked, hoping he'd done enough.

"His shields are holding."

Not his *shields*—mine. My *ship!*

Hawk-like, the Klingon vessel plunged past her again, brightening space with orange spheres that smashed into *Enterprise* and sent her bouncing off her course.

"Her shields are weakening!"

Picard mopped his brow with a wet sleeve as *Enterprise* spat back furious bars of bloody raw power, rocking the ship around him.

Eyes fixed on her sweeping lines as she curled around to fire another blast at her master, Picard yanked up his hand phaser and ordered, "Target aft shields and fire!"

He tapped his comm badge and looked away as the shots rang out. "Riker, stand by!"

The *Enterprise* captain swung back to the Hidran helm. "Well?"

"One more," Meliosh assured him.

"Fire then!"

Picard heard the energy scream from the ship—felt the wave of the blast.

"His aft shields are down!" Meliosh yelled.

Picard sucked in a breath of moist air and lifted his phaser to chest level. "Now, Riker! Now!"

* * *

Crewman Lopez was the first he'd found. Riker holstered the tricorder but kept his phaser in hand as he tried to position the unconscious man in what would be a comfortable position when he finally awoke.

The tricorder reopened, he checked again for any residual gas, then scanned for Data.

As soon as he beamed aboard the android had left the battle bridge. Probably changed course too. The Klingon and Hidran vessels would be left behind.

Enterprise was alone again, and Riker with it. If Picard's plan failed, Riker too would die at the hands of ten Klingon battle cruisers.

Data was difficult to scan with a tricorder. Riker couldn't link in to the ship's computer to get a tack from the android's comm badge, and he wasn't about to actually *ask* where Data was. Once again Picard had ordered no easy task.

Riker scratched at his leg—it only itched now— and continued up the corridor. He glanced down at the tricorder. "Faint energy readings," he mumbled. *Could mean anything.*

He ambled up the corridor, waiting for a sound, an indication, something that might give him an edge.

Suddenly the tricorder graph shot off the scale.

A smile tugged at his lips. An edge.

He adjusted the right buttons, and headed where it told him.

Twenty meters straight, ten left, another five left. At least that's what he figured—the tricorder didn't account for walls, it only told him linear direction.

He marched slowly, cautiously. Data could set a trap as easily as the next Starfleet officer. And the android had an advantage—the ship's computer at his disposal. He could move force fields and drop emergency bulkheads, effectively trapping Riker where he stood.

He looked down at the tricorder again. What if that was a force field reading?

No—it fluctuated, a wild lash across the graph.

He pressed on. There was no place else to go.

Up one corridor, vigilantly down the next.

Mumblings . . . No—yelling—up the hallway.

Riker stopped, listened a moment, then discreetly edged himself up the next corridor, careful not to trip over any crewmen that happened to have fallen in the path.

"You can't win, Data," Picard yelled, and Riker heard a phaser whine.

The only return argument was another phaser blast.

He poked his head around the corner, making sure to keep himself hidden from view. Picard was using a door alcove as cover at one end of the hall, Data was doing the same toward Riker's position.

Picard fired again, a bright orange lance sparking off the wall above Data and chipping the plasticine onto the android's head.

The captain's phaser was set to kill.

"You're alone, Data," Picard said. "The Klingon Empire will live a thousand years longer than you could hope to survive. Give up now while you still have the chance."

Data returned the fire and nearly connected with his target as Picard fell back into the darkness of the alcove.

Boldly, Picard rolled across the hall to another doorway, squeezing off two shots as he went. The deck in front of Data flared into smoke and spark, obscuring his view.

"Captain," Data said, his voice normal if somewhat muted, "I cannot give you this ship. I have sworn an oath and will not break it."

"There are no oaths," Picard said. "Starfleet is ours." The captain poked out of his cover and fired again. The dart of energy flew past Data and Riker had to yank his own head back as it glanced by.

Only a few meters apart, Data and Picard traded volleys again. Riker sank back against the wall, setting down the tricorder and resetting his phaser.

Stun. *Heavy* stun.

Picard fired once more, and the whine of his powerful setting whipped past again.

"Let us help you, Data," Picard yelled. "Put down the phaser and surrender control of the ship and you'll be kept alive—perhaps to fight another day. But stand in our way now, and we'll destroy you!"

One . . .

Riker tensed and pushed himself up to a squat.

Two . . .

He checked the phaser setting again, and also prepared to reset it to kill if he had to.

Three!

"No!" He leapt out—skid up the corridor—and fired.

An orange spear knocked Picard back into his alcove and through the door.

Riker dove, rolled onto a knee, and aimed at Picard's limp form—ready to fire again.

Breathing heavily he looked up at Data. "You okay?"

Eyebrows slightly arched, the android nodded. "Yes, sir."

"Our good captain here had me confined when I found out what was going on," Riker explained bitterly as he rose. "I escaped the Klingon brig—made it to their transporter room. I'm almost glad they knocked out your shields. I'm not sure where I would have gone."

Data pushed himself up from his crouched position. "I am pleased to see you are well, sir—"

"No time for that, Data." Riker gestured toward the nearest turbolift. "Report ship's status."

His phaser now at his side, Data began for the lift. "We are back on a course toward the Klingon Neutral Zone. Shields are down and I suggest—"

The android stiffened, his entire body gripped in energy.

He should have fallen . . . but didn't.

Riker fired again—

Data stumbled forward.

And again—

Energy cloaked Data as he tried to raise his weapon. He gurgled out a sound and turned his head. Riker tensed, ready to set the phaser higher.

The android turned against the beam, trembling with determination.

Another jolt, then another.

Data lifted his phaser arm, then collapsed to the deck. The weapon tumbled from his grip.

Riker sucked in a breath. What if Data couldn't be repaired this time?

He turned away, scowling at his phaser. What if he'd just killed his friend of so many—

A scraping sound.

Riker spun.

Data inched forward, toward his weapon.

One more blast—Riker fired.

Electrical filaments gripped Data's form for a moment . . . then he stiffened and finally lay peaceful.

Riker let out the breath he'd held, allowed his weapon to drop to his side.

He sighed again and looked from the captain, still crumpled into a heap up the corridor, back to Data, board straight at his feet.

Epilogue

"MY PEOPLE ARE STILL RETICENT, *Captain, but I assure you the agreement will be signed. I'll see to it myself.*"

A line of static flickered across the screen, bisecting Urosk's face.

Kadar had expressed the same sentiment when he'd left orbit—as furiously as they had both been against the accord, they now were vigorously for it.

Testing the strength of his stiff right arm, Picard leaned back into his desk chair.

"You're an individual of strong will, Captain. I have no doubt you'll be listened to."

Urosk nodded his appreciation, and the screen when black.

Picard tapped the desk console. "I'm waiting for that report, Mr. Riker."

Riker rose from his bed and tapped his comm badge. "On my way." He jabbed it off again, then grabbed Barbara's shoulders softly and pulled her closer. "I have to go."

She looked up at him, those green-hazel eyes still seeming to flash, even now. "I should be getting back too," she said.

"I'm sorry," he said softly, wishing he could make it sound like he actually felt, and not like something he always said. Which he did.

Barbara smiled. "For what? I only told you how I felt while you were missing because I wanted to be honest with you."

Riker frowned. "But, I'll be gone in a few hours and the honest chances of my return are—"

"Not important," she said, shaking her head. *"I* started this, Will. Not you. And I knew and expected it would only last a few days." She caressed his face. "I didn't tell you I was worried about you to make you feel guilty. I told you so that you'd know you had an effect on me, and that you're a special person." She stood on her toes and kissed him on the cheek, then pulled toward the cabin's door. "You're a great guy, Will, and I'm glad you're safe. That's all."

The corners of his mouth turned up and Riker returned her smile. Somehow he'd heard this before. Usually from his own lips. He and Barbara *did* have a lot in common. "Well, maybe I *will* get out this way again. Maybe we can . . ."

"Maybe," she said, winking. She stepped through the door. "But call first, okay?"

"Data?" Geordi stepped into Data's cabin.

"I'm here, Geordi."

He turned toward the android's desk, Data's voice being the only clue as to his location. He was probably sitting. "How are you," Geordi asked.

"I am . . . very sorry, my friend. Not only did I injure you, but I nearly began a war."

Geordi shook his head and tried to smile. "Dr. Crusher explained about the grain. Chances are you would have never gotten into Klingon space. The grain is only effective for a few days, and it takes longer than that to reach *Qo'noS*. You have nothing to be ashamed of." He heard Data rise and the proximity vest told him the android was stepping closer.

"That is not entirely correct," Data said. "The grain could not metabolize from my system. Its effects would not have worn off as they did with you. Had I not been stopped and treated—"

"The point is, you weren't in control, Data. You were under the same influence I was. You weren't responsible for your actions."

"Are we not always responsible for our actions?"

Data's question, in that almost childlike tone, seemed self-chiding.

Geordi sighed. "It's not that easy, Data. Not when there are outside influences forcing us to act against who we are. You were, as far as we can tell, caught in a logic loop caused by what is essentially a drug. You didn't know that would happen, and you couldn't think clearly when it did."

There was a pause, then Geordi felt Data's hand on his shoulder. "I am still sorry."

Geordi smiled. "I know. But look at it this way. Of all those beings who aren't rational, you had the best excuse of all—*you* were only sick, and you recovered."

"That is small consolation, considering that it cannot change what I have done."

"Data," Geordi said, reaching out and patting his friend's shoulder, "that *is* consolation—because it means you'll be more careful next time, don't you think?"

"Indeed," Data said. "I will. By the way . . ."

"What?"

"I just nodded. I thought you should know."

"Data," Geordi laughed, "it's good to have you back."

Picard's office door swished open.

Sporting a fresh uniform, Riker looked one hundred percent better. He stopped before the captain's desk and handed him a computer padd.

"Most of the crew is duty ready, sir. A few have reacted badly to the anesthetic and are being treated. Repairs will take another day, and Mr. La Forge assures me he *will* remember the longer password."

Nodding, Picard glanced over the padd. "How is Mr. La Forge doing?"

"Dr. Crusher said he'll be fine. She's already contacted the hospital that can re-implant the VISOR interface. We can drop him at Starbase Eighty-seven for transport, and he'll be back on duty within the month."

"Excellent." The captain looked up. "And Data?"

Riker hesitated. "Better. He won't stop apologizing. To me, to Geordi . . ."

Picard almost smiled.

"Bioengineering is clearing his system," Riker continued. "We think his system *was* trying to fight the grain as well. Dr. Hollitt has had access to the computers below the surface and informs me that the grain breaks down after a few days."

"No miracle cure," Picard said as he set the padd down on his desk.

"No. Dr. Crusher is in no danger of being replaced." Riker smiled and loosened his stance. "Barbara is a little disappointed—seems the grain can't be taken for any great length of time without taxing the body's normal immune system. She's thinking of suggesting it to her company as an occasional diet supplement or medicinal herb. She said you were very lucky you didn't eat any at the dinner."

Picard knitted his brows.

"Your artificial heart, sir."

The captain huffed. "Why? I can see why the grain wouldn't restore Geordi's eyes or allow Zhad to breath since those weren't natural conditions for them—but I *did* once have a heart."

Riker chuckled. "*I* believe you, sir. But even if the grain were that sophisticated, and there's no evidence it is, it would reject your artifical heart first and you'd die."

"Ah, I see. Most fortunate then. What about the planet's history?" Picard asked, gesturing Riker toward a seat.

The first officer only stepped toward the chair and leaned his arm against it.

"Nothing specific about the ancient civilization that she could find," he answered. "The grain is well described—powered by passive energy, usually the sun, but from our white-noise transmission for a while. In fact, that planet-wide tremor was the reaction of hundreds of thousands of machines suddenly having to shut down production once the white-noise jammer was gone. These machines learn well, though —there was no quake the second time we disengaged."

"Any specifics as to the grain's main function?"

"Seems to be toxin removal and minor cellular repair. Barbara won't be worrying too much—one way or another her company cleans up. Either they'll develop the grain as a cost effective medical tool, or they'll rent out plots to archeologists interested in the ancient Velexians."

Picard nodded. He wouldn't mind a look himself.

"How soon can Commander Data report for duty?"

Riker swiveled the chair under his palm. "Dr. Crusher says a few days, Bioengineering wants to wait a few extra until the grain-machines are definitely deactivated. As well, the nanites they're using to do that will have to be purged."

With a glance down at the padd and its casualty report, Picard sighed. "If only I'd noticed his condition sooner." The captain looked up, saw Riker was going to respond, and waved any comment off. "Have you shown this to him?"

Riker shook his head. "I haven't told him about any deaths. The Klingons aren't making an issue of it, and I thought it best to wait until he had his full . . . sense of reason."

How would Data react when he did find out? None of his shipmates perished, but that wouldn't matter to Data. Others died, and Data would have to deal with it. How? Logically, no doubt. The entire incident was an accident. But he still isn't quite back to his logical self.

"Agreed. If we haven't more pressing business planetside, let's get under way." The captain flashed his eyes. "Have we more business, Mr. Riker?"

The first officer shook his head. "No, sir. Dr. Hollitt has beamed down."

Picard allowed the slightest smile to pull at his lips. "Set course for Starbase Eighty-seven. Warp two as soon as she's ready."

"Aye, sir," he said, hesitating.

"Something, Number One?"

"Lieutenant Worf would like to see you, sir."

Picard shrugged. "Send him in."

The door opened and Worf entered after Riker walked past.

"Lieutenant," Picard greeted.

Worf was stoic. "Sir."

The captain stared and waited a moment for the Klingon to make some statement or ask a question.

"Can I help you, Lieutenant?" Picard said finally.

"I am ready to return to duty, sir," Worf answered as he looked straight over Picard's head.

"Splendid," Picard said.

Worf glared down.

"Oh, of course." Picard smiled. "My apologies, Mr. Worf. You are returned to duty. The Hidran have dropped all charges, and I regret the misunderstanding."

"Do not," Worf said, still laser-straight. "Even I thought it possible at one point that I had caused the ambassador's death."

The captain nodded. "At ease, Mr. Worf."

Relaxing slightly, Worf came to parade rest.

"I'm recommending you for a commendation regarding your brave, albeit unorthodox action on Velex."

"Thank you, sir."

Picard almost dismissed him, but decided to press one question before the Klingon returned to the bridge.

"Mr. Worf, did you hear what I said to Urosk and Kadar once you'd stabbed yourself?"

The Klingon's thick brow did not flinch, his eyes did not flicker. "I did, sir."

Picard rose, and tugged his uniform tunic into place as he walked around the desk, closing the distance between the two of them.

"I said there were no Klingons."

"Yes, sir."

No anger in that tone. In fact, nothing was in Worf's voice just now.

Picard glanced down at his boots a moment, then back up at that stern, ridged expression. "As a Klingon . . . did that offend you?"

The security chief—the Starfleet officer—tilted his head and met Picard's eyes.

"As Worf, sir, it could not."

Author's Note

There are a few people I have to mention for their help and support on this book. I know this stuff is boring if you're not listed, but I may just pick names at random at some point, so you might want to read anyway, just in case.

First and foremost I have to thank Gregory Brodeur. It would be too simple to say that I write the words and Greg plots the plot—the line is fuzzier than that. Let's just say that together, we are a writer.

I also owe my thanks to Greg's wife and regular collaborator, Diane Carey. She's a mentor, a big sister, and she does what no one else can do—kick me in the butt when I need it most. Thanks for letting me on your ship, Di. I'll always owe ya.

No softer shout of thanks goes to my parents. They've supported me (in more ways than one) through the tough times, and I'll always hold them dear. They're better than parents—they're friends.

A round of applause for Trek associate editor

John Ordover, please. He makes tough jobs easier (sometimes) and good books better (always).

Thanks also to Chuck Leibrand, who was stupid enough to listen to my early work, brave enough to tell me what he really thought, and smart enough to do it over the phone—out of throwing distance.

The same goes for Deborah Halford. Deb, I haven't known you long, but in ten years I trust I won't be saying that. Thanks for your kind words, and thanks for your not-so-kind ones as well.

Thank you also to Pat Julius and Peggy Eaton for their friendship and support.

These are the folks who, in their separate ways, have added to this book, my life, or both. I am forever in their debt, or at least until I become rich and famous and can drop them for people who have power and influence, whichever comes first. (Wonder if I'll get *any* Christmas cards now.)

To end on a more serious note, I began work on this novel the same week a friend lost his battle with cancer. Thoughts of him and his fiancée will always be with me as I reflect that I embarked on a new and enjoyable struggle, as he and his family lost to an older and uglier one.

This book is written in memory of Vincent Lloyd Whitenight, and in honor of his fiancée, Stacie Eaton, who will forever remind me that humanity's strength is in its courage, in the profundity of its spirit, and in the resilience of its will.

Dave Galanter